Praise for Aimée Carter and The Blackcoat Rebellion

"Corrupt leaders, graphic violence, rebellion, and first love, this title has it all... Carter (the Goddess Test trilogy) has created an engaging heroine to root for in Kitty and a page-turner full of twists and turns. Readers will look forward to the next book in the anticipated trilogy."

—*Booklist* on *Pawn*

"The tempo is brisk, the tension is deeply felt, the protagonist is a great reader's proxy, and the villains are smooth and terrifying. Kitty is a brash, imperfect hero, and readers will root for her every step of the way as she makes tough decisions."

—*School Library Journal* on *Pawn*

"Well-paced and readable."

—*Publishers Weekly* on *Pawn*

"*Pawn* is an intriguing political thriller that readers will want to finish in one night.... Filled with scheming, subterfuge, and the threat of being shipped off to Elsewhere, Carter has crafted a suspenseful mystery that will necessitate the purchase of the sequel."

—*VOYA*

"The plot twists and turns, with red herrings and a dynamic pace that will keep readers guessing. With even more political maneuvering, suspense, and romance, fans of the first book will not be disappointed."

—*School Library Journal* on *Captive*

"Readers will race through this and count the days until the final book is released."

—*Booklist* on *Captive*

"Carter's writing is smart; readers will feel as if they're really in Elsewhere experiencing Kitty's anguish, but these descriptions never take away from the rapid-fire plot. If you loved The Hunger Games and want your next dystopian YA fix, try this series now."

—*RT Book Reviews* on *Captive*

Also by
Aimée Carter

The Goddess Test Novels

in reading order:

THE GODDESS TEST
"The Goddess Hunt" (ebook)
GODDESS INTERRUPTED
THE GODDESS LEGACY
THE GODDESS INHERITANCE

The Blackcoat Rebellion

PAWN
CAPTIVE
QUEEN

PAWN

AIMÉE CARTER

HARLEQUIN® TEEN

ISBN-13: 978-0-373-21185-2

Pawn

This edition published by arrangement with Harlequin Books S.A.

For questions and comments about the quality of this book, please contact us at CustomerService@Harlequin.com.

Printed in U.S.A.

To Caitlin Straw, for reading every word.

I

UNLUCKY

Risking my life to steal an orange was a stupid thing to do, but today of all days, I didn't care about the consequences. If I were lucky, the Shields would throw me to the ground and put a bullet in my brain.

Dead at seventeen. It would be a relief.

As I hurried through the crowded market, I touched the back of my neck and tried not to wince. That morning, my skin had been pale and smooth, with only a freckle below my hairline. Now that noon had come and the test was over, my skin was marred with black ink that would never wash off and ridges that would never disappear.

III. At least it wasn't a II, though that wasn't much of a consolation.

"Kitty," called Benjy, my boyfriend. He tucked his long red hair behind his ears as he sauntered toward me, taller and more muscular than most of the others in the marketplace. Several women glanced at him as he passed, and I frowned.

I couldn't tell whether Benjy was oblivious or simply immune to my bad mood, but either way, he gave me a quick kiss and a mischievous look. "I have a birthday present for you."

"You do?" I said. Guilt washed over me. He didn't see the

orange in my hand or understand I was committing a crime. He should have been safe at school instead of here with me, but he'd insisted, and I had to do this. I'd had one chance to prove I could be worthwhile to society, and I'd failed. Now I was condemned to spend the rest of my life as something *less* than everyone in that market, all because of the tattoo on the back of my neck. Stealing a piece of fruit meant only for IVs and above wouldn't make my life any easier, but I needed one last moment of control, even if the Shields arrested me. Even if they really did kill me after all.

Benjy opened his hand and revealed a tiny purple blossom, no bigger than my thumbnail, nestled in his palm. "It's a violet," he said. "They're a perennial flower."

"I don't know what that means." I glanced around, searching for where he might have found it. Three tables down, next to a booth selling pictures of the Hart family, was one boasting colorful bottles of perfume. Tiny purple flowers covered the table. They were only decorations, not goods. Not anything that could get him killed or arrested and sent Elsewhere, like my orange. The seller must have let him take one.

"Perennial means that once they're planted, they keep growing year after year." He placed the flower in my palm and brushed his lips against mine. "They never give up, like someone I know."

I kissed him back, forcing myself to relax. "Thank you. It's beautiful." I sniffed the violet, but if it had a scent, it was lost in the smells surrounding us.

Despite the cool autumn day, it was sweltering inside the market. People were packed together, creating a stench that mingled with the sizzling meats, fresh fruit, and hundreds of other things the vendors tried to sell. I usually didn't mind, but today it made my stomach turn.

"We need to go," I said, cupping my fingers around the

flower to keep it safe. The orange in my other hand seemed to grow heavier with every passing second, and it wouldn't be long before someone noticed us. Benjy stood out in a crowd.

He glanced at the orange, but he said nothing as he followed me toward the exit, setting his hand on my back to guide me. I tensed at his touch, waiting for him to brush my hair away and spot my tattoo. He hadn't asked yet, but that courtesy wouldn't last forever.

I'd seen the posters and heard the speeches. Everyone had. We all had our rightful place in society, and it was up to us to decide what that was. Study hard, earn good grades, learn everything we could, and prove we were special. And when we turned seventeen and took the test, we would be rewarded with a good job, a nice place to live, and the satisfaction that we contributed to our society—everything we would ever need to lead a meaningful life.

That was all I'd ever wanted: to prove myself, to prove that I was better than the Extra I really was. To prove I deserved to exist even though I was a second child. To prove the government hadn't made a mistake not sending me Elsewhere.

Now my chance was over, and I hadn't even earned an average IV. Instead of living the meaningful life I'd been promised since before I could remember, I'd managed a III. There was nothing special about me—I was just another Extra who should never have been born in the first place.

I was a waste.

Worst of all, as much as I wanted to hate them for my III, it wasn't the government's fault. Everyone had an equal shot, and I'd blown mine. Now I had to live with the shame of having a permanent record of my failure tattooed onto the back of my neck for everyone to see, and I wasn't so sure I could do it.

Benjy and I had nearly reached the exit when a weedy man dressed in a gray Shield uniform stepped in front of me, his arm outstretched as he silently demanded my loot. The pistol holstered to his side left me no choice.

"I found it on the ground," I lied as I forked over the orange. "I was about to give it back to the merchant."

"Of course you were," said the Shield. He rotated his finger, a clear sign he wanted me to turn around. Benjy dropped his hand, and panic spread through me, white-hot and urging me to run.

But if I took off, he might blame Benjy, and all I could hope for now was that my stupid decision didn't affect him, too. Benjy had a month to go before he turned seventeen, and until then, he wouldn't be held responsible for his actions. Until that morning, I hadn't been, either.

At last I turned and pulled my dirty blond hair away from the nape of my neck. Even if I wanted to, I couldn't hide the mark or the angry red blotch surrounding it, still painful from the needle that had etched my rank into my skin.

Benjy stiffened at the sight of my III. I stared straight ahead, my face burning with shame. I'd let him down. I'd let both of us down. And now everything was going to change.

The man brushed his fingertips against the mark, feeling the three ridges underneath that proved it wasn't altered. Satisfied, he dropped his hand. "Is she telling the truth?" he said, and Benjy nodded, not missing a beat.

"Yes, sir. We were on our way to the stall now." Benjy twisted around to give him a glimpse of his bare neck. "We're only here to look around."

The Shield grunted, and he tossed the orange in the air and caught it. I scowled. Was he going to let me go or force me to my knees and shoot me? Less than five feet away, browned blood from another thief still stained the ground. I looked away. Maybe he'd send me Elsewhere instead, but I doubted it. The bastard looked trigger-happy.

"I see." He leaned in, and I wrinkled my nose at his sour breath. "Did you know your eyes are the same shade as Lila Hart's?"

I clenched my jaw. Lila Hart, the niece of the prime minister, was so wildly popular that hardly a week went by when someone didn't mention that the bizarre blue shade of my eyes matched hers.

"No," I said through gritted teeth. "Never heard that before in my life."

The Shield straightened. "What's your name?"

"Kitty Doe."

"Doe?" He eyed us both. "You're Extras?"

"Yes," I said, trying to keep the snarl out of my voice. No one with an ounce of self-preservation talked to a Shield like that, but after what had happened that morning, I didn't have it in me to kiss anyone's ass.

Out of the corner of my eye, I noticed Benjy frown, and I could almost hear his silent question. *What do you think you're doing?*

Stupidly risking my life, that's what.

The Shield stroked his pistol. "Stay put. Move, and I'll kill you, got it?"

I nodded mutely. But as soon as he turned away, Benjy touched my elbow, and our eyes met.

Without hesitating, we bolted.

Benjy and I pushed past the crowds, through the gates, and into the damp street. We sprinted between the aging buildings and ducked down alleyways, and as we passed a faded mural of Prime Minister Hart smiling down on us benevolently, I resisted the urge to spit on it.

We ran through a maze of side streets until we reached the border of the Heights, the easternmost suburb of the District of Columbia. And the poorest. I searched for any signs of the

IIs that populated the area, anyone who might be willing to snitch on us for a fresh loaf of bread, but during the day, while everyone was working at the docks or in the factories, the street was deserted.

After the workday ended, adults and children spilled into the overcrowded streets, begging for food. I usually had to elbow my way down the sidewalks and weave between men and women who couldn't be more than twenty years older than me, but already their hair had grayed and their skin turned to leather—the results of decades of hard labor and struggling to make ends meet. My life wouldn't be much better. As a IV, I could have counted on reaching sixty. Now, as a III, I would be lucky to hit forty. If I wasn't careful, I would also be out on the streets begging for more than the government had decided I was worth.

As we dashed around a corner, I spotted a sewer entrance a few feet away and sighed with relief. We were safe.

I shimmied through the opening on the edge of the sidewalk, and a minute later, Benjy climbed down from a manhole nearby. The sewer was dark and smelled like rust and rot, but it was the only place our conversation would be private. Even the empty streets didn't offer that guarantee. Shields were everywhere, waiting for their chance to pounce the moment they heard a word against the Harts or the Ministers of the Union. According to Nina, the matron of our group home, they got bonuses for each arrest they made, and they had families to feed, too. Didn't mean I hated them any less, though.

That morning, before I'd left, she'd said we all had our roles to play. It just so happened that some were better than others. We couldn't all be VIs and VIIs, and all any of us could hope for was food in our bellies and a place to call our own. I would have a roof over my head; the government made sure of that. But now, with my III, I would be outrageously lucky if it didn't leak.

In the speeches we watched from first grade on, Prime Minister Daxton Hart promised us that as privileged American citizens, we would be taken care of all our lives, so long as we gave back to the society that needed us. If we worked hard and gave it our all, we would get what we deserved. We were masters of our own fate.

Up until today, I'd believed him.

"What were you doing back there?" said Benjy. "You could've been killed."

"That was kind of the point," I muttered. "Better than being a III for the rest of my life."

Benjy sighed and reached for me, but I sidestepped him. I couldn't take his disappointment, too.

He slouched. "I don't understand—sixty-eight percent of all people tested are IVs."

"Yeah, well, guess I'm dumber than sixty-eight percent of the population." I kicked a puddle of rancid rainwater, splashing a few rats that squeaked in protest.

"Eighty-four percent, actually, including the Vs and above," said Benjy, and he added quickly, "but you're not. I mean, you're smart. You know you are. You outwitted that Shield back there."

"That wasn't smart. That was reckless. I told him my real name."

"You had no choice. If he'd found out you were lying, he would have killed you for sure," said Benjy. He stopped and faced me, cupping my chin in his hand. "I don't care what the test said. You're one of the smartest people I know, all right?"

"Not the kind of smart that matters." Not like Benjy was. He read everything he could get his hands on, and he forced me to watch the news with him every night. By the time we were nine, he'd read the entire group home library twice. I could recite whole articles seconds after he read them to me, but I couldn't read them to myself.

"Nina was wrong," I added. "You don't get extra time if they read the questions to you. The parts I reached were easy, but the reader was slow, and I didn't finish. And they docked points because I can't read."

Benjy opened and shut his mouth. "You should have told me before we left the testing center," he said, and I shook my head.

"There's nothing you could have done." A lump formed in my throat, and I swallowed hard. All of the studying, the preparation, the hope—it was all for nothing. "I'm a III. I'm a stupid, worthless—"

"You are not worthless." Benjy stepped closer, so close I could feel the heat radiating from his body. He wrapped his arms around me, and I buried my face in his chest, refusing to cry. "You're strong. You're brilliant. You're perfect exactly the way you are, and no matter what, you'll always have me, okay?"

"You'd be better off without me and you know it," I muttered into his sweater.

He pulled away enough to look at me, his blue eyes searching mine. After a long moment, he leaned down and kissed me again, this time lingering. "I'm never better off without you," he said. "We're in this together. I love you, and that's never going to change, all right? I'm yours no matter what your rank is. You could be a I, and I would go Elsewhere just to find you."

I tried to laugh, but it came out as more of a choking sob. The rank of I was only given to the people who couldn't work or contribute to society, and once they were sent Elsewhere, no one ever saw them again. "If I were a I, we probably never would've met in the first place."

"Doesn't matter," he murmured, running his fingers through my hair. "I would know something was missing. I would know my life was pointless, even if I never understood why. Even if we'd never met, even if you never existed, I would still love you beyond all reason for the rest of my life."

I kissed him, pouring every ounce of my frustration and anger into it. The sewer wasn't exactly romantic, but with Benjy there, I didn't care. He understood. He always understood, and in that moment, I needed him more than I could ever explain. The government might not have thought I was worth anything, but I was worth something to Benjy, and that should've been all that mattered.

At last I pulled away and cleared my throat. The lump was gone. "You won't have any problem with it," I promised. "You'll finish early and still get a VI."

"If you couldn't get a IV, then there's no hope for me," said Benjy. I snorted.

"Please. Someday we'll all be bowing and scraping and calling you Minister." If anyone from our group home got a VI, the highest rank a citizen could receive, it was Benjy. The test wasn't designed for my kind of intelligence, but it was tailor-made for his.

He slipped his arm around my waist and led me farther through the sewer, but he didn't disagree. Even he knew how smart he was. "Did you get your assignment?"

"Sewage maintenance."

"That's not so bad. We're down here all the time anyway," he said, slipping his hand under the hem of my shirt. I pushed it away.

"In Denver."

Benjy said nothing. Denver was so far away that neither of us knew where it was. To the west, more than likely, because the only thing east of D.C. was the ocean, but I'd never seen a map of anything bigger than the city. The only bright side was that Denver couldn't possibly be as crowded as it was here.

"I'm going to talk to Tabs," I said, and Benjy stopped cold in his tracks.

"Don't. Wait until I take my test. Nina will let you stay at the group home, and then I can support you."

"Nina won't commit assignment fraud for me, and I won't let you do it, either," I said. "If they find out you're hiding me, they'll send me Elsewhere and kill you in front of the entire country. It's not happening."

"Then Nina can give me permission to get married," he said, and my mouth dropped open.

"Are you *crazy?*"

"No," he said. "I love you, and I won't let them separate us. If that means getting married earlier than I'd planned, then so be it." He paused. "Do you not want to marry me?"

"Of course I want to marry you, but you haven't even taken the test yet, and what if being married to a III affects your rank? I can't do that to you, Benjy. You deserve better than that."

"What do I deserve, Kitty? To lose you? I don't care about the consequences."

At least he hadn't fooled himself into thinking there wouldn't be any. "You'd never let me risk myself like that for you, so I can't let you, either," I said, fighting to keep my voice even. "I've already made my decision."

"Kitty." He held his arm up to stop me, and when I started to move past him, he wrapped it around my waist again and pulled me closer. "I'm not going to let you do this to yourself."

I tried to push him away, but his grip tightened. "I'm the one who has to clean up shit for a living, not you. You don't get a say."

"We can run away," he said. "We can go somewhere warm. Have our own cottage, grow our own food—"

"Neither of us knows anything about farming. Besides, if a place like that exists, the Harts would have claimed it by now."

"You don't know that for sure. There's hope, Kitty. There's always hope. Please," he said quietly. "For me."

The way he watched me, silently begging me to say yes, almost made me change my mind, but I couldn't do that to him. Running away would mean he would miss his test, and no mark at all was as good as a I.

I'd failed, but he still had his chance, and I couldn't let him throw his life away for me.

"I'm sorry," I said. His face crumpled, and he turned away, dropping his arm. The cold seeped in where he'd touched me only moments before, and my heart sank. I would have done anything to make him happy, but because of my stupid III, I was going to hurt him no matter what I did. At least this way I would be the one risking everything, not him.

Every bone in my body screamed at me to run away with him, to get as far from D.C. as we could, but as we climbed the ladder to the manhole that opened up half a block from the group home, I knew two things for certain: Benjy would spend the entire afternoon trying to talk me into not going with Tabs, and I would do it anyway.

Nina was waiting for us in the kitchen of our group home, spatula in hand. It was still early enough that everyone was at school—everyone except me, now that I was seventeen, and Benjy, who wouldn't have missed today for anything. Having Nina to ourselves was a rare treat, but all I wanted to do was climb into my bunk and hide.

"How'd it go?" she chirped, but her smile fell the moment she saw Benjy. She looked to me for an explanation, and I stared at the floor, feeling even worse now than I had when I'd received my results. Nina was the only mother I'd ever known, and even though her attention was split between forty of us, she always seemed to have time for me. The last thing I'd wanted was to disappoint her.

"They didn't give me extra time," I finally said.

Without saying a word, she handed her spatula to Benjy and embraced me. All I could do was bury my face in her hair and swallow the sob that had been threatening to escape since the needle had first touched my skin.

"It's okay," she murmured. "It wasn't what you wanted, but you still have your whole life ahead of you, and good things will come your way."

She brushed her fingers against the back of my neck to see what my rank was, and I flinched. Nina sighed and held me a little tighter, but I knew what she was thinking: at least it wasn't a II. At least my life was worth a job that wouldn't kill me and enough food not to starve.

But I'd been stupid enough to hope for happiness and something more than mucking around in the sewers for the rest of my life, and now the ache in my chest was the price I had to pay.

Before today, I had never questioned the ranking system. It was there to give us what we deserved so we could make the most of our natural abilities. The smartest members of society could help people in ways that IIs and IIIs couldn't, so they earned more. It was fair, and without the test, someone who had grown up in a disadvantaged family might never have their talents recognized. This way, no one would fall through the cracks. No one who deserved a VI would have to live the grim existence of a II, and the people who weren't happy with their ranks only had themselves to blame.

Benjy was right, though; I wasn't stupid. I could do complicated math problems in my head, recite stories and poems and talk about what they meant—I just couldn't make sense of written words. If the tester had bothered to talk to me, she would've seen that. Maybe I didn't deserve a VI, but I didn't want a VI anyway. All I wanted was to prove I wasn't a waste.

A long moment passed before Benjy broke the silence. "She was assigned to Denver."

Nina released me. "That's halfway across the country," she said, stunned.

In other words, I would never see Benjy again if I got on that train. My resolve hardened.

"Tabs is stopping by this afternoon," I said, clearing my throat. "I'm going to talk to her."

A muscle in Benjy's jaw twitched. "I can't do this," he said, glaring at a spot on the floor. "If you change your mind, you know where to find me."

Setting the spatula down on the counter, he walked away, and the soft click of the kitchen door made me wince. I watched it, willing him to come back, but the door stayed shut.

"He'll come around eventually," said Nina as she went back to mixing. "Don't you worry."

"I hope he doesn't," I mumbled. "It'd be better for him."

"None of that," she said. "You need to focus on what you're going to do, not how Benjy feels."

"I'm going with Tabs," I said, perching on the edge of the worn countertop. "It's not a bad life, and she seems to like it."

"Tabs is Tabs. That life might suit her, but that's not the kind of trouble you're built for. And don't let her fool you—it's a hard life. It might have its perks, but the things you give up...it isn't worth it. Not for you."

"What would you know about it anyway?" I said, trying to snatch an apple from the fruit bowl. She slapped my hand away.

"I know enough to be sure you'd be better off in Denver than sleeping with strange men."

My stomach clenched uncomfortably. "Tabs said she doesn't have to do it that often. It's mostly going to parties and clubs and stuff."

"Yeah? Did Tabs also mention that for recruiting you, she gets a cut of your pay?"

I blinked. "She never told me that."

"Of course she didn't, dear. And of course she's going to pretend like it's a good life. It's hers, and she's in too deep to walk away." Nina touched my cheek with her flour-covered fingers. "Misery loves company, Kitty. Maybe she's telling the truth and most of it isn't so bad. But some of it will be, and those men will never see you as a person, not the way Benjy does. Not the way I do. You deserve better than that."

"I don't deserve anything," I said. "I'm a III."

"You're more than the mark on your neck, and you damn well know it," said Nina. "It might feel like a death sentence, but you'll see soon enough that you can have a good life no matter where you're ranked."

"Easy for you to say," I muttered. "You're a IV."

"And look at me now." She gestured widely. "Cooking dinner for forty children who never have enough. What a grand life I lead."

"Oh, please. You love it. You love all of us."

"I do." Her voice softened. "But because I love you, I feel it every time you hurt and every time you're disappointed. I understand how upset you are, Kitty. But it's your life, not the government's, and you can make something of yourself no matter what they tell you."

I stared at my hands and picked at a ragged nail. I wanted to believe her. I did. But how could I when everything was a mess? "Benjy's going to hate me for doing this, isn't he?"

"I don't think that boy could hate you even if you killed him," she said. "Though if you get yourself killed, I suppose he might hate you for that."

I frowned. She was right. Of course she was right, which only made the unease in the pit of my stomach grow. "I did something stupid today."

"Stupider than usual?" she said, but there was a hint of amusement in her voice. At least one of us thought this was funny.

"I tried to steal an orange from the market," I said. "A Shield caught us, and we ran. I told him my name, so he knows I'm an Extra." All Extras—second children of IVs and below, who were only allowed to have one—had the last name of Doe. Benjy did. Tabs did. Even Nina did. And because most Extras were sent Elsewhere when their parents couldn't pay the fine, there were only a few group homes scattered throughout D.C. Nina's was the only one within five miles of the market.

"I doubt he'll come all this way for an orange," she said as she tapped her spatula against the side of the bowl. That was what I loved most about Nina: she'd heard it all, and nothing any of us threw at her ever surprised her. "You know, once upon a time, everyone could walk into a market and buy anything they wanted."

I snorted. "Fairy tales start with 'once upon a time,' Nina."

"It was a fairy tale of sorts, but that didn't make it any less real," she said, lowering the bowl to focus on me. "It's frightening how much things change in seventy-one years."

"Yeah, and in another seventy-one, they won't bother giving IIs and IIIs jobs," I said. "They'll take us out back and shoot us instead."

"There will always be a need for people to perform menial labor." She crossed my path to get to the sink and gave me a kiss on the cheek. "The Harts won't always be in power. They're flesh and blood just like us. Things will change."

"Not in my lifetime," I said, and a chill ran down my spine. Talking about the Harts like this was treason. I had nothing left to lose, but forty kids relied on Nina.

"The world doesn't exist because you gave it permission," she said. "Things happen all the time that you and I and every other citizen who trusts the media never hear about, things the Harts don't want you to know."

"Like what? If anything important happened, everyone would be talking about it."

"Not the people who want to live to see next week. The deaths of Yvonne and Jameson Hart, for instance."

"They died in a car accident."

"Did they?" said Nina, eyebrow raised. "Or is that what the media told you?"

I eyed her. The prime minister's wife and elder son's funerals the year before had been mandatory viewing. Seeing the Harts gathered under black umbrellas and watching the coffins being lowered into the ground—it was the only time I'd ever felt sorry for them. "Are you saying it wasn't a car accident?"

"I'm saying even if it was, you would never know. But the world is out there, and it understands that the illusion of knowledge and freedom is not the same as the real thing. Eventually it will fade, and there are those who will do whatever it takes to make that happen sooner rather than later." She set her hands on my shoulders, staring me straight in the eye. "Listen to me, because I will only say this once. You have a choice. You can choose to accept the hand the Harts dealt you, or you can pick yourself up and do something about it."

"What, like scream and protest and get myself killed? It'd be better than this, that's for damn sure."

"If you're going to shun the role the government gave you

and live your life underground, then why not do something to change all of this, as well?"

"Nothing I do will make this better. My rank's already there, and it's not going away."

"It only means something because the Harts decided it did, and we went along with it," she said. "You are more than the number on the back of your neck, Kitty. Never forget that."

Never forget that if I'd been born a hundred years earlier, I would never have had to deal with any of this? "I won't."

"Good girl." She patted my cheek. "I trust you not to tell any of the kids about this. Not even Benjy. It's safer for him that way, and I know you don't want to get him into trouble. But you're an adult now, and it's time you learned what's really going on. If you want to do something worthwhile with your life, all you have to do is say the word, and I'll put you in touch with people who can help."

I hesitated. "Who—"

A loud knock on the door made me jump. Nina wiped her hands on her apron and muttered a curse, and the tension in the air disappeared. "Don't you dare touch anything," she said, bustling into the hallway.

The moment she turned the corner, I dipped my finger into the bowl and hooked a gob of dough. It melted in my mouth, and I let out a contented sigh, the weight of our conversation forgotten. My last meal in the only home I'd ever known would include my favorite biscuits. That was a nice surprise. And all I wanted today were nice surprises, not the kind that could get me killed. Maybe once Benjy had his VI and was safe, I would talk to Nina. Right now the only thing I could think about was how I was going to survive the next month.

"Can I help you, gentlemen?" Nina's voice floated through the hallway and into the kitchen, and I could tell by her tone that it wasn't someone she knew.

"Nina Doe?" said an authoritative voice. Moving silently across the kitchen, I peeked around the corner, and a gasp caught in my throat.

An official dressed in black and silver stood in the doorway. Beside him, with a deep scowl on his face, stood the Shield from the market.

II

AUCTION

"Is there something you need?" said Nina briskly to the men.

I pressed my back against the wall and frantically searched for a way out. I could escape through the back door, but there was a chance they'd brought others. Besides, the fence was too high to jump without Benjy giving me a boost, and I'd have to go around the front way anyway.

I was trapped.

"Ma'am, I'm Colonel Jeremiah Sampson. I'm looking for Kitty Doe," said the official, and I forced myself to take a deep breath. Panicking wouldn't help. There had to be somewhere I could hide.

My gaze fell on the cabinet underneath the sink, and I hurried toward it. It would be tight, but there was a chance they wouldn't look there. I slipped inside and closed the door seconds before three sets of footsteps entered the kitchen.

"I'm sorry, but she isn't here," said Nina. "May I ask what this is regarding?"

"Government business," said the Shield, and he didn't need to elaborate. Nina and I both knew what that meant: a bullet with my name on it. But why was the official in the strange uniform there? Surely the Shield from the market was more than capable of pulling the trigger himself.

The footsteps grew nearer, and I held my breath, keeping as still as I could. My back pressed up against a pipe, and I had to curl into a ball to avoid hitting the sink above me. The chemical scent of cleaner burned my nose, and my heart pounded against my rib cage, trying to get in every last beat it could before it stopped.

The footsteps paused in front of the sink, and I winced at the rush of water when someone turned on the faucet.

"I'm happy to tell her you dropped by when she comes home," said Nina, her voice distorted from the water, but nearby. She was in front of the sink, blocking the cabinet. Did she know where I was hiding?

"Do you mind if we look around?" said Sampson.

Nina shut off the water. "Since when do you people ask permission?"

Another shuffle of footsteps, this time from the other side of the kitchen. "Nina? What's going on?"

Benjy. My body went numb, and I groped around for some kind of weapon to use. If they touched him, if they even so much as looked at him the wrong way—

"These men would like to know where Kitty is," said Nina tartly.

"Couldn't say," said Benjy, and his footsteps grew louder as he neared the sink. I heard a light slap of skin against skin. He must have gone for the biscuits. "We got separated."

"Turn around," said the Shield, and for one awful moment I thought he was going to arrest Benjy. He couldn't, though—Benjy was still underage.

"Still as blank as it was an hour ago," said Benjy. His neck. The Shield was checking his rank. "She's not stupid enough to come back here, so if you want to find her, I'd recommend waiting at the train station. Or possibly the clubs," he added. "She's considering that, as well."

I opened and shut my mouth, horrified. Did he really hate the idea so much that he was willing to risk me being killed over it?

"Very well," said Sampson. "Thank you for your cooperation. If you don't mind, we will have a look around before leaving."

"By all means," said Nina. The men's footsteps echoed out of the kitchen and down the hall, and above me I heard Nina mutter, "Politest bastard I've ever met. Is she back there?"

Benjy must've shook his head, and she sighed. "Then let's hope she manages to get out of here before they see her."

I didn't announce my presence while the men searched, in case something was going on that I couldn't see. Occasionally I heard the low murmur of them speaking in another room, and I froze whenever they sounded like they were coming back, but they never searched the kitchen. "Rotten, uppity nuisances," said Nina after the front door opened and shut, and I knew the coast was clear. "Promise me that when you're marked, you won't turn into one of those VIs that thinks he's better than the rest of us."

"You mean there's another kind?" I said.

I pushed open the cabinet. Benjy stumbled backward, and Nina dropped her spatula on the floor.

"You were in there the whole time?" said Benjy, and I nodded. "How did you fit?"

"I'm flexible," I said. "I need to get out of here before they come back. Tabs said she'd be here by the time the kids got home."

I gave Nina a kiss on the cheek and headed into one of the two large rooms filled with bunk beds that the forty of us shared. Benjy stormed after me, but I resolutely stared straight ahead.

"Kitty— *Kitty.* You had this planned before today?" He took me by the elbow, and I spun around to face him.

"Yes," I said hotly, wrenching my arm away from him. "Because unlike you, we don't all have superbrains to fall back on." I hurried to my bunk, where my half-empty duffel bag sat waiting for me. I thought I'd be taking it into a better part of the city that evening, not Denver, and certainly not the club where Tabs lived. But I'd planned for the worst, thinking that when she arrived to pick me up, I'd tell her that I wouldn't be going with her after all. Not this.

"Fine," he called, disappearing into the boys' bunk. Half a minute later, he appeared in the doorway holding his backpack. "I'm coming with you."

I shoved my shirt into my bag. "What are you going to do in a club, Benjy?"

"We're not going to the club," he said. "We're running away."

"No, we're not. I'm not going to let you do that to yourself."

"I already told you. If you only earned a III, there's no hope for me." He grabbed a sweatshirt I'd borrowed from him and stuffed it into his backpack. "You're just as clever as me and you know it."

"No, I'm not," I said, my face burning as I struggled not to cry. I hadn't cried in years, not since Tabs had gone underground and we hadn't heard a word from her for six months. By the time she'd finally waltzed back into our lives, I'd convinced myself she was dead in a ditch somewhere. "Either way, you can read."

Before today, I'd managed to get by all right. Benjy had attempted to teach me to read for years, and while I could recite the alphabet, words didn't make sense to me. We'd been seven when Benjy had taken pity on me after our teacher had mocked me for not being able to spell my own name. He'd been there ever since, shielding me again and again. He even had two kinds of handwriting: his own and the handwriting he used on my homework when he wrote down the answers I gave him. But this wasn't something that Benjy could protect me from, no matter how hard he tried.

"Come here," he said, and I walked into his open arms. He ran his fingers through my hair and stood there silently, and I refused to let myself cry. It wouldn't solve anything, and the last thing I wanted was to let Benjy see how upset I really was. As long as I pretended to be strong enough to take this, I would have a way to keep him from doing something stupid.

"You can't go with me. I'll be okay," I said, my voice muffled by his shirt. I wished I could believe my own words.

"I would rather have you and no mark than a VI and lose you," he said. "I don't care if it means we'll be hunted. I won't let you go."

I took a shaky breath. "Please don't do that to me. Don't make me be the reason your life is ruined. You won't lose me, I promise. I'll come see you every day, and when you turn seventeen, you can take your test, and then we'll both be okay."

"You're my girlfriend," he said roughly. "I don't want those pigs touching you."

"I'm not exactly happy with the idea, either," I said, rubbing his back. "But I won't let Nina risk the kids by hiding me, and I'm not going to Denver."

"Can't you see if they'll place you in a position here?" said Benjy.

"I already asked when I got my assignment. They said—they said Extras from D.C. who score low always get placed in other cities. The Heights are too crowded, and we don't have any family holding us here."

"Yes, you do," he said. "You have me."

I swallowed hard. "They don't care. They said I'm lucky I wasn't sent Elsewhere when I was little, and I should take what I can get. I'm not going, Benjy. I know you think it'll be better, but it can't be. Not without you, okay? And Tabs is my only option."

He slipped his hand underneath my shirt and traced an invisible pattern around my navel. "There has to be another way."

"If you can think of something, I'm all ears."

He kissed me, his lips warm against mine as he gently nudged me backward onto the bed. "Maybe, before you go..."

I sat down on the edge of my bunk, but I set my hand against his chest, holding him at a distance. "I'm sorry," I said softly. "Tabs said they'll take better care of me if we've never..." I trailed off.

"I should be your first," said Benjy, sitting beside me and lacing his fingers in mine.

"And you will be."

"No, I won't. Not if you go with Tabs."

I shook my head. "They won't count. They will never count. It's just you, and it will always be just you, okay? You'll be the first I love and the only one that ever matters."

He rested his forehead against mine and squeezed his eyes shut. "If something happens to you—"

"That's what the club's there for," I said. "To protect me."

"They didn't do a very good job with Tabs."

"Tabs does extra stuff on the side," I lied. "I'll be okay. It's one month, and then it'll be over, and it'll be me and you for the rest of our lives, okay? Maybe no one will even want me."

Benjy gave me a look, his eyes rimmed with red. "If they don't want you, they're crazy."

I kissed him again, this time chastely. "Just forget about

this part and think about what it'll be like when you get your VI, okay?"

"I can't," he said, his voice breaking. "It isn't fair to me, Kitty, and it isn't fair to you. I love you, and nothing will ever change that, but I can't sit here and do nothing while they—while they—" He shook his head, and the cords in his neck strained. "I can't."

"Then don't," I said, my chest tightening. "If it'll make it better—"

"Nothing is going to make this better. You have no idea what you're getting into."

"I know," I whispered. "But I have to. And by the time it's over, we'll have enough saved up to get out of here. Go anywhere we want. You'll have your pick of assignments, and we'll never have to worry about any of this again. Until then..." My mouth went dry, and I tightened my grip on his hand. "Until then, I think we should break up."

Benjy stiffened beside me, but he didn't say a word. He didn't have to.

"You're right," I said. "You deserve better than this. Better than having me as a girlfriend. Better than having me ruin your life. So—let's not anymore. Not until it's over. When you're a VI, if you still want me..."

"I'll always want you," he said, and he looked at me, his face red and his eyes filled with tears. "I will always want you no matter what rank I am, no matter what rank you are, and no matter what you have to do to survive."

I brought his hand up to my lips and kissed his knuckles. "Then when you're a VI, you can choose me. But you deserve to have that choice in the first place. So—so I'm giving it to you."

"By breaking up with me." It wasn't a question, but I nodded anyway.

"Until you're ranked. And then you can choose what kind of life you want. One of us should."

His shoulders slumped, and he leaned toward me. "Kitty..."

The sharp rap of knuckles against the front door made us both jump. They were back.

Benjy and I exchanged a look. Without a word, he went to shove a chair underneath the doorknob while I grabbed my duffel bag and climbed a bunk to reach the nearest window. If I was lucky, they wouldn't have the whole place surrounded. If I wasn't—

"Tabs!" Nina's greeting echoed through the thin walls. I relaxed and jumped from the bed, landing with a thud.

"It's her," I said, trying to reach around Benjy for the door. "I have to go."

He didn't move. I tried again, and he still didn't budge.

"Please, Benjy—this is the only way," I said. "It's only a month, and then everything will be better."

"You don't know that for sure," he muttered, his arms crossed tightly over his chest.

"No, but I know that whatever happens, it'll be better than going to Denver and losing you forever. Please."

I set my hand on his and watched him, silently begging him to move. I didn't want this. If I'd had my way, I would be a IV, and everything would be okay. But I'd failed a single test—the only test that ever mattered—and now I had to face the consequences. And because Benjy loved me, he did, too.

At first he didn't respond. After a few seconds, however, he gave in and hugged me.

"Come see me tomorrow," he said. "Wait for me outside the school, and we'll go to the beach. We'll swim and watch the sunset and forget this ever happened. Promise me."

I nodded. If I didn't, he would try to track me down anyway, and Tabs with her big mouth would probably be more than happy to tell him exactly where I was. "I will. I love you."

Finally he stepped aside. I gave him a lingering kiss and touched his clenched jaw, and before he could say goodbye, I was gone.

The night air was cool on my bare skin, and I followed Tabs through an alleyway full of overflowing trash cans and leering men. Now that I was marked, I could leave home after dark, and there was a sense of tension that unnerved me.

Shields patrolled the streets, scanning every face that passed. I kept my eyes glued to the ground and my hair in my face as I followed Tabs, who balanced precariously on stiletto heels that made her bare legs look longer, all the way up to the few inches of skirt she'd squeezed into. I was dressed similarly, but because I was half a foot shorter, the skirt covered me to midthigh. She wore red lipstick and charcoal around her eyes that made them stand out, but I'd refused when she'd tried to do mine. Her dark hair was curled, and it was so long that it nearly touched her skirt. I'd run a comb through mine, but that was it.

"Is this typical at night?" I said quietly as we passed another Shield who kept his hand on his gun holster. "So many Shields and all?"

"Sometimes," she said with a shrug. "People drink too much and get rowdy. It gets really bad on the weekends."

"Today's Tuesday."

"Whatever." She eyed me. "You and Benjy didn't do it last night as some sort of screwed-up goodbye, did you?"

I shook my head. "I broke up with him."

"Good. It's easier when you don't have an angry boyfriend getting in the way." She stopped at a door and knocked four times. In the moment that passed, she must have seen the look on my face, because she pulled me into a quick hug. "It'll be fine, Kitty. It's scary your first time, but there's really nothing to it at all. You're not actually afraid he won't forgive you, are you? Because he will. He's Benjy."

The door opened before I could answer, revealing a man with a pointy chin. His eyes took in the curves Tabs was flaunting, and when he focused on me, it was all I could do not to glare.

"'Lo, Tabs. Who's your friend?"

"Fresh meat." She flashed him a flirty smile. "Going to let us in? Marion's expecting us."

He glanced over our shoulders, undoubtedly to check for Shields, and then stepped aside. Tabs took me by the elbow as we entered a narrow hallway, and the door slammed shut behind us. "Welcome to the Red Star Inn," said the man, and he grinned to reveal a missing tooth. I averted my eyes as Tabs pulled me past him.

As a IV, Tabs must have been given a perfectly ordinary assignment and the chance to live a normal life. Tabs was anything but normal, though, and instead she'd chosen this.

There was no audition for this job. Anyone brave enough to risk it could find a place at one of the clubs scattered around the city, and even though it was highly illegal, everyone knew that the VIs who made up the governing body of society frequented these places. No matter how many laws were written forbidding it, it was a reliable lifestyle, at least until you grew too old to be wanted. I didn't know what happened then, but at that moment all I cared about was staying in the Heights until Benjy turned seventeen.

Tabs introduced me to Marion, a graceful woman who must have done this at some point, but had been successful enough to start her own club. She directed me to a cramped dressing room and gestured for me to take a seat.

"A III, hmm?" She riffled through the rack of clothes pushed against a wall. "Bet you wish it was a VI."

"I'm not exactly VI material," I muttered. "A IV would've been nice, though."

"We all want to be something we're not, don't we?" She pulled a purple outfit off the rack and showed it to me. I wrinkled my nose. A bikini had more fabric. Marion replaced it. "There's no point in fighting who you are. You can only survive it. We all have our place in the world, and grumbling about it won't get you anything but a one-way ticket Elsewhere. Coming here, though—that'll change your life. Aha!"

She handed me a sleeveless white dress. I held it up to my body, and the hemline reached my knees. Marion beamed.

"Perfect. The auction starts soon. Tabs explained how you'll get a percentage of the profits and a room above the club?"

"Yeah. And I only have to—to be with men I choose, right?"

"Other than whoever buys you tonight, yes. But if you plan on making any money at this, I wouldn't be so picky if I were you." Marion eyed me. "Tabs said you're a virgin?"

I nodded, struggling to keep a neutral expression as my face grew hot. She either didn't notice or didn't care.

"Good. That's worth a small fortune these days. Get ready. I'll be back for you when it starts."

Marion left, and once we were alone, Tabs squeezed my hand. "She's wrong, you know. You're better than a III. She doesn't want you to change your mind, that's all."

"I don't exactly have much of a choice," I said. "But she's right anyway. I'm a III, and nothing's going to change that." And all I could do was try to survive it.

"It doesn't matter anyway," said Tabs. "You're not a III down here. You're the gorgeous and desirable Kitty, and you're in control of your own life now."

I would never be gorgeous or desirable, not like Tabs, but I nodded anyway. "Does it hurt?"

"Not nearly as much as losing Benjy forever would," she said. "Don't worry about any of it, okay? You'll be fine. I'll pick you up tomorrow morning, and you can tell me all about it then."

Tabs kissed my cheek, and I couldn't look her in the eye. For her, this was about liberation. All I wanted was to buy myself an extra month, and I didn't enjoy feeling like I was lying to her. Benjy was my freedom, not this.

"Are you really getting a cut of my profits on the side?" I said, and Tabs stopped in the doorway.

"Who told you that?"

"Nina."

She sighed dramatically. "I'm doing this so you can stay here with me and Benjy, not because I need the money. I make plenty on my own, and you will, too. But if it'll make you feel better, I'll give you my share."

"No, that's fine," I said, staring at my ragged fingernails. "I just wanted to know. Thanks, though—for helping me, I mean."

She flashed me a dazzling smile. "Anytime. Love you," she said as she flounced back into the hallway.

"Love you, too," I mumbled before she closed the door.

I sat on the stool and stared at my face in the mirror, trying to imagine the men who would bid on me. According to Tabs, most of the people who frequented these kinds of places weren't especially attractive, but that wasn't what I was worried about. Tomorrow, when I met Benjy in front of the school, what would he say? Would he even touch me anymore? Would he look at me the same way? Or would I be different—too different for him to love anymore, at least the way he loved me now?

And was losing him really worth it?

Yes, I decided. Benjy deserved better than this. He deserved better than me. But if by some miracle he still wanted me when this was over, then I would be here for him. I wasn't going to leave him, or Tabs, or Nina, no matter what it cost me.

In a month, Benjy would choose what life he wanted and if I would be in it. But this—right here, right now—*this* was my choice to make sure I'd still be here when he did.

The wait was torture. There were no clocks or televisions in the room, and by the time Marion came to get me, I had bitten my ragged nails so short that they bled. She took one look at my hands and dragged me to a bathroom across the hall.

"You'll have to stop that before you ruin your hands. Completely unattractive," she said as she ran a trickle of cold water over my fingertips. I hissed at the pain, but she didn't let go until they were clean. "There we go. Now c'mon, they're waiting."

Taking me by the arm, Marion led me down the narrow corridor until we reached a velvet curtain. Behind it I could hear the buzz of conversation and laughter, and warm light spilled out from underneath.

"You don't have to say anything," she said. "I'll handle the bidding, and after it's over, I'll escort you to the room. It's simple."

There was nothing simple about any of this. As I wiped my sweaty palms on my dress, all I could think of was Benjy. He might hate me for this. He might never look at me the same way. But this would give him a chance at a real future, and it was worth it.

When I stepped through the curtain, the crowd quieted, and a hundred pairs of eyes focused on me. Marion nudged me forward onto the small stage, and above us, a blinding light warmed my skin.

"Good evening, my loves," she said, and the sea of people in front of me clapped and hooted. "You've all been waiting so patiently for this very special moment, and as promised, one of you lucky gentlemen will be richly rewarded. For those of you who are interested—and don't be coy, we know you all are—tonight's bidding will start at one thousand gold pieces."

The air whooshed out of my lungs. One thousand gold pieces was more than I would have made in ten years as a III. There was nothing about me that made one night in my bed worth that much money. Maybe I was right—maybe no one would want to bid for me. Maybe this would be a bust, and I'd have to go back to the group home, or Tabs's place, and I'd get to apologize to Benjy and—

"One thousand gold pieces!" a booming voice from the back of the room called, and I closed my eyes, fighting the urge to be sick.

Over the next few minutes, the bids steadily climbed into absurdly high amounts, and eventually it came down to two men: a mustached whale in the front near the stage, and another who was too far back to see. By then the sum was astronomical, and when the number hit thirty thousand gold pieces, the mustached bidder in the front backed down, leaving my fate to the man whose face I couldn't see.

Wild applause filled the club, and Marion took me by the arm again, trembling with excitement as she led me through the curtain. "No one has ever outbid Minister Bradley before," she said, stunned. "Thirty thousand—I've never—can you believe—and for *you,* of all people—"

For me, of all people. I wanted to be offended, but she was right. "How much of that is mine?" I said, my voice shaking.

"Half. I've never had a girl make that much her first year,

let alone her first night." She stopped in the hallway and faced me, her nose an inch from mine. "You will treat the winner with the respect that kind of money deserves, do you understand me? You will give him whatever he wants, and you will make sure you do it with a smile on your face. He paid for something special, and you will give him something special."

I nodded, my mouth dry. The full impact of what this meant hadn't hit me until now, and my insides clenched uncomfortably as I followed her upstairs. This was really happening, and there was no backing out now.

Marion escorted me to a luxurious bedroom with a four-poster bed so wide there was barely enough space to walk beside it. Just like the dressing room, there were no windows, and the only door was the one she closed behind me. Once again I had to wait.

I sat on the edge of the bed and drew my knees to my chin, and I tried to pretend I was somewhere else. At home with Benjy, curled up underneath a quilt as he read to me. Sitting in front of him at school as he tossed me drawings, our way of passing notes. Even walking through the rancid sewers, so long as he was with me and I wasn't in this room, waiting for a stranger to do whatever he wanted to me.

I took a deep breath and tried to calm my racing heart. It would be all right. Tabs did this all the time, and she was fine. Countless girls did. And for a hell of a lot less than fifteen thousand gold pieces, too. With that kind of money, I didn't have to stay here. In the morning, I could pack my things, take the money, and run. Find a room to rent and stay there until Benjy was ranked. After seventeen years of never having a say in my own life, I'd finally be the one in control. I would put a smile on my face and pretend that I was having the best night of my life if that's what it took to make that happen.

The door opened, and my breath caught in my throat.

The Shield from the market stood in the hallway, flanked by a pair of men wearing the same black-and-silver uniform from before. One was a stranger, but the other I recognized from the group home. Sampson.

Instead of saying anything, the Shield stepped inside the tiny room and bent down, looking me straight in the eye. I stared back at him, refusing to smile or wink or any other cutesy gesture Tabs might do to get out of this situation. Several seconds passed before he straightened and nodded to the men behind him. "It's her."

One of them mumbled a few words into his cuff, and the Shield from the market gestured for me to stay put. Had he been the one to buy me? How could he have possibly afforded me on a Shield's salary?

Instead of taking a seat next to me, however, he stood by the door, facing me but not looking at me. The urge to ask what he was waiting for bubbled up inside me, but the words caught in my throat. It was obvious what he was doing; he was making sure I didn't escape.

This time there was a clock in the room, and over forty minutes passed before I heard a shuffle in the hallway. The men outside the door saluted in crisp unison, and they stepped aside. A tall man in a black overcoat entered the room.

I froze.

"Hello," he said with a voice that everyone in the country would recognize. "What's your name?"

I clutched my dress so tightly that the fabric began to rip. "Kitty," I croaked.

The corners of his dark eyes crinkled in amusement. He removed his hat, revealing a high forehead, bushy eyebrows, and dark hair that was graying at the temples. If I'd had any doubts before, now I was positive.

Prime Minister Daxton Hart. The position was supposed to

be temporary, but when the elections came every four years, there was only one name on the ballot.

"Kitty," he said, as if he was testing out my name. "Is that short for something?"

"Yeah," I said. "It's short for 'my mother was insane and had a thing for cats.'"

Silence filled the room, and the Shield stared at me as if he couldn't believe I'd talked back to the prime minister. My mouth went dry, but I held my ground and refused to flinch.

A few seconds passed, and to my surprise, Daxton laughed. "I *like* you. You have spunk. Though with a name like Kitty Doe, we both know you never knew your parents."

My cheeks grew warm. "If you already knew my name, then why did you ask for it in the first place?"

He shrugged. "Courtesy, my dear. Though I daresay you will not ask for mine. May I?" He gestured to my neck, and while the thought of anyone touching me made my skin crawl, I nodded. It was the least he would do tonight.

He brushed his fingers against the ridges and frowned. "A III," he said gravely. "And a fresh one at that. You must not be very happy."

"My choices in life have now been reduced to cleaning sewers or whoring myself out to strangers. It isn't exactly what I had in mind."

"What did you have in mind?" he said.

"None of your business."

The guards shifted uneasily, but Daxton sighed. "You're right, it isn't. Such a pity. I do like you."

He drummed his fingers against his elbow, and we stared at each other. I refused to be the first to look away.

"Tell you what, Kitty," he said, and he leaned in closer to me. "How would you like to be a VII?"

I blinked, and for a second I was positive I'd misheard him.

Only the Harts were granted VIIs. Not even the twelve Ministers of the Union were ranked so high.

"I'm a III," I said, as if that settled it, because it did. No one changed rank. No one. Everyone took the test, and everyone was marked accordingly. There was no special treatment, no taking it over again. Everyone had the same shot as everyone else. The only exceptions were the Harts, who didn't take the test at all. "I'm already marked."

"Yes, I can see that." Daxton straightened and adjusted his overcoat. "I will only offer this once, and I need your answer immediately. If you say yes, you will leave with me tonight, and your mark will be replaced."

"And if I say no?" I said.

"I think we both know what happens then." Daxton checked his gold watch. "My offer is good for the next thirty seconds."

I stared at him openly, but his eyes were focused on the time. His finger tapped the watch face as each second ticked by, and with every tap, my throat seemed to close up a little more.

A VII. A real VII from the prime minister himself. Wealth, power, and prestige, endless resources and beautiful things, never again having to worry about being arrested and sent Elsewhere—

Benjy.

What would happen to him? What would he do when he found out I'd disappeared? I couldn't leave him. A VII was worth a lot, but it wasn't worth losing one of the few people in my life who really mattered.

"Do I get to stay in D.C.?" I blurted, and Daxton gave me his trademark benevolent smile.

"I don't see why you wouldn't," he said. "We have many

homes across the country, but the one in Somerset is by far the most lavish."

Somerset. That was on the opposite end of the District of Columbia, where the Vs and VIs lived. I wouldn't have to live in a club. I wouldn't have to work in the sewers. I wouldn't even have to leave the city. I'd get to see Benjy whenever I wanted, and when he got his VI—

What would he say when he saw a fresh VII on the back of my neck? A VII would guarantee me riches beyond imagining, things that would make the perfumes and fruits and silks that were sold in the markets look like worthless trinkets instead of the treasures they were. A mark that meant we wouldn't have to break the law to stay together.

So what if I had to be the prime minister's mistress? He probably had dozens of them. He'd grow tired of me eventually, and then I'd be free to be with Benjy. And I would still be a VII.

Not a III, not a IV, but a VII.

"What's the catch?"

His lower eyelid twitched, but his expression didn't change. "Your time is almost up."

Whatever the catch was, it was worth thirty thousand gold pieces and a VII. I was stupid for hesitating.

"Five," he said, counting down. "Four, three, two—"

"Yes." I couldn't get the word out fast enough. I pictured Benjy's face when he found out we could stay together, and I had to bite the inside of my cheek to keep from grinning.

A VII. A real VII.

Daxton's lips twisted into a strange hybrid of a smirk and a smile. "I cannot tell you how pleased I am to hear that. There is a car waiting. Shall we?"

He offered me his hand, and his skin was smooth and cool against my damp palm. When we stepped out of the room, half a dozen guards surrounded us, and all of them eyed me. I hunched my shoulders in an attempt to make myself as small as possible.

"What's the catch?" I said again.

"Why on earth do you assume there's a catch?" said Daxton, and I didn't answer. Of course there was a catch. No one changed ranks, ever.

I rushed to keep up with his long strides, and the guards were so close behind us that I couldn't stop and take a breath. Daxton ushered me down a narrow flight of stairs and through a series of dank hallways, and finally I spotted the exit into the alleyway. Butterflies fluttered in my stomach. How was I supposed to let Benjy know I was safe? Daxton had to let me send word. Or did he expect me to cut all ties with my old life completely?

No. I wasn't going to abandon Benjy, no matter what he offered me.

To my left a door opened. Tabs poked her head out in time to see the prime minister walking beside me, and her mouth dropped open. "Kitty?"

Relief rushed through me. "Let Benjy know I'm okay," I said. "Go tonight if you can and tell him—"

"Nothing to see here," said a guard behind us. He stepped in front of Tabs, blocking her view, and Daxton marched me past her.

"Let me— Tabs! Tell him!" I called, but she didn't respond.

"Come on," said Daxton, and he pushed me into the alleyway. I shivered. The temperature had dropped several degrees, and my flimsy white dress didn't provide much protection from the cold. Daxton removed his overcoat, still warm from his body, and draped it over my shoulders.

"Thanks," I said. How many times had he done this before? How many mistresses had he bought and enticed with a VII?

The thought of sleeping with him made me sick to my stomach, but there was nothing I wouldn't have done to change my III. Benjy would hate it, but he had to understand. This way, I wouldn't be putting him in danger. This way, he wouldn't have to spend his life hiding me. This way, I wouldn't be forcing him to risk his life just so we could be together.

We turned into another alleyway, where a sleek black car waited for us. It stretched the length of three normal-sized cars, and I had to fight to keep my mouth from dropping open. I'd never seen such a big one up close before. Only Vs and above were allowed to own a car, and one this big must have been made especially for the Harts.

Daxton noticed me staring, and he chuckled. I pulled myself together and stood as straight as I could. I might never have been in a car before, but that didn't give him the right to laugh at me.

A guard opened the door, and Daxton gestured for me to go first. I was halfway inside when I heard it.

Bang.

My heart leaped into my throat. "What was that?"

"Nothing to worry your pretty little head about," said Daxton, and another pair of hands pushed me into the seat. I struggled to see, but Daxton slid in next to me, blocking my view, and the car door slammed shut. "It's a long trip to our destination, so I hope you don't mind that I've taken the liberty of making arrangements to ensure that your stomach doesn't get the best of you." He winked. "Leather seats. You understand."

I didn't understand, since Somerset couldn't have been more than twenty miles away, but I didn't care, either. I craned my neck so I could see around him and into the alleyway.

Through the weak light, I made out two men leaving the club, dragging the body of a girl behind them. We were too far away for me to see her face, but her long dark hair was unmistakable.

“Tabs?” I choked. “What—”

“Shh,” murmured Daxton, brushing my hair aside. Before I could push him away, a needle pricked my neck, and everything went black.

III

CELIA

Beep. Beep. Beep.

I groaned. It couldn't be morning already. The need to sleep weighed me down, and my head pounded. Maybe Nina would let me stay home from school today.

Beep. Beep. Beep.

I tried to turn over, but something held me in place. With monumental effort, I opened my eyes. As my vision swam into focus, I made out a small crystal chandelier hanging above me, casting rainbows across the white walls.

This wasn't the group home.

Everything that had happened the night before slammed into my consciousness. The auction. Daxton. The VII.

Tabs.

I struggled to move, but I couldn't so much as wiggle my fingers. I searched the unfamiliar room for anything that might help, squinting against the bright overhead lights. No visible windows. One door. Lots of open space. If anyone came in, I'd be trapped.

The beeping caught my attention again. It wasn't an alarm clock; a machine sat beside my bed, measuring my pulse with a green flashing light. Someone had stuck a plastic tube in my arm, and it was connected to a bag of clear fluid.

A hospital room, maybe? If it was, it was the strangest hospital I'd ever seen. If anything, it looked like a bedroom. A very large bedroom with a fireplace in the corner and white everything with gold trim, but still a bedroom.

"Ah, I see you're finally awake."

My heart pounded, and the frequency of the beeping increased. Out of the corner of my eye, I spotted Daxton sitting on a white sofa, holding a drink in his hand. I gritted my teeth. Whatever they were giving me through that tube, it clouded my mind and made my vision blurry, but no amount of medication could make me forget what I'd seen driving away from the club.

"You killed Tabs." It was hard to speak. My voice sounded deeper and hoarse, and I tried to clear my throat without success.

"No, I didn't," said Daxton, walking around the bed until I could see him without straining. "My guards did."

Again I told my body to move, but I was stuck. If something held me down, I couldn't feel it, and horror spread through me. Was I paralyzed?

I swallowed. Panicking wouldn't help. "Why?"

"Because she stuck her nose where it didn't belong." He took a sip from his cup. "Oh, don't look at me like that. She was nobody."

"She was my friend." He was lucky I couldn't move, else my hands would have been wrapped around his throat, treason or not. "And she was a IV."

"She was a prostitute," said Daxton, but that was a load of bull. Prostitutes on the streets, desperate to make their families a little extra money, were sent Elsewhere when they were caught. But in the clubs, especially clubs frequented by government officials and the ministers themselves—

"Would you like to see your new mark?"

I didn't answer. This was my fault. Tabs had been killed because she'd seen me with Daxton. There was no other explanation.

Pulling something from his pocket, Daxton held a small screen a foot away from my face, and with his other hand he slid something cold between the pillow and my skin. It must have been a camera, because the back of my neck appeared on the screen, and I could clearly see the new letters.

VII, marked in black ink that stood out against my pale skin. I looked away. It wasn't worth Tabs's life.

Daxton sighed. "It is a tragedy, what happened to your friend, and because it hurt you, I am so very sorry that it was necessary. But she knew the dangers that came with her profession, and she chose to do it anyway. You cannot blame me for upholding the law."

I closed my eyes and swallowed the lump in my throat. As much as I hated to admit it, Daxton was right. Tabs knew the risks. We all knew stepping one toe out of line could mean a bullet to the brain, yet instead of accepting her perfectly normal IV, Tabs had turned to prostitution. I'd tried to steal that orange. Benjy had offered to run away with me.

We all dodged bullets from the moment we turned seventeen. Sometimes they caught up with us, and there was nothing I could do about it. Feeling sorry for myself and for Tabs wouldn't bring her back, and if she'd known what was happening, that I was getting a VII—

She would've smacked me upside the head for risking it all because of her, especially when nothing I did would change what had happened.

People died and were sent Elsewhere all the time. It hurt

like hell when it happened close to home, but what made Tabs any different from the others who were punished for breaking the law? I hadn't cried for them. I never thought twice about the articles Benjy read to me about executions. People were there one day and gone the next, and they were the ones who'd risked it.

It was different when it was my friend, but at the same time it wasn't. Life still went on. Daxton still ruled the country, and I was nobody. At least now I was a nobody with a VII.

Tabs shouldn't have opened that door. And I shouldn't have talked to her.

A lock of my hair on the screen caught my eye. Instead of dirty blond, it was the color of wheat and blended in with the pillow.

"What did you do to my hair?" I said. The small mole on my neck was gone, as well.

"You wanted to be a VII," said Daxton as he switched the camera off. "Did you think I would just hand it to you because you were pretty?"

No, of course not. A snarl rose from the back of my throat, but when I let it out, it sounded more like a whimper than the roar I needed it to be. "What did you do to me?"

"I didn't do anything to you. You agreed to our arrangement, and now that it's done, you have two choices. You can accept it, or you can join your friend."

"What are you talking about?"

He perched on the bed. "I have also lost someone quite close to me recently," he said, lacing his fingers together. "My dear niece, Lila, was killed while on a skiing trip in the mountains last week."

The beeping beside me slowed. "She did? But I didn't hear about it on the news."

"The media does not know. No one does."

I stared at him. "I don't understand."

He shifted on the bed until he was facing me. "Do you know why I picked you?"

"Picked me for what? To be your mistress?"

"My mistress?" Daxton chuckled, but it was a humorless laugh. "Whatever gave you that idea?"

"You—you bought me," I said, at a loss.

"I did buy you, but not to be my mistress."

My mind raced. What other reason did he have to spend thirty thousand gold pieces on me? "I don't understand."

He leaned in close enough for me to smell the coffee on his breath and count the pores on his nose. "We have searched a long time for someone like you, Kitty. So long that I had begun to give up hope. When my officials told me someone with your unique features had been spotted, I had to come see you for myself. And there you were. Perfect in every way that mattered." His smile was so cold I wanted to shiver. "Did you know that eye color is the one thing we cannot change? Experiments have been done, of course, but ninety percent of those who attempt the alteration are instantly blinded. The other ten percent go blind within a year."

I had no idea what he was talking about, so I stayed silent. Daxton didn't seem to care.

"Tell me," he said, cupping my cheek. "Have you ever thought about how much better your life would be if you were a Hart?"

Before I could answer—or spit in his face, because I was still deciding—the door on the other side of the room swung open. A pair of guards entered, followed by a woman I'd only seen in photographs and on television.

Celia Hart, Daxton's younger sister and Lila's mother.

Pictures didn't do her justice. Like her daughter, Celia was stunning. Her face, so perfect it must have been surgically altered, was set in a smooth mask, but her eyes burned as she glared at me. "What the hell do you think you're doing?"

Thinking she meant me, I opened my mouth to answer—honestly, did she think I'd paralyzed myself on purpose?—but Daxton cut me off. "What does it look like I'm doing?"

"Playing God." She waved her hand, and her guards disappeared through the door. "Who is she?"

"A nobody. Some tramp I found in a club in the city," he said, and I hissed.

"I'm not a tramp. *You're* the one who bought my virginity."

"And yet you still have it," he said. "Hold your tongue, Kitty, or I'll have it numbed, as well."

"Do it, then," I said, not feeling half as brave as I sounded. "I have a right to know what's going on."

"Your rights extend as far as I let them." Daxton opened a drawer in the bedside table and pulled out a syringe. "This might sting."

Celia snatched it away before he could uncap it. "Don't you dare."

"But she's talking," he said.

Celia tapped the tip of the syringe against his throat. "So are you. Unless you start telling me what I want to hear, I'll freeze your vocal cords, and who knows how long that'll last?"

Daxton scoffed, but I could see his hands tighten into fists. "We need a replacement to undo the damage she caused. Mother thought it best if we take advantage of this opportunity."

"Opportunity?" sputtered Celia. "My daughter's *dead*."

Daxton shrugged. "It is of course a shame, what happened to Lila—"

"Don't you dare act like you aren't responsible," said Celia. "You murdered my daughter, and you think you can replace her without any consequences?"

Replace her?

"I didn't touch a hair on her head," said Daxton patiently. "Your conspiracy theories are growing tiresome, Celia. It was a freak avalanche."

"You're lying," she said, her voice shaking with anger. "You planned this. I know you did."

"You just lost your child. Your grief is getting the better of you. Once you've had time to adjust, you'll see the madness in your accusations."

Her expression darkened. "I'm not crazy. First my husband, now my daughter—"

"Your husband was a traitor," said Daxton. "Lila was seventeen. No matter how poorly you think of me, dear sister, I do not execute teenagers."

"No, of course not," she snapped. "Wouldn't want to risk making her a martyr, would you? Who knows what kind of revolution that would lead to?"

I cleared my throat, and both Harts focused their glares on me. Terrific.

"As fascinating as all of this has been, what does it have to do with me?" I said.

Celia turned toward Daxton in astonishment. "You haven't told her? She's lying here like this, and she doesn't know?"

Daxton shrugged, and thc beeps of the heart monitor next to my bed increased. "What d'you mean, lying here like this?" I said.

"I can't *believe* you," Celia all but exploded. "I know better than to think you'd ask me first, but you didn't ask her, either?"

"Yes, well." Daxton swallowed, his Adam's apple bobbing nervously. "Desperate times, you know. Couldn't wait. By the time you came out of seclusion..." He gestured at me. "If you'd rather have her killed, it could be arranged."

"What?" Using every ounce of willpower I had, I finally managed to lift my head from the pillow. "Listen, if it's all the same to you, I'd rather not die."

"You will not murder her," said Celia fiercely. "You did this, and now you're going to have to live with the consequences."

"What consequences?" I said. "What did he do to me? Why can't I move?"

She jerked her head to the side, and Daxton slouched toward the corner and dropped onto one of the white couches. Celia began searching the drawers. "Your name's Kitty?"

"Yeah," I said, watching her closely.

"It's not short for anything," said Daxton, but Celia gave him a look so poisonous that he fell silent.

"How old are you, Kitty?" She gave up her search and leaned in toward me. Her cool fingers brushed the back of my neck, and she must have seen the VII, because she pressed her lips together and straightened.

"Seventeen." My voice cracked. "My birthday was yesterday."

"Two weeks ago," said Daxton. "Enough time for the swelling to go down."

I'd lost two weeks? "What— But you said Lila died a week ago."

Celia rounded on him. "You *planned* this?"

Daxton shrugged and held up his hands innocently. "An unfortunate coincidence, I assure you. Mother is the one who came up with the idea. I'm merely following instructions."

"Of course Mother's behind it," she said. "You're too weak to think of anything like this yourself."

"Would someone *please* explain what's going on?" I said.

"Daxton, give me your camera," she demanded, holding out her hand. He grudgingly fished it out of his pocket and tossed it across the room as if it were nothing. Celia caught it and fumbled with the pieces.

"He's already shown me the back of my neck," I said. "He promised me a VII for going with him."

"Did he?" she said. "Well, you certainly have your VII now, don't you?" She steadied the camera in front of my face with one hand, and with the other she held up the screen for me to see.

At first I didn't understand. They were my eyes staring back at me, as clear and blue as ever, but nothing else was the same. My skin was paler and freckle-free. My hair had gone from dirty blond to the same wheat-blond I'd seen earlier. My cheekbones were higher, my eyebrows thinner, my nose smaller, and my lips fuller—even the shape of my face had gone from a square to an oval. And somehow my forehead, which had always been a little too small, was now perfect.

I gazed at the image for several seconds before it dawned on me. This wasn't just a gorgeous face where mine was supposed to be.

I stared into the camera, and Lila Hart stared back.

IV

KNOX

I couldn't breathe. The room spun around me, and the edges of my vision faded until all I could see was Lila's face where mine should have been. No matter how many times I blinked, it didn't change back. I was her. She was me.

Daxton had turned me into Lila Hart.

"What did you *do* to me?" I cried.

"You were Masked. A simple procedure," said Daxton from across the room. "Nothing more than a few alterations."

"Masked?" I said, choking on the word. What had they done, removed Lila's face and put it on mine? "I don't even *look* like me anymore."

Celia turned the camera off, her brow furrowed with anger. "There's nothing simple about it. Being Masked is rare and supposed to be done with the entire family's permission." She took a slow breath, like she was trying to keep calm. "It's more than a few alterations. Typically we use it for a body double, but in your case, my dear mother and brother always intended on you taking over my daughter's life, no matter how innocent Daxton pretends to be."

The pair of them exchanged venomous looks, and my

mouth went dry. Taking over Lila's life? "You mean I'm—you expect me to be—"

"It means that your VII has a few strings attached," said Daxton. "You can fight it and suffer the consequences, or you can accept it and all of the perks that come along with being one of us. It is, of course, your choice, but I've honestly no idea what in your past life is worth holding on to. You'd be a fool to refuse us."

A dead fool at that. I was nothing but collateral damage to Daxton. The only thing keeping me alive was my face. But Daxton was wrong; Benjy was the one thing in my life worth holding on to.

Daxton smoothed the front of his unwrinkled shirt. "It won't be so bad," he added, his voice a mockery of comfort. "You'll be waited on hand and foot, and you'll never want for anything again in your life. You, my dear, will be the most powerful girl in the country. You'll be one of us, and what more could you ask for?"

I closed my eyes as my mind raced. If I refused, I was dead. But if I said yes—then what? I would be Lila Hart. For the rest of my life, I would have someone else's face, answer to someone else's name, live someone else's life.

But at least I would be alive. I breathed in slowly, forcing myself not to panic. I was still me, wasn't I? I still felt like me. I still thought like me. They couldn't take that away no matter what they did to my body. I might have looked like Lila Hart, but I was still Kitty Doe.

Then why did it feel like Kitty Doe was lying alongside Tabs in a ditch somewhere?

"Besides," added Daxton, "it won't last forever."

I opened my eyes, the only part of me that was still me. "What d'you mean, it won't last forever?"

"It would be silly of us to expect you to give up your *whole* life, now, wouldn't it?"

That was exactly what they wanted me to do, though. "Can you—undo it?" I said.

"We can't give you your old face, but if you pretend to be Lila for as long as we need you to be, we can give you a new one," he said. "Do what we ask, and you can even keep your VII once it's over."

I glanced at Celia for reassurance, and she refused to look at me.

So Daxton was lying. I would be Lila for the rest of my life, and the only choice I had would be how long it lasted. I could call him on it, or I could pretend to be the fool he thought I was and play along. Only one option meant staying alive and in his good graces.

"And you won't kill me?" I said.

"Do what we want, and there will be no need for anyone to die," he said. "I promise."

It was the voice he used when he promised a better life for IIs and IIIs. When he promised new opportunities and chances for those who were stuck serving and cleaning up after the rich and powerful. It was the same voice he used every time he swore that if we worked hard and did our best, we would get the rank—the *life* we deserved.

Even if I did this, they would kill me eventually, but I would have a few more months or years to figure out how to escape. I couldn't change what they'd done to me, but I could use Lila's privilege to find a way out of it. And a way back to Benjy.

"Are you—are you all right with this?" I said to Celia.

"Seems I have about as much choice as you do," she said frostily. "But if you're asking if I will help, yes. Enough people have died for my dear brother's ambitions. No need to add to the body count."

Daxton set his hand over the place where his heart would have been if he'd had one. "I'm wounded, Celia, truly. If you have a problem with it, talk to Mother, not me. I'm merely following her instructions."

"Of course you are," said Celia. She set the camera down on my bedside table and reached toward me. For a moment I thought she was going to touch my face—Lila's face—but her hand stopped short, and she pulled away. "Once the medication has run its course, I will help you learn all you need to know. Knox must be told, as well," she added, directing that at Daxton. "And your son, if you haven't told him yet."

"I won't be telling Greyson," said Daxton shortly. "And neither will you."

"Of course not," said Celia. "Wouldn't want him knowing you killed his cousin so soon after the deaths of his mother and brother, would we?"

A wave of dizziness hit me. I'd have to deal with Greyson, Daxton's eighteen-year-old son, along with every other member of the Hart family. I'd grown up seeing their faces on television and hearing their voices on the news, and now I wouldn't just be meeting them. I'd be one of them.

Originally Jameson, Greyson's older brother, had been set to inherit the country. But now, once Daxton died, Greyson's name would replace his father's as the only one on the ballot every four years. I didn't know why Daxton didn't want to tell him about me, and I didn't care, but I couldn't remember a Knox in the news articles Benjy read to me every morning.

"Who's Knox?"

"Lennox Creed," said Celia. "He prefers Knox."

The beeping next to my bed accelerated. Lennox Creed was famous not for his father, who was one of the Ministers of the Union, but for his antics inside the exclusive night-clubs and parties that no V could ever dream of getting into, let alone a III.

And he was Lila's fiancé.

"Do I still have to—"

"Yes," said Daxton, cutting me off. "Like it or not, darling, from here on out, you're Lila until I tell you otherwise. Hold up your end of the bargain, and I'll hold up mine. Sound fair?"

When the end resulted in my death no matter what I said—no, it didn't. "Doesn't seem like I have much of a choice," I said, echoing Celia's words. When Daxton continued to watch me expectantly, I swallowed. "Sounds fair."

Celia sniffed and stared down her nose at me. "If you're going to do this, you might as well do it right. Is the tattoo there?"

"The VII?" I said. "It's there."

"Not that one," she said, and she faced Daxton. I closed my eyes and ignored them as they discussed every tiny detail of Lila's body, and their voices faded into the background.

A VII for life, but it wouldn't last long. One less sanitation worker wasn't anything for the Harts to cry about, and when they didn't need me anymore, that would be the end of it. The only chance I had at survival was to make sure they needed me until I was ready to make a break for it.

Stay alive. Stay safe. Make Daxton think I was his, and one day I would find a way out of this and back to Benjy. Those were the things that mattered. Whatever Daxton made me do in the meantime would be worth it.

But what was so important that they had to keep Lila alive through me? The people loved her, but tragedies happened. What had she done to make her life so indispensable?

And why had Daxton killed her in the first place?

I didn't mean to fall asleep. When I woke up, Daxton was gone, and sunlight streamed into the room through a window behind me that I hadn't noticed earlier. All I could see through it was blue sky, but at least now I had another way out of here if I needed it.

I rolled over to shield my eyes from the bright sunlight, and I noticed the white couch on the other side of the room. With a jolt I remembered what had happened. I touched my face—Lila's face—and felt the strange angles and curves. Even her skin was smoother than mine had ever been.

My neck itched, and as I started to scratch it, I froze.

I could move.

I stared at my hands. The skin was so white I looked like I'd never been outside, my nails were perfect and smooth, and when I pressed my fingertips together, they throbbed. Now that the medication had worn off, I could feel every little thing they'd done, and my face wasn't the only thing they'd changed.

Pushing the blanket from my body, I examined the skin exposed around my flimsy hospital gown. So much paler than my own, without a single freckle or mole. My hip felt tender, and when I pulled up the gown, I saw a delicate tattoo of a butterfly.

So that was what Celia had been talking about. The media would've had a field day if they'd known their precious Lila had had it.

"See something you like?" said an unfamiliar voice, and I yanked the blanket back over my lap. Leaning against the doorway, with his arms crossed and his dark hair tousled as if he'd just stepped indoors on a windy day, was Lennox Creed.

Knox. Lila's fiancé. *My* fiancé.

I scowled. "She has a tattoo."

"We all do." Knox rubbed the back of his neck, and a small thrill ran through me. Did I outrank him? Outranking IIs was nothing, but if he really was a VI...

"On her hip," I said. "Of a butterfly."

"Ah, that one." He stepped into the room and pulled off his jacket. By the time he reached my bedside, I could smell the cold leather. "She had a lot of secrets."

"Were any bad enough that the prime minister decided she couldn't die properly like the rest of us?"

Knox smiled grimly. "Apparently."

At a loss for what to say, I stared at him instead. He stared back. "You're Knox," I said.

"And you're not Lila." He made himself comfortable on the edge of the mattress. "Celia said your name's Kitty. True?"

"Yeah," I said, trying to keep an edge in my voice. It still sounded funny to me—had they somehow made me sound like Lila, too? They must have, else I didn't see how they expected me to pull this off. "What do you want?"

Instead of answering, he stuck out his hand for me to shake. I eyed him as I took it. There was something about him I didn't trust. It wasn't every day some strange girl showed up with the face of his fiancée, and he was being too nice, too—*casual* with this.

"You have a strong grip," he said. "You'll need to fix that before you go out in public. Lila was always very delicate."

"I'll work on it." I hesitated. Knox had obviously been close to Lila, and he could be my ticket to pulling off this charade. It wouldn't hurt to talk to him. "Is that why you're here? To criticize my grip?"

"Partially," he said drily. "Celia and I have agreed to work with you to make sure you transition to Lila's life as seamlessly as possible, so you'll be seeing plenty of both of us. In the meantime, I thought I'd introduce myself, since we're going to be married in a few months and all."

My stomach cramped. Daxton had mentioned I still had to marry him, but part of me had hoped that Knox wouldn't go along with it now that he wouldn't be marrying Lila. "I didn't—" My voice broke, and I cleared my throat. "The prime minister said it was only temporary—"

"Not that temporary," he said. "The wedding's set for New Year's Eve. Lila didn't do much to help with planning, so you've got a lot of work ahead of you."

"And what if I don't want to marry you?" I said. "Do I get a say in this?"

The corners of his mouth tugged upward into a darkly amused smile. "Considering Lila didn't want to marry me either, I'd say no."

Terrific. On top of everything else, now I had to worry about explaining this to Benjy. "I have a boyfriend."

"Yes, you do," he said. "Me."

"One I actually like."

"You'll learn to like me eventually," said Knox. "Most people do."

I bit back a retort and ran my tongue over my teeth. They were different, too—straighter, and my front teeth were smaller now. I touched my new face again, mapping out the new contours, and instinctively I brushed my fingertips against the back of my neck to reassure myself of my new mark. Except—

My blood ran cold. Three ridges to indicate a III, not the VII that should have been there. I pulled my hair away from my neck and turned so Knox could see it. "What's there?" I said urgently. "What rank?"

"A VII," he said, the confusion in his voice clear. When I turned back around, I must've looked as panicked as I felt, because he reached forward without asking. I leaned away, clutching the sheets. He paused. "I'm not going to hurt you. May I?"

Wordlessly I nodded, and he ran his fingers against my mark.

"You were a III?" he said. "Christ, that's rotten."

He could tell. The ink said I was a VII, just like Daxton had promised, but the ridges underneath my skin were still there. And if Knox could tell, anyone could. My heart hammered. "They said I'd be a VII, not—"

"Insurance," said Knox. "They need a way to control you and prove you're not Lila if they have to. Don't worry about it, though. It won't come to that, and no one in their right mind will check your rank."

I forced myself to breathe steadily. It would be a problem after I ran, but until then, Knox was right. There was no reason for anyone to think I wasn't Lila, nothing to connect her to an Extra III who was supposed to be in Denver. No one but Tabs, and she was already dead.

No, Tabs wasn't the only person who knew where I'd been. Daxton had no way of knowing about Benjy, though. He couldn't.

But what if he did?

I pushed the blanket away and swung my legs around to the side of the bed, ignoring the sharp pain as my feet touched the floor. Something felt off, but whatever else they'd done to me didn't matter. I had to find a way to warn Benjy.

I pushed myself off the bed and stood. No, not stood—I swayed, seconds away from falling, and my legs shook under the stress of bearing my weight. *Shit.*

"Whoa, what do you think you're doing?" Knox reached out to steady me, and when I tried to take a step, my foot caught on the lush carpet. Yes, something was definitely wrong.

"What does it look like I'm doing?" I clumsily fell back onto the bed. When I stuck my legs out to see what was wrong with them, my mouth dropped open. They were several inches longer. And thinner.

It wasn't just my face and my hands and my hip. I was taller, too.

Knox sat down beside me. "They did a good job on you," he said, glancing at my legs. "If I didn't know, I wouldn't be able to tell."

"Good for them," I said faintly. "I need some air."

"Excellent idea. I could use some myself."

Gritting my teeth, I forced myself to stand on my unsteady legs. This time I knew what to expect.

"Let me," said Knox, offering me his arm. I pushed it away and shuffled across the carpet. I needed to do this on my own.

By the time I finally reached the door, I was panting, my muscles burned, and a bead of sweat trickled down my forehead. Knox had left it open, and I poked my head around the corner, only to see a long white hallway that looked about a mile long. My heart sank.

"Stubborn little thing, aren't you?" Knox reappeared beside me with a wheelchair. "You really should learn when to ask for help. There's no shame in it, you know."

"I'm not letting you push me around in that thing," I said flatly.

"You have two choices—stay in this tiny room all day and mope, or go for a ride." He paused. "Well, you could also try to walk farther than you already have, but I wouldn't recommend it. Doubt the doctors would, either."

I didn't particularly care about what the doctors thought—or the fact that Knox thought the bedroom was tiny—but my legs were shaking so badly underneath me that my knees were practically knocking together. A wheelchair might have been embarrassing, but it had to be better than collapsing.

"Promise to take me wherever I want to go?" I said.

Knox placed his hand over his heart. "You have my word as your loving and devoted fiancé."

I rolled my eyes and eased myself down into the chair. My legs ached with pain beyond anything I'd ever felt before, and I could feel where they'd elongated the bones and tissue. No wonder they'd kept me unconscious.

"Where to, Your Highness?" said Knox as he handed me a blanket. I tucked it in around my lap, grateful for the warmth.

"Think you can manage a tour?" He'd never let me leave the building, but I might as well learn the layout.

Knox pushed me forward. "I'll see what I can do."

The long hallway was only the start of it. Knox wheeled me down another one, then another, and another, and I struggled to remember where we'd turned. It wasn't until I started imagining the hallways as the sewers that I figured out a way to keep track. I knew the sewer system better than most city workers, and it was dangerous to get lost down there. I was willing to bet it wasn't half as dangerous as it would be getting lost in this place, though.

"Where are the exits?" I said. The doors all blended into the walls, and none of them looked like they would lead to the streets.

"Thinking about leaving us so soon?" said Knox.

"There might be a fire," I said lamely, and I could practically hear his grin as he pushed me into an elevator. They were rare in the Heights, most being rickety and the sort that broke down once a week, and I hated the way I felt trapped inside them. But I was stuck in the chair for now, and I doubted this elevator broke down much at all. It was exquisite, with the ceiling made of white molding and buttons that shone like gold. Mirrors surrounded us on all four sides, and I saw the scowl on my unfamiliar face. Lila even looked pretty when she was miserable.

That was also the first good look I had at my new body. As the elevator flew upward, I stared at myself, trying to find any connection to my real appearance. Everything from my hair to my feet had been changed into an exact copy of Lila's, and the harder I looked, the more I realized even I couldn't tell the difference.

My eyes widened as I caught sight of my chest, and my hands flew upward. "You gave me *implants?*"

In the mirrors I could see Knox struggling to keep a straight face. "*I* didn't do anything, and I doubt they're implants. Those haven't been done in years. Chances are they're as real as your old ones."

I didn't find that very comforting. "What was wrong with mine?"

"They weren't Lila's."

"Yeah, but there wasn't that much of a difference, was there? Who spends so much time staring at Lila's chest that they'd notice?"

Knox smirked. "Roughly half the population."

My face turned scarlet, and I was still trying to come up with some kind of retort when the doors glided open, flooding the elevator with sunlight.

For a moment I thought I was imagining things. Clear blue sky stretched out before me, nothing like the smoggy skies of the District of Columbia, and white peaks loomed in the distance. Mountains.

"This is the exit," said Knox, wheeling me forward so we were close to the edge of the roof. The bitter wind whipped around me, but I was too dazed to worry about the cold. We were in a compound that seemed to be carved out of the mountain itself. When I stood on my shaky legs to look around, there were no towns or houses or anything in sight. Just the roof and snowy peaks.

"You didn't think we'd keep you in the city while we made the alterations, did you?" said a voice behind me. Daxton.

He sauntered toward us, wearing a crisp black suit that made him look as if he'd come from some extravagant event. Behind him stood a jet with the Hart family crest stamped on the tail, and the air around it seemed to ripple from the heat of the engines.

"Where are we?" I said, wishing my voice wasn't trembling as much as my knees. I grabbed the rail to steady myself.

"Somewhere no one will find you," said Daxton, smiling as he removed his leather gloves. "The family calls it the Stronghold, and its location is quite secret. You understand." He winked. "We thought this was the safest place for you until you've adjusted."

Until there was no chance I'd give away their game publicly, he meant. "How long will that be?"

"That, my dear, is entirely up to you." He unwound his scarf and stepped toward me. I flinched, but he gently wrapped it around my neck. "Wouldn't want you to catch cold in this chill."

"I'll take her back inside," said Knox, and he touched my elbow. I stood my ground, refusing to let go of the frozen rail.

"What do you want from me before I'm not your prisoner anymore?"

"My dear," said Daxton, his eyes wide with mock concern. "You're not my prisoner. If you really wish to go, we won't keep you here, but do understand that there will be consequences if you choose to leave."

Like a bullet with my name on it. "Yeah, I know."

Knox cleared his throat. "Sir, I believe she means how long she's stuck here until she can take over for Lila."

Daxton's lips curled upward into a leering smile. "Have you decided not to fight us after all? What pleasant news. Mother will be thrilled to hear it."

I dug my nails into the steel railing. "I'm not going to fight you. Tell me what I need to do to get out of this place, and I'll do it."

Daxton cupped my cheek, his hand like fire in the icy wind. "I am so very happy to hear that, darling. I understand how difficult this must be for you, and we are all here to help you. I will have Knox and Celia begin working with you tomorrow. Only your progress will dictate how long it will take. I am hoping for a few weeks, but it will last as long as it must."

Unless I was hopeless. Then I had no doubt it would be easy enough to replace me.

"When we're certain you will pass muster, you will meet Mother," he continued. "She will be the final judge."

I tightened my grip on the railing and tried not to sway. Nina called Augusta Hart the Bitch Queen, and with good reason. There hadn't been a single photograph taken of her since before I was born that showed her smiling, and she was notoriously unforgiving with both the people and her own family. It was common gossip that her husband, Edward, had just been a figurehead while she ruled the country with an iron fist, and apparently the same was true for Daxton.

Knox helped me into my chair, and I struggled to hold back the horror building inside me. Pretending to be a VII was one thing, but I would've had an easier time making an elephant tap dance than gaining Augusta's approval. Any hope I had at outsmarting them faded, and the only thing I had left was staying alive long enough to make sure they didn't hurt Benjy.

V

AUGUSTA

Lila was right-handed.

Normally this wouldn't have been a problem, but even though I barely knew the shapes of the cursive letters that formed my name, I could draw. I'd been holding markers and crayons since I was big enough to steal them from the supply cabinets in the group home, and everything I'd ever done had been with my left hand.

It wasn't just learning how to mimic the curves that formed Lila's signature. I had to learn to eat with my right hand as well, and the Harts seemed to have an endless stream of rules I had to follow in the dining room alone. Sit up straight, use the correct fork without hesitation, hold my pinkie up as I took a sip of water—everything Lila did instinctively, I had to learn from the ground up. It was a well-rehearsed show, as if Celia and Knox expected the cameras to be on me constantly, and I couldn't ignore the possibility that they were right. I would have no second chance.

"Get the basics down, and you'll be fine," said Knox on the first day of my training. "The trick isn't to convince them you're Lila—it's not to do anything to make them question it."

That probably held some special distinction for Knox that

was supposed to make it easier on me, but I didn't know enough about Lila to mimic her. Everything I did, from the way I walked to the way I spoke, was different. I had an accent she didn't. I'd never worn a pair of heels before, and those were all Lila seemed to wear. The foods she ate were ones I hated, which made maintaining her slight weight easy enough, but it also made the urge to sneak into the kitchens for a real meal gnaw at me unbearably.

I didn't, though, and not just because I could barely find a bathroom in the Stronghold, let alone the kitchens. If I were caught, or if they had any reason to suspect I wasn't going along with their plan, I had no idea what they would do to me. Knox at least seemed to pretend he was on my side, but Celia—she never looked me in the eye. Not that I could blame her, but it did little to make me feel like any less of a pariah. To her credit, she didn't seem to take it out on me. She grew more and more distant as the days passed, but she was never cruel. She was as stuck as I was, and the most either of us could do was pretend not to hurt as much as we did.

The one problem that wasn't going to be solved anytime soon was the fact that I couldn't read. Lila had loved books, and according to Celia, she had an entire library to herself in their New York home. She had constantly carried an old-fashioned paperback around with her to read in her spare moments, and many of the speeches she gave were read off glass screens in the middle of the crowd. Teleprompters, Celia said. Knox called them cheat sheets.

That wouldn't work for me, though. I had to learn how to repeat a speech fed to me through an earpiece, which I quickly discovered was much harder than it sounded. I tried again and again, but it never got easier. Worse, Lila sounded exactly like Celia, her voice rich and much more adult than mine. Some sort of technology had been implanted in my voice box to copy hers, but it wasn't really the sound of her voice that tripped me up. It was the way she talked and formed sentences. After a week, I still didn't have it down. When she spoke, she sounded like she had the answers to everything, and there was something about her that made even me want to follow her off a cliff. I couldn't mimic that no matter how hard I tried.

Celia also made the mistake of trying to teach me how to read, even though I insisted it was useless. It wasn't that I was stupid or wasn't trying. Letters strung together had simply never made sense to me. I knew what words meant, and because Benjy had read to me every night, I knew my favorite stories by heart. But while I had a talent for remembering what I'd heard, something about reading didn't work in my head. Celia tried to keep her cool, but eventually she gave up.

"I'll record your speeches for you," she said after a disastrous lesson using one of Lila's favorite childhood books. "You can memorize them instead."

This worked for me, and once we figured it out, things gradually grew easier. Whether I liked it or not, I was slowly turning into Lila Hart.

It took me eleven days to learn everything I needed to fool the casual observer into thinking I was Lila. Every moment I wasn't sleeping or receiving lessons from Knox and Celia, I watched recordings of her. Speech after speech after speech, public appearances, family recordings from when she was an infant onward—by the time those eleven days were over, if there was something to know about Lila, I knew it. She didn't eat red meat; she preferred music so old that the songs were sung by people, not by digitally created voices; her eyes never crinkled when she smiled; and according to Knox, she'd gotten that butterfly tattoo only months before she died. It had been an act of rebellion that she'd purposely revealed during a formal dinner between her uncle, her grandmother, and the leaders of foreign nations I'd never heard of. Even Celia, who stared blankly at her hands while the speeches were playing, managed a smile at the memory.

But those were only snapshots. Glimpses of who she was. Facts. In a way, it felt like the more I learned, the less I knew her. And I was no closer to having a conversation with her than I had been before Daxton had found me.

The speeches she gave were dangerous and full of reasons why there should be equality among the people like there had been during the early twenty-first century—when no one was marked or assigned careers, when freedom meant more than being able to walk down designated streets at night. When one person's entire life wasn't determined by a single test; when you had the chance to be whatever you wanted to be and live the kind of life you wanted without being told what to do. When we all had a choice. A *real* choice.

My entire life, I'd been told that the ranks were there for a reason. Everyone had their place, and the only way society could function was if we all respected the system. We were all equals when we took the test, and we were all scored the same way.

But in the speeches Lila gave, she said that the children who grew up in the neighborhoods meant for IIs and IIIs weren't given the same opportunities as the others. At first I didn't understand—there was only so much you could learn, right? Who cared where the schools were or what kind of supplies we had?

And then she talked about the education the children of Vs and VIs received.

"Some kids have tutors to help them with the test?" I said, stunned. "Isn't that cheating?" Getting five minutes with my teachers had been next to impossible, let alone anything more. It wasn't their fault, not really—there were dozens of us crammed into a classroom. Most days the teachers were lucky if they got everyone to shut up at the same time.

Celia pressed a few buttons on the remote. "I wouldn't call it cheating. It's more...teaching to the test, shall we say?"

"Most of the highly sought-after tutors are people who have worked in the testing centers," said Knox. "If your family has enough money, they'll hire one."

"Yeah, but only VIs can afford that," I said. He shrugged.

After that, I made a point of listening to what Lila was saying, not just the way she said it. If the government lied to everyone about the so-called equality of the test, then what else were they lying about?

None of the speeches Lila gave were televised. Instead they were recorded on handheld devices like the one Daxton had, some so shaky that I had to look away, but it wasn't what she looked like that mattered. She talked about doing away with Elsewhere and reverting to the system of government America had used before the Ministers of the Union had been formed, one where the elections were real and not a way for the Harts to legitimize their stranglehold over the country.

It was political treason, and if she'd been anyone other than a Hart, she would have been shot on sight. She was questioning the very system that was responsible for her family's power and the VII on the back of her neck. She was leading a rebellion.

School didn't teach us anything about the time before the ranks. There were mentions of the past, the World Wars and long-dead kings of countries across the oceans, but as far as the textbooks were concerned, history began seventy-one years ago, when the first citizen of the union was marked and Daxton's grandfather became prime minister. Years before I was born, there had been people who'd remembered a time before, but now everyone over the age of sixty was sent Elsewhere and never heard from again.

Maybe instead of killing me, that was what Daxton had in mind. I'd be as good as dead anyway, since no one knew where Elsewhere was. Presumably someplace warm where people could grow old and die, where they wouldn't take up space in already crowded cities and could keep an eye on the criminals who were sent there as well, banished from society for the smallest of crimes. That wouldn't be so bad, except for the part where I wouldn't have Benjy.

But something about the way Lila spoke—she believed in her message. There was no need to tell IIs and IIIs that something crucial was missing from their lives, but judging by the well-dressed crowds, few members of the audiences were below a V. Not only was she speaking to the population about her traitorous ideas, but she was convincing the smart and the powerful.

No wonder Daxton and Augusta had had her killed.

The door handle rattled one afternoon as I watched the last recording of her, a rousing demand that the rank and assignment system be demolished in favor of freedom and choice. Knox, who sat beside me, jumped up and turned off the screen. From the other side of the room, Celia launched herself toward the door.

I expected her to chew out whoever was on the other side, but instead she stepped back and opened it all the way. Daxton entered, and behind him walked a woman with chin-length white hair and a face so smooth it looked like she was made of marble. She held her shoulders back with such perfect posture that my spine ached just looking at her, and as a member of the only family exempt from going Elsewhere at age sixty, she was by far the oldest person I'd ever seen.

Augusta Hart.

"Good afternoon, Mother," said Celia. "We weren't expecting you for another two hours." The bitterness in her tone was obvious to me, but Augusta didn't seem to notice. If she did, she didn't care.

"My schedule freed up unexpectedly," said Augusta, her voice as cold as her expression. She stared at me, as if she could see right through Lila's face to the person I was underneath. I held her gaze, but she said nothing to me.

Daxton hesitated. "Mother, this is Kitty. Lila's replacement."

"Stand-in," corrected Augusta. "What have you been teaching her?"

"Everything," I said. "How Lila talked, how she acted, how she walked and what she ate—"

"Celia," interrupted Augusta, as if I hadn't said anything at all. "I asked you a question."

My face grew warm as I glowered at her, and a muscle in Celia's jaw twitched. "We've been teaching her exactly what you told us to, Mother. The basics and enough to help her fully adjust. Nothing more." She flipped on the television screen Knox had turned off in such a rush. Somehow Lila's last speech had been replaced by a recording of her running around as a child while wearing a frilly tutu and a crown I wasn't so sure was plastic.

Augusta nodded curtly, still watching me as if I were a piece of furniture instead of a living, breathing human being. "If she passes tonight's test, she will be taken back to the city and will resume her duties. If not, you will all remain in the Stronghold until she is ready."

"Of course," said Celia, and Augusta sniffed.

"If all goes well, the media will be informed of your return from vacation tomorrow, so no one will have a chance to speculate," she added, as if the Harts hadn't controlled the media and public opinion for decades. "You holidayed in Aspen. Do prepare her for that, as well."

Augusta turned to leave the room, and I tightened my fists. "It was nice to meet you," I said before I could stop myself.

She stopped dead in her tracks. Seconds ticked by, and my heart pounded as I waited for her to say something. Maybe I was nothing more than a pawn to her, a nameless piece in whatever twisted game she was playing, but she had to acknowledge me eventually.

Finally Augusta stepped toward the door, and Daxton held it open for her. "Don't be silly, dear," she said. "You've known me your whole life."

Celia spent the next two hours preparing me for dinner. She stuffed me into a dress and painful high heels, and while she did my hair, she drilled me on everything I'd learned over the past eleven days. No matter how hard I tried, nothing I said was exactly right.

"No, no, no," she snapped, yanking my hair. "She named her cat Missy, not Misty, and her favorite color's chartreuse, not green." She let out a frustrated groan and turned to Knox, who sat on the couch watching the whole production. "She's going to fail, and it'll be our asses on the line."

Knox stood and crossed the room. He took my hair from her and nudged her aside, his gentle fingers expertly finishing the intricate hairstyle. How many times had he done this for Lila?

"All you can do is your best," said Knox patiently to me while Celia collapsed in a huff on the sofa. "If you aren't there yet, we'll keep at it until you have it down. No one can expect you to learn how to be a completely different person in less than two weeks."

Apparently Augusta did, and her opinion was the only one

that mattered. "What's she going to ask me?" I said, using my loose dialect instead of stumbling over Lila's prim and proper accent. If anything screwed me up, it'd be that.

"I don't know," he said, tying off a twisted braid. "Just remember what we've taught you, and you'll do fine."

"Whatever you do, don't mention the speeches," added Celia, and Knox shot her a look. She returned it. "She needs to know she can't talk about them, else Mother will have all our heads."

So the speeches they'd shown me hadn't been on Augusta's approved teaching list after all. Somehow that didn't surprise me. "I won't," I said, glancing at Knox in the mirror. "Don't worry about it."

"That's not the only thing we have to worry about," he muttered. He finished up my hair quickly, and to my surprise, it looked good on Lila. On me.

He offered me his hand, but I ignored it and took one last look at my new face. This would have to be enough for tonight. "Let's get this over with."

Knox and Celia led the way to the dining room. Everything I'd been taught seemed to drain from my mind as we made our way down the hallway, leaving me feeling empty. My hands shook, and I could barely remember my own name, let alone Lila's.

I took a deep breath, and another, and another, trying to calm my nerves, but nothing worked. My heart raced, and no amount of silently reassuring myself helped. I was screwed. I might have looked like Lila, but I wasn't her. And no amount of training would ever change that.

Halfway there, Knox set his hand on my shoulder and offered me a smile that didn't reach his eyes. "You can fake anything as long as you have Lila's attitude. Hold your head high and act like you're pretending nothing bothers you when everything does, and you'll be golden."

"You say that like it's the easiest thing in the world," I said.

"For Lila, it was." Knox offered me his arm. I thought about not taking it, but my dress was made of silk, and I would never have forgiven myself if I'd fallen and ripped something so exquisite. I slid my arm into his and straightened. Lila wouldn't have been caught dead slouching.

"How did we meet?" I said, using Lila's accent. It sounded fake to my ears, but Celia didn't comment, so it couldn't have been too bad.

"Has your memory gone now, as well?" he said, eyebrow raised. "Or were you more drugged than I thought?"

I glared at him. "I'm not talking about me. I'm talking about Lila. How did you two meet?"

"We've known each other since we were kids, and we've been engaged since she turned seventeen. My father's the minister of ranking, so my family's close with the VIIs. It was pretty much a done deal as soon as she was born."

"So you're not a VII?" I said. "I mean, I know only Harts have VIIs, but since you're going to marry her—" Marry *me.* I cringed. "I thought they might have given one to you, too."

Knox turned down his collar so I could see his tattoo. A black VI stood out against his skin, and I bit my lip to stop myself from grinning. I outranked Lennox Creed. "No one who wasn't born and raised a Hart has a VII. Except for you, of course." He smirked. "Lucky you."

"Lucky me." If Knox wasn't going to have a VII even after he married Lila—married me—did that mean Augusta was a VI, as well? It almost seemed too good to be true. "You must be smarter than you look."

"How do you mean?" he said.

"Your test," I said. "To get a VI."

"Oh, you mean the aptitude exam," said Knox. "I didn't take it. Wouldn't do for the next minister of ranking to have a IV or a V, would it?"

I stopped dead in my tracks. "You didn't take it?" I said, stunned. "But—that's not fair!"

Knox tugged me forward, but when I dug my heels into the marble floor, Celia stepped up beside me and took my other elbow. "All Ministry positions are inherited," she said. "All of the Harts are given VIIs, and all the children of ministers are given VIs."

Together they dragged me down the hall, and I gave in, too horrified to fight. "So what, the whole line about everyone having an equal chance is really a bunch of bull?" I spat.

"Yes," said Celia. "I'm surprised anyone still believes that."

Everyone still believed it. What else did we have to justify our miserable lives? And for the kids who hadn't taken it yet, they still had hope they could make something of themselves. It was the same hope I'd lost the day I'd been marked a III.

"What if there's someone out there better qualified?" I said. "What if you're really a II and suddenly you run the entire country?"

Knox smiled grimly. "I'm not a II, and I've trained my whole life for that job. When my father turns sixty, no one will be better prepared for it than me."

"It's still not fair," I said, and he shrugged.

"Most things aren't. That's just the way the world works. If you don't like it, then do something about it."

I gritted my teeth. There wasn't anything I could do; that was the problem. I might have had a VII, but that gave me no power or privilege that Daxton hadn't already approved. If I opened my mouth, I'd be risking more than my new rank, and no matter how mad I got, I couldn't forget that my only job right now was to convince the world I was Lila.

I had to grin and bear it. Lila might have gotten away with speaking out against her family for a little while, but I wasn't Lila, and look what had happened to her in the end. I refused to let that happen to me, too.

The dining room was bathed in a warm golden glow from the crystal chandelier. The table was covered with a scarlet tablecloth, and the furniture was made of dark wood, giving the room a rich, homey feel. Whatever I'd been expecting, it hadn't been this. A cold, bright room where I'd be quizzed on every aspect of Lila's life, sure. But not something this comfortable.

Daxton sat at the end of the table closest to the door, and across from him, Augusta watched me over her wine. My feet didn't want to move, but Knox led me around to the side of the table, and we both sat down. I was two chairs away from Augusta, and I averted my eyes to avoid her burning stare.

"Good evening, Mother," said Celia. "Daxton."

Knox echoed her greeting, and they both looked at me expectantly. I swallowed, wishing I'd paid more attention in the lessons about protocol. These people were supposed to be my family, my uncle and grandmother and mother and—fiancé, so bowing wasn't necessary. But a polite hello probably was.

"Good evening," I said, forcing a small smile. This seemed to be enough, and they all unfolded their napkins to lay them across their laps. Before this, when I was Kitty instead of the strange fusion of myself and Lila, there was no point using a napkin like that. Nothing I owned was expensive enough to warrant protection from something as simple as broth or water. Now, with the silk I wore and the red wine in my glass, I wished I had a bib.

"We've missed you, Lila," said Augusta in a clipped voice, and I tensed. Underneath the table, Knox set his hand over mine and squeezed it. I didn't dare look at him, unsure if he meant to reassure me or if this was a natural gesture between him and Lila. "How was your vacation?"

Right. Our cover story—not a lie, really, except the fact that the real Lila had died on the slopes. "Cold," I said as servants dressed in black began to set dishes in front of us. Lettuce with bits of chicken and drizzled sauce that made my stomach turn, but remembering my training, I picked up the fork farthest from the plate and nibbled on a piece. It tasted as bad as it smelled.

"And?" said Augusta, eyebrow raised. Clearly she expected something more, but I'd never been there, so how was I supposed to report on an unfamiliar place? Lie, I supposed. Convincingly. A little practice wouldn't hurt.

"Skiing was enjoyable," I said in Lila's prim accent. She used a more common dialect when she spoke to the crowds, but I wasn't supposed to know about those speeches. "I spent so much time on the slopes that I can hardly walk, but nights at the lodge were relaxing."

This seemed to satisfy Augusta, because Daxton spoke up next. "How are plans for the wedding coming along?"

I didn't even want to think about it, let alone talk about it, and thankfully Celia jumped in and saved me. "The plans are coming along nicely, thank you for asking," she said, and I noticed she hadn't touched her salad. "Everything is on schedule for New Year's Eve. I hear you're going on another hunting expedition tomorrow."

"I am, and I was thinking of taking Lila with me, since it's only a day trip."

Beside me, Knox tensed. "I'm sure she could use a few days of rest—"

"No, she should go," said Celia. She stabbed her salad with enough force to chip the delicate china, though she still didn't take a bite. "It'd be good for her to see what you do to amuse yourself."

Knox's hand tightened around mine. Hunting wouldn't be so bad, though. The idea of spending the day with Daxton made my skin crawl, but he needed to see that I was willing to do whatever he wanted, and this was the perfect opportunity.

"I agree," said Augusta. "She should go. Perhaps it will help her better understand how things work." She eyed me over her wineglass, and I hastily looked down at my plate.

With each new course came questions, and I answered them as best I could. A look from Celia or a squeeze of the hand from Knox told me when I'd made a mistake, and I back-tracked quickly.

Augusta and Daxton brought up everything from plans for Lila's eighteenth birthday celebration in December to her last charity event, where she had worn a dress made by an up-and-coming designer whose name I'd never heard. With each answer I gave, Augusta either nodded or scowled, and I hung on her every gesture, too nervous to eat much. Most of it looked inedible anyway, and anything that tasted good came in such small portions that it hardly made a dent.

By the time a servant set the main course in front of me, I was starving. My mouth watered at the scent of seasoned beef that reminded me of Nina's cooking, but as I picked up my knife to begin cutting, I remembered that Lila didn't eat red meat. Maybe Daxton's plan was to starve me to death instead.

Despite my growling stomach, I set my knife down, and once it became clear I wasn't going to eat it, my plate was replaced with some kind of vegetable and pork in a sauce that smelled even worse than the salad. But Augusta nodded, and it was worth it.

After what felt like a dozen courses and more questions than I could count, the servants cleared our dessert plates. Augusta set her napkin back on the table and stood. Everyone followed suit, and I mimicked their actions, lacing my fingers together as I waited for the verdict.

"Well," she said, her focus now entirely on me. "I am pleased you have finally decided to rejoin us, Lila. Do enjoy your hunting trip with Daxton tomorrow, and I shall see you back in Washington in the evening. Your schedule will be sent to you, and I expect you to follow it to the letter."

For a second I thought I'd heard her wrong. I couldn't possibly be ready, not this quickly—I'd slipped up at least seven times that I'd noticed, and surely there had been other mistakes I hadn't realized I'd made.

But I'd heard her right. After only eleven days of training, I was expected to step into a pair of the most closely watched shoes in the country, and I had to be flawless.

Everyone in the room stared at me, waiting for a response. I nodded tightly as my dinner threatened to come back up. "Of course."

Knox took my arm again and led me out of the dining room. Celia followed closely behind. Once we'd turned the corner, he sighed with relief and loosened his grip.

"I passed," I whispered. "I actually passed."

"Yes," said Celia dully as she strode past us. "Congratulations."

There was no warmth or pleasure in her voice, only cold hatred I didn't understand. Instead of coming back to my room with us, she hurried down another hallway, her heels clicking sharply against the floor. I looked up at Knox, expecting some kind of explanation, but he shook his head and forced a small smile.

"Congratulations," he echoed. "I'd enjoy tonight if I were you. It's the last chance you'll have to be yourself."

Without warning, my stomach lurched, and I took off toward the nearest bathroom. After slamming the door, I sank to my knees next to the toilet and hid my face in my hands. On the other side, Knox knocked and called out, and I slid the lock into place.

The moment I stepped out of the Stronghold, any part of me that was still Kitty Doe would cease to exist, and I would be Lila until the day they didn't need me anymore. And when that happened, all I would be was dead.

VI

HUNTING

Celia shook me awake the next morning. Despite her chilliness the day before, she fussed over me as if I really were her daughter. I stood awkwardly in the middle of the bedroom while she dressed me in warm bundles of luxurious fur and leather, clothes I wouldn't have been allowed to touch as a III, let alone wear.

"Don't upset Daxton," she said. "Do exactly what he tells you no matter what you see. Don't talk back, and whatever you do, don't step off the platform. Promise me."

I had no idea what she was talking about. "I promise."

Celia stepped back and eyed her handiwork. "You're my responsibility now, and I won't let anything happen to you if I can help it. Those speeches you saw..." She paused. "Lila was doing a good thing. A great thing."

"I know," I said. Probably better than Celia did.

"If you want..." She hesitated. "You can continue the work she did. All the good that Daxton wants to die with her—it doesn't have to, and that's completely within your power. No one else's."

Was she joking? This had to be some sort of trap—another

test to see if I would agree to commit treason. I watched her warily, refusing to say a word.

"I will only ask you this once," said Celia. "You don't have to give me an answer immediately. I want you to think about it. You have no reason to trust me, and I don't expect you to, but I swear on everything I am and everything I believe that I am on your side. Do you understand?"

Again I nodded. Whether or not I trusted her was irrelevant; I had no choice but to do what Daxton told me.

"Good." Her expression softened, and she reached toward me as if she were going to set her hands on my shoulders, but she faltered and let them fall back to her sides. "Have you ever played chess, Kitty?"

I eyed her. What did a board game have to do with this? "Not really."

"You and I should play sometime. I think you would like it," she said. "It's a game of strategy, mostly. The strong pieces are in the back row, while the weak pieces—the pawns—are all in the front, ready to take the brunt of the attack. Because of their limited movement and vulnerability, most people underestimate them and only use them to protect the more powerful pieces. But when I play, I protect my pawns."

"Why?" I said, not entirely sure where this conversation was going. "If they're weak, then what's the point?"

"They may be weak when the game begins, but their potential is remarkable. Most of the time, they'll be taken by the other side and held captive until the end of the game. But if you're careful—if you keep your eyes open and pay attention to what your opponent is doing, if you protect your pawns and they reach the other side of the board, do you know what happens then?"

I shook my head, and she smiled.

"Your pawn becomes a queen." She touched my cheek, her

fingers cold as ice. "Because they kept moving forward and triumphed against impossible odds, they become the most powerful piece in the game. Never forget that, all right? Never forget the potential one solitary pawn has to change the entire game."

I toyed with the zipper on my coat. I understood what she meant, of course, but I couldn't play the game she wanted me to no matter how many promises she made. I wasn't her pawn. I was Daxton's. And she didn't want me to reach her side of the board.

"What's going to happen today?" I said, and she pressed her lips together.

"I don't know, not for sure. Just keep your head down and your mouth shut, and you'll be all right."

She did know. She just didn't want to tell me. "I will. Thanks."

"Don't thank me," she said, and for a moment she turned away. When she faced me again, her eyes were rimmed with red. "Right. I'll take you to the jet, and I'll be back in Washington by the time you arrive tonight."

Waiting for my answer, no doubt, but I already knew what it was going to be. I wasn't impersonating Lila to do the same things she'd done and die the same way she had. Daxton was in charge, and as long as I followed his lead, as long as I played his game, I'd be safe. As long as he still needed me, I would be alive. That was what mattered, not Lila's speeches or Celia's need for revenge. No matter what good they were trying to do, the Harts had ruined enough of my life already. I wasn't going to get involved in some twisted game between them regardless of what I believed. Because above all, I was one person, and all I had was my life. I wasn't going to do anything to give that up again.

We reached the elevator a few minutes later, and as it rose,

I watched Celia in the mirrored wall. What if it was a trap? What if Celia or Daxton saw my not giving an answer as a sign that I could turn?

I already knew what it was going to be anyway. There was no point in waiting to tell her.

"Celia?" I said, steeling myself against her anger. "What happened to your daughter is terrible, and I don't blame you for wanting to do—whatever it is you want to do to Daxton. But I can't help you. I'm sorry."

Instead of getting upset, Celia met my gaze in the mirror, her expression impassive. "All right. If you change your mind, you know where I'll be."

"I'm not going to," I said. No matter how bad I felt for her, staying alive for Benjy was much more important. "Can I ask you something?"

"If you must."

I hesitated. "Why didn't you kill Daxton when you found out what he'd done to Lila?"

For a long moment, she said nothing. At last she met my eyes, and to my surprise, she wore a small smile. "Who says I didn't try?"

I didn't respond. Whether she'd tried or not, I didn't see how she could sit across a table from the people who had murdered her daughter and act like nothing had happened. I had a hard enough time looking Daxton in the eye, knowing he'd had Tabs killed.

The elevator door opened to reveal the rooftop, and a blast of cold air hit my face. It was still so early that the sky was painted a warm rainbow of colors, and something tugged inside me. On clear mornings, Benjy and I would climb onto the roof of our group home to watch the sunrise, and it made each day a little more bearable. Now all it did was remind me of what I would never have again.

Daxton was waiting for us in front of the jet, wearing his usual winning smile. "I'll have her back by sunset," he promised, taking my arm from Celia. She scowled, and before I could say goodbye, Daxton ushered me up a narrow flight of steps and into the interior of the jet.

I'd never been on a plane before, and my stomach flip-flopped nervously. It was larger than I'd imagined from the outside. White leather armchairs were scattered throughout the cabin, and three of them faced a fireplace dancing with colorful flames that almost looked real. Other seats surrounded a table firmly attached to the floor, and a huge television screen covered a wall halfway down the length of the plane. Beside it was a narrow passageway that led to another door.

"What's that?" I said, peering down the corridor.

"A bedroom," said Daxton offhandedly, as if having a place to sleep in the middle of the sky was no big deal. It probably wasn't to him, since he'd grown up with this kind of luxury. Never mind the fact that it could undoubtedly have kept the entire population of the Heights in food and clothing meant for VIs for the rest of their lives.

No, I couldn't think like that—the way Celia wanted me to, the way Lila had before she'd been killed. I wasn't them. I hadn't been born into endless privilege, and I was making the right decision. Sticking with Daxton would buy me enough time to contact Benjy and come up with a plan to get out of this mess. At the first hint that Daxton was done with me, I would disappear, and all of this would be nothing more than a bad memory.

Daxton settled into an armchair and focused on a glowing screen embedded into the table, pointedly ignoring me. As the jet took off, I gazed out the window, enchanted. I'd never seen this kind of sky before—endless and blue, stretching on for miles over mountaintops. For a moment, I couldn't wait to tell Benjy about it. Until I remembered I'd be lucky if I ever spoke to him again.

I fell asleep an hour into the flight, and by the time I woke up, we'd landed. I refused Daxton's arm as we descended the stairs and stepped out onto the runway, and after my eyes adjusted to the bright sunlight, I saw red and orange trees in every direction.

"Where are we?" I said. There was a small cluster of buildings nearby, but otherwise it looked like we'd landed in the middle of a clearing in the woods.

Daxton beamed and spread his arms open wide. "Welcome to the best hunting grounds in the entire country."

What made hunting grounds good or bad, I had no idea, but I didn't ask. Beckoning for me to follow, Daxton stepped forward to meet a group of uniformed guards heading our way. Each carried a pistol, and my pulse quickened.

This place was different from the market, I reminded myself. I was Lila now, and none of the guards would dare point one of those at a Hart. The only person I had to worry about was the one standing beside me.

"Your Excellency. Miss Hart," said the man I assumed was the head guard. He wore a white uniform to the others' black, and he bowed deeply when he reached me and Daxton. "We have arranged for your visit, and your usual vehicle is ready. Your requested game has been herded into Zone Four, as well."

"Fantastic, Mercer," said Daxton, clapping the head guard on the back. "Is there anyone else here today?"

"Minister Bradley, sir," he said. "He is in the lodge."

The name Bradley stirred up a memory, and it took me a few seconds to remember he was the mustached man who'd lost the auction. No doubt I wouldn't have wound up a Hart if he'd won.

"Come, Lila," said Daxton, taking me by the elbow. Instead of heading to the nearest building, we walked through the crisp autumn air toward a smaller structure across the asphalt.

Once I was sure the guards weren't close enough to hear us, I said quietly, "Do all the ministers come here to hunt?"

"Yes," said Daxton, not bothering to keep his voice down. "You remember from our visit last year, of course, when Minister Creed hunted with us."

Minister Creed. Knox's father. "Of course," I said as we entered the second building. So Lila had hunted with him before. If she'd survived it, maybe I would, too.

The building was full of circular metal platforms with railings, and connected to them were vehicles that looked like cars with the top half missing. As I tried to figure out what it was for, Daxton greeted another man dressed in a uniform with different shades of green splashed across the fabric. Everyone knew who Daxton was, naturally, but the stunning part was that he seemed to know who they were, too.

"Your weapon, sir. Fully loaded," said the man dressed in green, and he handed Daxton a rifle. He didn't bother to offer me one.

"Ah, perfect. Lila, after you," said Daxton, gesturing for me to step up onto the circular platform. He followed, closing the gate behind us. With one hand he held his rifle, and with the other he gripped the railing. I hung on as well, and the platform hummed to life and floated off the ground.

My eyes widened, and I had to bite my tongue to stop myself from commenting. Lila would have known what to expect, and Daxton stood calmly beside me, as if nothing strange were happening. I clung to the metal bar so tightly that my knuckles turned white, but even though we were floating in midair, the platform didn't wobble.

"Ready?" called the driver, and Daxton nodded. I resisted

the urge to squeeze my eyes shut, and instead I watched as he steered us out of the building, past the clearing, and into the forest.

The faster we went, the higher the platform floated, giving me a view of the surrounding forest. We had plenty of run-down parks in the Heights, but they were nothing like this. Thick with autumn foliage, the trees were colorful and the moss on the ground was the most vivid green I'd ever seen. The air here was cleaner, too, and everything seemed brighter.

The driver weaved between the trees expertly, and the bitter wind made me grateful Celia had bundled me up. Once I was positive I wasn't going to fall off or lose my balance, I loosened my grip on the railing. I could see why Daxton enjoyed it so much. Besides the chill, it was almost fun.

After nearly fifteen minutes, we reached a massive chain-link fence guarded by dozens of Shields with guns that looked even more deadly than the one Daxton held. The gate opened for us, and I frowned.

"To sort the game I requested," said Daxton, answering my unspoken question. "Wouldn't want anyone to get hurt, would we?"

He flashed me a dazzling smile, and I looked away, keeping my eyes peeled for any signs of movement on the ground.

A minute later, Daxton raised his rifle and aimed. As I craned my neck to see what it was, he pulled the trigger, and the sound was deafening. I clamped my hands over my ears, but the noise didn't seem to bother Daxton. Cursing to himself, he lowered his rifle and instructed the driver to slow down.

Shortly after, he raised his rifle again, and this time I was ready. I covered my ears as something pale flashed in the distance. A rabbit, maybe, or a light-colored deer. I couldn't see well enough to be sure.

"You should watch," said Daxton, his eyes shining. "You'll like this."

I obediently leaned against the rail to get a better look. He held his gun at the ready, his finger on the trigger as he waited, but nothing appeared.

"What—" I said, but Daxton shook his head, and I fell silent. We'd all but stopped now, and the hum of the platform was barely audible. I noticed something out of the corner of my eye, but by the time I turned my head, it was gone.

"Aha," said Daxton. "There!"

The driver pulled the platform around, and finally I saw what had caused the flash of something pale.

Crouched in the bushes, her face dirty and her clothes torn, was a woman.

I blinked. Was that—

It couldn't be.

"Nina?"

Without thinking, I sprang forward. I was halfway over the railing when Daxton grabbed my wrist and pulled me back onto the platform. "Don't move."

I struggled against his bruising grip, and when he let go, cold metal bit into my skin. He'd handcuffed me to the railing.

"Nina!" I shouted, yanking against the chain. "Over here!"

Instead of running toward us, she froze in fear, her eyes wide as she stared at us. As she stared at *me.*

"Please don't," she cried as tears streamed down her face. "I'll do anything."

For a moment our eyes locked, and all the air left my lungs. Desperation and fear were written all over her face, and she clung to the tree beside her as if it would protect her.

I didn't understand. Why wasn't she coming toward us?

"Lila," she choked. "Please."

"Nina," I said, stretching my free hand out toward her. "It's safe up here, come on—"

"Keep watching, Lila," said Daxton as he aimed. "I want you to remember this moment."

"But—"

And then it dawned on me.

I launched myself toward Daxton, but the cuff bit into my skin and nearly wrenched my shoulder out of place. "Stop!" I cried. "She's—"

Bang.

The tree behind her splattered red with blood, and Nina crumpled to the ground.

She was dead.

"Got it," he said, smirking as he started to reload. The world spun around me, and I leaned over the railing and retched.

"Welcome," said Daxton, "to Elsewhere."

VII

TRUST

Time seemed to slow down as the platform raced through the forest, away from Nina's dead body.

She was gone. Nina was gone, and it was my fault. Her being here today, Daxton killing her—

I couldn't breathe. The trees felt as if they were closing in around us, slowly suffocating me as reality set in.

Nina was dead. She was really dead.

The only thing that kept me from kicking the life out of Daxton was what Celia had told me that morning. If I upset him, I would become one of them for sure, no matter who I looked like. And it wouldn't change anything anyway.

I buried my face in my free hand and sobbed. Celia had known this was going to happen. Maybe she'd even known about Nina. She'd known, and she hadn't warned me. She really was no better than Daxton.

For the rest of the afternoon I sat on the edge of the platform, closed my eyes, and tried to ignore the shots from the rifle and the howls of joy that followed. I tried not to picture their faces. I tried to forget watching Nina die and not think about what she could've possibly done to wind up here—what any of them could have done. Steal an orange, maybe, except they hadn't been lucky enough to have Lila's eyes and get away with it.

Daxton unshackled me before we returned to the lodge, a rustic building full of overstuffed armchairs and trophies in cases. I didn't wait for him to show me around. The moment I spotted the door, I headed outside and back to the plane. Daxton didn't stop me, and as soon as I was alone in the jet, I went into the bathroom and was sick.

This was Elsewhere. All those elderly people, all the criminals, all the people who weren't smart enough to meet the standards of the government—this was their fate, to be sent Elsewhere and hunted like animals.

Lying there on the cool tile floor, I wondered how many people knew about this place and had never said anything. Lila had been here, and Celia knew, as well. This was why she'd wanted me to go, I realized. This was why she'd wanted me to think about her offer before I answered—so I would see this and understand exactly how twisted Daxton was.

It wasn't only Daxton, though. It was Minister Bradley, too, and Minister Creed. Every minister, as far as I knew—would Knox one day stand on the same platform and hunt people whose only crime had been to speak their mind or steal a pair of shoes when theirs fell apart? Had he done so already?

No. I refused to believe he could have gone along with this. If he hunted, Daxton would have invited him along. Besides, Knox had been there when I'd watched Lila's speeches. He was as much a part of that as Celia.

But how many children of ministers changed their tune once they had power? How many stopped caring when they no longer had to worry about becoming one of the hunted?

By the time Daxton returned, I was curled up in the armchair in front of the fire, shivering despite my layers of fur.

He said nothing as the jet took off, and it wasn't until we were well on our way that he settled into the seat next to mine.

"How did you get a III?"

The sound of his voice made my stomach churn again, but there wasn't anything left to come up. I stared resolutely at the fire.

"You seem too clever for it," he continued. "I was sure Mother would make us wait another few weeks for you to get more practice, but you're perfect as Lila. No one there suspected a thing. Did you throw the aptitude test on purpose?"

I shook my head, dumbfounded. "Do you not get how important that test is to your people? Do you really think someone would ever purposely *fail?*"

Daxton drummed his fingers against the arm of his chair, perfectly calm. "Then what was it?"

"I ran out of time," I said through gritted teeth. If Celia and Knox hadn't told him I couldn't read, I wasn't about to give him something else to hold over my head. "I had to leave a third of it blank."

His eyebrows shot up. "You left a third of it blank and still received a III?"

My nails dug into the soft leather of the chair. "You want to talk about my test when you just killed the only mother I've ever had?"

"You have Celia now," he said. "You are in need of a mother, and she is in need of a daughter. It's a perfect fit."

"What about the other people you killed? What about their mothers and daughters?"

"They were criminals," he said. "Ones who were warned ahead of time what the penalty of their crimes would be."

"What did they do? Steal a bit of food? Talk back to a Shield? What did Nina do to deserve to die?"

"She hid you," said Daxton, and he might as well have

punched me in the gut. "You think I don't know about that? I know about everything, Kitty, and you would be wise never to forget that."

I struggled for air, and the walls of the plane pressed in on me like the trees had done in the forest. It really was my fault. All she'd done was try to protect me, and she'd died for it.

Oh God. Benjy.

"Did you know," said Daxton as he folded his hands and studied me, "that if we did not punish every criminal, there wouldn't be enough to feed everyone?"

"Then why don't you sell the damn jet and buy more food?" I choked, my eyes watering with anger. What if Benjy was there, too? Had he been one of the others Daxton had killed?

He shook his head. "You don't understand. Shortly after my grandfather was elected into office, our economy collapsed, and everyone was destitute—no one had enough, and people were starving. The country had—still has—a finite number of resources. There is only so much food and drinking water. There are only so many teachers, so many doctors, and so many scientists. The mediocre and the dim vastly outnumber the intelligent, and it has been that way for far too long. We outgrew ourselves. Our economy suffered, and so did our people. Crime was astronomical, and no one had any hope of a better life. That is why he helped turn the ruins of the United States into the shining beacon it is today."

"At least then you didn't get shot for stepping out of line," I spat.

"At least now you have enough food to eat," he said. "At least now you can sleep safe in your bed and not fear your neighbors ransacking your home and murdering your entire family."

"Why would I fear my neighbors when my government does it for them?"

Daxton took a deep breath. "I did not make the laws. My grandfather did, and he did so with the welfare of the entire country in mind. Without Elsewhere, the overpopulation would be so bad that we would still be where we were seventy-one years ago—too many mouths, too little food, and no one had enough. There was no clean water. The currency was useless, and everyone had to fend for themselves. Do you understand what kind of chaos that brings?"

I knew what kind of chaos this government brought, and that was enough for me.

"We needed a way to help average out the country," said Daxton once it was clear I wasn't going to answer. "Yes, there are winners and losers. Yes, it is difficult for those who are at the bottom of the heap and those who lose loved ones to Elsewhere. But our society must make those sacrifices in order to survive."

"Like the Harts make sacrifices?" I muttered.

"Someone must rule, and it is imperative that those who do know the ins and outs of the country. America has thrived under my family's reign. This world exists because my grandfather had the courage to step up and give everything he had to fixing this country. Now, because of him, we have a controlled population whose value is decided through identical measurements, and they are given resources to equal their worth. Everyone contributes what they can. As a III, you could never hope to do the work of a VI."

"But I can be a VII."

"Yes, because VII is inherited, not earned." He patted me on the knee, and I jerked away.

"Don't touch me."

Daxton leaned in close enough for me to smell the faint trace of whiskey on his breath. "Like it or not, this is how it's been for decades, and this is how it's going to stay. Everyone gets what they deserve based on what they're worth, and if they do anything to take away from our society, they pay the price. The elderly can no longer do the jobs the young people can do, so they go. The criminals choose to take that risk, and when they're caught, it's usually not their first offense anyway. And the Is—" He shook his head. "Useless, drooling idiots, the lot of them. Some of them show signs of worth, and they're kept in special facilities until we can determine that. But the vast majority do nothing but eat, sleep, and use up resources they do not earn. They have no place within society."

"So you kill them." It wasn't a question. "Not even humanely, but as entertainment."

He shrugged. "Occasionally, if they're still alive after we harvest their organs."

Sickened, I stood. Before I could storm off, however, Daxton grabbed my arm and held me in place. Remembering Celia's words, I didn't struggle. As much as I wanted to kill him for what he'd done to Nina, the price was my life, and she wouldn't have wanted me to die because of her.

"Let's get something straight," he said in a low voice that slithered through me, chilling me to the bone. "You might have a VII on the back of your neck, but it only entitles you to the privileges that come with it as long as I say so. You aren't here to change the world, Kitty. You're here to do what I tell you. Don't mistake your face with who you really are and what you're worth to society. You are just as replaceable as Lila."

"You think I don't get that?" I said. "I know you own me. You didn't need to kill Nina to prove it."

His grip tightened, and I hissed in pain. "Do you know how we found you at that filthy club?" His eyes glittered with malevolence, and every trace of his usual charming facade was gone. "We looked you up, Kitty Doe. We tracked you down. We went to your group home, and your matron lied for you. Now she's paid the price, and you only have yourself to blame."

I blinked back tears, refusing to give him the satisfaction of making me cry.

"Luckily we did manage to find someone who knew where you were going," said Daxton. "Benjamin Doe."

All the blood drained from my face, and my knees buckled. "What did you do to him?"

His lips twisted into a calculating smile. "I see I've hit a nerve. How fascinating."

"Tell me what you did to him, or I'll throw you out of this jet."

He chuckled. "I would love to see you try. We've done nothing to him yet. He shows quite a bit of promise, and we are of course keeping an eye on him, but he's safe for the time being. You have my word that as long as you behave, he will live a long and happy life."

So that was it. As sure as I'd been that they couldn't possibly have known about Benjy, they knew anyway, and now his life was directly attached to how well I could sit, stay, and roll over.

There was nothing Daxton could possibly do that could ever make me hurt Benjy. Even if it meant putting up with this and staying silent about the things Lila had the courage to fight, Daxton had me, and he knew it.

When the jet landed and the pilot welcomed us back to the District of Columbia, I was so worn down and weary that I allowed Daxton to take my arm and lead me down the steps. Just like every other decent thing Daxton did, I knew it was only to show a waiting Celia that he had me, and her expression hardened as we walked toward the cars.

"Have a nice hunt?" she said. Daxton released me, and Celia wrapped her arm protectively around my shoulders.

"Lovely," said Daxton as a guard opened the door for him. "I'm afraid all the excitement seems to have worn Lila out, though, so as soon as we get back to Somerset, you may want to put the poor dear to bed."

"I'll make sure to do that," said Celia coldly. After Daxton got into the first car, Celia ushered me into the second, where Knox was waiting. I said nothing until the door was closed and we were driving away.

"Why didn't you warn me?"

Celia fixed a drink from some sort of icebox in the side of the car, and she thrust the cold glass into my hand. "Because you needed to see it for yourself. Drink."

"He killed Nina," I said. "She was practically my mother."

"I'm sorry," said Celia. "Truly. But there's nothing we can do about that now, and you need to calm down. You're shaking. Please, drink."

No, but there was something she could've done about it that morning. I took a sip and nearly spat the burning liquid out. "That's disgusting."

"It's brandy," she said. "It'll help calm your nerves."

I wrinkled my nose and set the drink aside. "What I need is a damn phone."

"Don't say *damn,*" she said, and Knox wordlessly fished something out of his pocket and offered it to me.

"What is that?" I said, taking it warily. It was a piece of glass roughly the size of my little finger, and it was so thin that I was afraid I would snap it in two.

"A phone," he said. "Touch the screen."

I brushed my fingertip against the surface. It lit up with blue symbols, and there were so many that I didn't know which to press first. "How do I dial?"

Celia snatched it from me. "Who are you calling?"

"None of your damn business," I said. She narrowed her eyes.

"I'm not trying to stop you. Tell me the number and I'll dial it for you, but first I want to know who you're calling."

"A friend," I snapped. "To make sure he's still alive. Is that all right with you?"

Knox grabbed his phone. "Both of you, stop it. Kitty, what's the number?"

I rattled off the number of the group home, and he dialed and pushed a button so I could hear it. Instead of ringing, however, the line clicked, and a cheerful voice spoke. "We're sorry, but the number you have dialed is no longer in service."

Knox pressed another button, and the blue light went dark. "Are you sure that's the right number?"

"Positive," I said numbly. "I've known it forever. Can you—can you try again?"

I repeated the number slowly, but the same message played. My chest tightened as if someone were squeezing a fist around my heart. "I don't understand. It was working before."

"Any number of things could have happened," said Knox. "Nina was the matron of your group home, right? They probably shut it down after she was arrested and sent the kids somewhere else."

"They wouldn't hurt him, would they?" I said. "He's not even seventeen yet."

Celia sat across from us, her legs crossed and her foot bobbing up and down as she studied me. "What did Daxton say to you?"

"Does it matter?" Knowing Daxton, Benjy was probably already dead.

"It matters a great deal," she said. "If there's something I can do to help you, I will."

"You've done a great job so far, seeing as how I'm stuck in this situation to begin with."

"You're the one who agreed to this mess, Kitty, not me,

and whining about it isn't going to change a thing. You've been given an incredible opportunity, and if you waste it by letting Daxton blackmail you into being his puppet, I will kill you myself. So tell me," she said. "What did he say to you?"

I turned away and rested my forehead against the cool window. It was tinted so that no one outside could see us, but I could see everything through the waning light of dusk. We drove through a part of the city I'd never been to before. Shining glass buildings rose high above us, and everything looked brand-new. Even the streetlamps were so bright that I had to squint. The wealth in this section, undoubtedly meant for Vs and VIs, was obvious. The buildings in the Heights were squat, made of brick, and older than any citizen who occupied them. There was no newness, only old that was no longer needed and could be handed down to us, the people who weren't valuable enough to merit glass skyscrapers or shiny cars or fruit that wasn't hours away from rotting.

Benjy would have loved this. And if Celia could help make sure he lived long enough to see it, then I had no choice but to tell her.

"I have a boyfriend," I said at last. "Had a boyfriend, I guess. Daxton said he'd send him Elsewhere if I didn't cooperate."

Beside me, I heard Knox exhale, and when he tried to set his hand on my shoulder, I shrugged it off. "What's his name?" he said.

"Benjamin Doe," I said hollowly. "Everyone calls him Benjy."

Celia pulled out another electronic device I didn't recognize and pushed a few buttons. "I'll make sure nothing happens to him. Daxton thinks he has all of us cornered, but he overestimates his own power."

And I was sure Celia overestimated hers. "How?" I said bitterly. "Are you going to have him followed? Assign him personal protection?"

"Something like that."

Knox fixed another drink and offered it to me. "It's just water," he said, and reluctantly I took it from him and sipped. I hadn't had anything to eat or drink since breakfast. "How did you meet Benjy?"

When Knox said his name, I gulped down the contents of the glass to buy myself a few moments. The idea of sharing Benjy with them made my skin crawl. No matter how much Celia and Knox pretended to care about me, it was clear they were using me as much as Daxton was. The only question was for what.

"We grew up in the same group home," I said, staring at my drink. "We played together sometimes, and when we were seven, he did my writing homework for me without being asked—"

I stopped. They didn't care, or if they did, it was only to use him against me. Instead of moving on, however, Knox shifted so he was facing me. When I glanced at him, I saw real interest in his eyes. Something about him was less intimidating than Celia, so as he silently encouraged me to go on, I focused on him and tried to forget that she was listening, as well.

"He knew I was struggling in class, and the teacher liked to pick on me." It had seemed like such a big deal at the time, what Benjy had done for me, but he would have done the same thing for anyone else. He was that kind of person—the same kind who offered to run away with me and destroy the rest of his life so mine might be easier. "So he started doing my homework for me. He read to me every night, and eventually we just..." I shrugged.

Knox smiled faintly. "It sounds like you have a good friend in him."

"He probably thinks I'm in Denver by now," I mumbled.

"I doubt that," said Celia, and Knox gave her a murderous look. "What?" she added. "She has a right to know."

"A right to know what?" I said, and when they seemed too busy glaring at each other to answer me, I raised my voice. "A right to know *what?*"

Knox looked away, clutching his glass so tightly that I thought it would shatter. "Kitty Doe was legally declared dead the day after you arrived at the Stronghold."

I opened and shut my mouth, but there was nothing to say. Benjy thought I was dead. First Tabs, then Nina, then me—it wasn't just my life I'd destroyed. It was his, too. The pain and worry I'd felt for him had to be nothing compared to what he was going through. Did he blame himself? After telling the Shields where I'd gone, he must have. But it wasn't his fault. I was the one who'd done this to him. Not the Shields, not Daxton, but me.

"What's the date?" I said suddenly.

"The twentieth of October," said Celia. "Why?"

I didn't answer. Benjy's birthday was the twenty-second, which meant I had two days until he took his test.

"Kitty—" said Knox, but I shook my head.

"Don't," I said softly. "Please."

Two days. I had two days to find him until he would be gone forever, and I would never have the chance to tell him that it wasn't his fault.

I spent the rest of the drive to Somerset in silence, staring out the window. Everything here was *more* than I had ever seen before. There were television screens everywhere: in shop windows, mounted on the sides of buildings, even scrolls that ran around intersections broadcasting words I couldn't read. Instead of sidewalks, this section of the city had motorized walkways, and even though it was nearly nightfall, the rich and the powerful stood still as the walkways carried them wherever they wanted to go. How could a world like this exist so close to the Heights?

The car glided through a gate in a brick wall covered with ivy, and the world outside transformed into a lush green lawn that seemed to go on forever. I sat up straighter. A row of trees bordered the drive, their leaves brilliant shades of gold and ruby, and in the distance I noticed the edge of a looming mansion.

"We're almost here," said Celia. "So answer me this, Kitty—are you all right with what you've seen today? Do you think it's acceptable for people to be treated no better than game?"

Still stinging from the news that Benjy thought I was dead, I glared at her. "Of course not. What do you think I am, a monster?"

"No," said Knox. "If we thought you would go along with Daxton and Augusta, we wouldn't be talking to you now. But you have spunk, Kitty, and there's so much good you could do now that you have Lila's face. Things even Lila wasn't able to do."

Spunk. Daxton had said the very same thing to me. I pressed myself against the door, ready to spring free. I knew what was coming, and the car began to feel like a cage.

"You saw the speeches my daughter made," said Celia. "She was starting a revolution right under Daxton's nose."

"And that's how she wound up dead in the first place," I said. "I'm not your puppet. I won't dance because you tell me to."

For a moment I thought I saw a flash of guilt cross her face, but it was gone as quickly as it'd come. "No, I suppose you won't," said Celia. "Whose puppet are you, Kitty? Daxton's and my mother's? Because from where I'm sitting, that's exactly what it's beginning to look like."

"I'm not—" I began, but she cut me off.

"What do you intend to do with your life? With my daughter's life? Will you waste it doing their bidding?"

"What, when I could be doing yours?"

Her expression hardened, but before she could say anything, Knox held up a hand. "We know you didn't ask for this, but no matter how unfair it is, that's the way your life is going to go from here on out. You have a choice. You can let Daxton control you and tell you what to do, you can rebel and get yourself killed, or you can listen to us and do something worthwhile. Something other than just be Lila's replacement."

He said that like it was easy, like there were no consequences, but each choice had a price I would have to pay one way or the other.

Knox leaned toward me, and the leather squeaked underneath him. "They gave you a III because they thought you would never amount to anything more. Are you going to prove them right?"

I scowled. I wasn't a coward. I wasn't afraid of dying. I didn't want to, but I wasn't afraid of it. What I was afraid of was getting Benjy killed, and that fear was paralyzing.

Celia must have sensed my hesitation, because she said, "If it's your friend you're worried about, you have my word that he will be protected."

"The same way you protected Lila?" I said, but there was no venom in my voice.

She flinched anyway, and Knox quickly cut in. "What happened to Lila was terrible, and it's a mistake we won't make again."

I swallowed. Celia wouldn't meet my eyes, and I couldn't blame her. "You're asking me to trust you when I don't even know you."

"No, you don't," said Knox. "But you do know Daxton

and what he's capable of. You have my word—*our* word that no matter what you decide and no matter what happens to you, we will protect your friend to the best of our ability." He glanced at Celia, and she nodded wearily. "Even if you decide to play it safe and do what Daxton wants, we won't let anything happen to Benjy."

I covered my face with my hands and took a deep breath. There was no way for me to know if they were lying or not, and either way, I'd be pissing someone off. I wanted to believe that Knox and Celia would protect Benjy, but Celia had let her daughter die. She couldn't guarantee Benjy his safety any more than she could guarantee me mine.

I might have lost my identity, but this was still my life, and the thought of taking orders from Daxton until he decided I was better off dead made me sick to my stomach. He'd killed Nina to show me what would happen if I didn't behave. He'd threatened Benjy. Once he was dead, what would Daxton do to control me? Find my real parents and kill them, too?

With Daxton, the bloodshed would never end. With Celia and Knox, I could at least pretend that not everyone I loved would die for my mistakes.

The image of Nina's blood spattered against the tree flashed in my mind, and I dug my nails into my palms. Daxton had had me until that morning. I would've done anything he wanted as long as it bought me time and kept me alive, and he'd known it. He'd killed Nina not to control me, but to lord over me—to prove how much power he had and how little I possessed. And now Celia and Knox were offering me a way to get some of my own. It might not have been much, but if Daxton wanted a pissing contest, then that was exactly what I would give him.

"All right," I said. "I'll do it as long as you keep Benjy safe. But you have to be honest with me, too. No keeping things from me, no bossing me around, and don't treat me like I'm stupid, all right?"

Celia nodded, and Knox moved to pat my shoulder again. This time I let him. "You've got yourself a deal," he said.

Except as we drove down the winding drive, I was all too aware that there was only one way this could end, and it wouldn't be with Celia or Knox taking the fall for me.

VIII

SOMERSET

As a III, I would have never been allowed to set foot into Somerset. While thousands of people were crammed within the borders of the Heights, Somerset was equally as large and catered solely to the Harts. The only way for anyone else to get inside was to work there or be invited by a member of the family. The armed guards that patrolled the gates made sure of it.

As we drove up to the mansion, I tried not to gawk, but it was impossible. Standing five stories high, the outside was painted a shimmering white that reflected the deep hues of the sunset. A massive glass wall offered a glimpse into the luxurious atrium, and I craned my neck to get a better look.

"Is this for real?" I stepped out of the car, and the gravel drive crunched beneath my boots. "This is a house?"

"This is home," said Celia, looping her arm in mine. Two guards opened the double doors for us, and we stepped inside, Knox trailing behind us.

The entrance hall gleamed with brilliant whites and silvers, crystal and glass, and there was even an elevator that rose through the atrium. Off to the side I spotted a sitting room, richly decorated in blue and gold, and in the opposite direction I saw a door that led into a magnificent dining room.

Unlike the one in the Stronghold, it could easily have held fifty or more.

As Celia led me to the elevator, I noticed paintings of people I didn't recognize. Their eyes seemed to follow us, and a shiver ran through me. Despite my success in convincing the people in Elsewhere that I was Lila, now that I was in her home, I was no longer confident. Something as simple as putting my shoes in the wrong place could give me away.

"Welcome home, Lila," said a voice above us. Daxton leaned against the railing two stories up. "I've already checked with the staff, and they assure me your suite has been aired out and prepared for your arrival. Mother has scheduled you for a luncheon tomorrow for the grand opening of St. George Hospital. Celia, if you will, Mother requests you accompany her."

"Of course," said Celia. "Knox will be staying with us for the foreseeable future, so if you would also tell the staff to prepare his room, I would be much obliged."

"Already done," said Daxton. "On that note, that little problem we discussed earlier, Lila—Knox will help you with it."

I gave Knox a puzzled look, and he bent down to whisper in my ear, "He wants me to teach you to read."

"Oh." How had he found out so quickly? I shoved my hands in my pockets and nodded up toward Daxton. Good luck with that one.

Lila's rooms were on the fourth floor, across from Celia's. Along with a guest room Knox would be using, they took up an entire wing of the mansion. Lila's suite alone included a sitting room, two bedrooms, two bathrooms, a kitchen nook, and worst of all, a door that led into an empty room.

"Your future nursery," said Celia. "For after you're married."

I made a face. Terrific.

Everything from her bedspread to the sofa to the rug laid out in front of a gigantic fireplace was made of white furs—fake, Celia informed me, but I couldn't tell the difference. I took my boots off, and the hardwood floor was cool against my bare feet. The windows were wide and faced the sunset, and in the distance I could see the buildings that made up the wealthy downtown area.

The bathrooms were decorated with swirling marble floors and counters, and they were full of soaps that smelled like flowers and fruits and things I couldn't name. I explored the suite under the guise of making sure everything was in place, and once I was done, I collapsed on the sofa and ran my hand over the fur.

"Get some rest," said Celia, standing in the doorway. Knox lurked behind her. "I'll be down the hall if you need me."

With one final warning look, Celia shooed the servants away and closed the door behind her, leaving me alone in Lila's suite.

No matter how lavish it was, I was standing in the middle of my prison cell. I'd noticed locks on the door coming in, and the only window that opened was the small one in the bathroom. Even if I could squeeze through it, I was several stories up, and dropping from that height would mean broken bones at the very least, if not a painful death.

Looking up at the ceiling, I noticed the opening to a vent in the corner. It wasn't very big, but with some squirming, I might fit. I pushed an end table underneath it and climbed. Using the bookcase beside it as another step, I managed to move the grate aside and get a good grip.

My muscles strained as I pulled myself up and tried not to tip the bookcase over. Finally I made it into the vent, which was made of plastic and surprisingly clean. More important, it extended past Lila's suite in either direction.

It was a tight squeeze, but no different from shimmying through sewer openings. Easier, even, because unlike the concrete, which rubbed and cut my skin, the plastic didn't hurt. The vent extended in front of me with no visible end, though that wasn't saying much considering the only light came from the grates. With effort I wriggled through it until I reached the next one, and I peered through the thin slits.

Directly below me, Knox sat at a desk, hunched over a folder full of documents. Relief washed over me. At least now I had a way out if I needed one.

I started to slide back to Lila's suite, but a faint knock stopped me cold. "Come in," said Knox, and his door opened and shut. He stood and removed his reading glasses, and I strained to see who was there.

"Knox. So good to see you."

I cringed. Daxton.

"Sir. I hear your hunting trip was successful."

"Ah, so she told you, did she?" I could hear the smugness in Daxton's voice. "What else did she say?"

Knox cleared his throat, and I tensed. He wouldn't tell Daxton about my deal with Celia, would he? He couldn't. He'd be incriminating himself, too.

"She's upset with you, and with good reason," said Knox, a hint of annoyance in his voice. "You had her already, Daxton. You didn't have to kill that woman."

"I know," he said with a dramatic sigh. "But it was so much *fun,* and there's nothing quite like a bullet to make my point for me, now, is there?"

"There were subtler ways," said Knox. "You're better than that."

"If you insist. Do let me know if there's anything to report, will you?"

"Don't expect much. She's scared to blink the wrong way, let alone disobey you."

"Good," he said. "Peaceful and controlled, just the way I like it." I heard his footsteps as he walked to the door, but before it opened, he paused. "No hard feelings about what happened to Lila, yes? It was a shame, but I tried to warn her. She knew the dangers of what she was doing. So did Celia."

Knox was silent for a long moment. "Nothing's changed," he finally said. "Thank you for allowing my father to tell me ahead of time."

"Of course," said Daxton. "You're a good man, Knox. You deserved the chance to say goodbye." He paused. "Don't forget, poker next Thursday."

Knox nodded, and after the door opened and shut, he sank into his chair and buried his face in his hands.

He'd known. He'd known Lila was going to die, and he hadn't done a damn thing to stop it. Had their entire relationship been for show? Had he been using Lila as much as Daxton was using him?

I shimmied back through the vent. He hadn't snitched on me. That was the important part. And Lila— I forced myself to take a mental step back. What could he have done? Lila had one of the most famous faces in the country. Hiding her would have been impossible, and warning her would undoubtedly have cost him his life. Maybe he had tried anyway. Maybe he'd failed. I had no way of knowing what had really happened.

After returning to Lila's suite, I used one of the pokers next to the fire to move the grate back to its proper position. Once I was done, I pushed the end table back into place and surveyed the corner. Even if someone noticed something was different, they would probably assume I'd done some redecorating, that was all.

Spreading out on the sofa, I shut my eyes. This was as hellish as I'd thought it would be, but at least now I knew who my real friends were. Daxton could try to secure my cooperation by threatening me and giving me things I would have never had as a III, but I would never trust him. Knox had lied for me. I didn't have to know what had happened to Lila to feel confident that he wouldn't let it happen to me.

He'd said he wouldn't make the same mistake twice. Now I understood what he'd meant.

A loud pounding on the door shook me from my fading dreams. I was still spread out on the sofa with my head at a strange angle, giving me a crick in my neck. I rubbed it, and my hand brushed the three telltale ridges. I sat up.

"Who is it?" I said. It was dark now, and all that remained of the fire were glowing embers.

The door burst open, and half a dozen guards entered my suite. I stood, adrenaline chasing away all traces of exhaustion. Were they here for me? Had I done something wrong? Had Daxton somehow found out about my deal with Celia?

"You have to come with us, Miss Hart," said one of the guards. "It's urgent."

I nodded and swallowed the lump in my throat. Silently I followed them out of the room, and it was only when I saw Knox being led out of his that I let myself breathe again. So it wasn't just me.

Unless they'd discovered Knox had lied.

"What's going on?" I said as the guards surrounded us. My face grew hot when I noticed he was wearing pajama bottoms and not much else, but being half-naked didn't seem to bother him.

"I don't know," he said, his brow furrowed. "Did you hear the rumbling earlier?"

I shook my head. I could sleep through practically anything after sharing a room with nineteen other girls my entire life.

Celia soon joined us, but she had no more of an idea of what was going on than we did. The guards led us down to the basement and through a maze of hallways I mapped out mentally. The one who had spoken, a man dressed in a black-and-silver uniform, stopped in front of a metal door and punched in a long series of symbols. The screen turned green and the lock clicked, and he pushed it open. So we were being arrested after all.

The door was at least two feet thick, and on the other side was a screen to unlock it from the inside. Without the password, however, it would be impossible to escape. It had no windows, and unlike the rooms I'd seen earlier, it was practically bare in comparison. Only a few couches and chairs were scattered throughout, with a kitchenette and what looked like a small bathroom in opposite corners, and cabinets that went from floor to ceiling lined the walls. I subtly searched for a vent, but I didn't spot anything big enough to be useful.

"The safe room," said Knox in a low voice as we were ushered inside. "This place could withstand a nuclear attack. Wouldn't recommend trying to break in. Or out, for that matter. Three tries and you'd alert half the city."

I had no idea what a nuclear attack was, but I didn't doubt him. The room was impenetrable. I sat stiffly on the edge of the sofa, and Knox and Celia took a seat nearby. As we waited, I closed my eyes and counted the seconds in an attempt to calm myself down, but it didn't stop my pulse from racing.

Finally Daxton joined us. Instead of telling us anything, he sat down next to me, so close I could smell his soap. Greyson, Daxton's son, trailed behind him, his shoulders slumped and a book tucked underneath his arm. He was tall and blond and reminded me of Benjy, but I pushed that thought aside. It hurt too much to think about him right now.

Greyson ignored the rest of us and sat as far away from the group as he could. Even though he was eighteen, he looked younger with his furrowed brow and guarded eyes. I thought I spotted him staring at me, but when I looked at him, he was focused on his book.

The last to join us was Augusta, wearing a silk dressing gown and a scowl. Daxton stood when his mother entered, and she gestured for him to sit back down.

"There has been an attack," she said, her voice steady. "In what looks to be a coordinated effort, seventeen government buildings have been bombed in various cities across the country, including three in the District of Columbia. Two of our ministries were targeted directly. So far we have no numbers on casualties, but because of the late hour, they are not expected to be more than a hundred or so."

I clasped my hands together, stunned. Across from me, Celia paled. "Has anyone taken credit?" she said.

Augusta pursed her lips. "The Blackcoats."

Beside me, Daxton scoffed. "Impossible. My advisers insist they don't have the manpower or the resources."

"Obviously they do," snapped Celia. Augusta gave her a look I didn't understand, but Celia kept her glare on Daxton.

"How?" he said. "None of the terrorists we've dealt with before had the capability or the means to pull off something like this. It takes resources that the lower ranks don't have."

"Clearly you must have pissed off the wrong people this time," she said.

"Enough." Augusta sat beside Greyson and smoothed the wrinkles of her dressing gown. Instead of moving away from her, like I expected, Greyson leaned against her, and she rubbed his back. "They are demanding you step aside as prime minister and allow real elections. Abolish the rank system. Allow the elderly and helpless to remain in society. The same absurdities as last time."

I chanced a look at Celia, but her expression was as blank as ever. Those were the things that Lila had talked about in her speeches.

"I'll have the Shields on it in the morning," said Daxton. "It should be easy enough to track them down and squash all of this nonsense."

Greyson sighed. "So why do we have to stay in the safe room? It's not like they can get past the guards."

"Caution, my dear," said Augusta. "It would do us no good to purposely ignore the threat. Besides, if something happened to you, we would have no heir."

"You'd have Lila," he said. Apparently no one had bothered to tell him after all.

I watched him openly now, able to see in person similarities to the other Harts that weren't evident in pictures or film. The way the corners of his mouth turned downward when he wasn't talking. The way his forehead furrowed to make him look much more serious than his voice let on. He was definitely his father's son, but there was a glint in his eyes that Daxton didn't have, an intelligence that seemed to take in everything. Including the fact that I was staring.

I looked down at my hands, but it was too late. He'd already noticed.

"Perhaps," said Augusta with a sniff. "However, you are my only remaining grandson, and I will not compromise your safety so you can waste the night tinkering with your toys."

"They're not toys," he said, sitting up straighter now and shifting away from her. "They're inventions, and they work. If you'd just come to my workshop for a few minutes and look—"

She raised her hand, and even though his anger was palpable, he fell silent, as if he'd expected her to cut him off. A father like Daxton and a grandmother like Augusta. At least I'd had Nina.

"I'd like to see your new inventions sometime, if you'll let me," said Celia warmly. "You must have come up with some interesting things in the past few weeks."

"It's been a while for me," said Knox. "Lila, too."

The way Knox looked at me made it clear I was expected to chime in. "Right," I said, clearing my throat. "I'd like to see them, too." I couldn't imagine what Greyson could have invented that didn't already exist, but that was why he was the one making things and I wasn't.

Greyson bit his lip. "Yeah, all right. If they ever let us out of here."

"Patience," said Augusta. "It will do you a world of good."

"Maybe so, but I still say we don't get out of here until morning."

Unfortunately Greyson was right. I managed a few restless hours of dozing, curled up in an uncomfortable position with Daxton snoring next to me, but as the night wore on, he inched closer and closer. When he threw his arm across my chest and settled his head on my shoulder, I gave up hope of getting any sleep.

It was nearly dawn by the time we were escorted back to our rooms with a stern warning from Augusta that none of us were to leave Somerset. My time to find Benjy before his seventeenth birthday was dwindling, and without a way out, I would have no chance at all.

Exhausted, I followed Knox and the guards up to the fourth floor, but it wasn't until we'd reached Knox's room that I tried to work up the courage to speak. Instead of heading toward Lila's suite, I stood in front of him with my arms folded and the weight of a sleepless night on my shoulders. How was I supposed to say this in front of the guards?

Knox picked up on my uncertainty and gestured for them to leave us. Once they were gone, he held open his door for me, and I shook my head. I wasn't going anywhere private with him.

"Who are the Blackcoats?" I said softly. Knox leaned down to answer, and his lips brushed against my ear.

"The people who bombed the ministries last night," he said. "Why are we whispering?"

He was determined to make this difficult, and I was too tired to play games. "Was—I—involved with them?"

Knox straightened, his eyes narrowing as he studied me. "Why do you ask?"

"Because they wanted the same things I talked about."

Several seconds passed, and I dug my toes into the carpet, wondering if I should walk away now before he lied and told me no. It was too much of a coincidence: Lila dying, me replacing her, the bombings—they had to be connected.

"Those are the same things every rebellion has been about for the past seventy-one years," said Knox at last. "Groups have tried again and again to take down the Harts, but you've seen how well that worked out."

"Except when Daxton's wife and son died," I blurted, remembering the conversation I'd had with Nina the day I'd received my III. She hadn't outright told me they'd been killed by rebels, but she might as well have.

Knox paused, his gaze unfocused. "Jameson and Yvonne died in a car accident. There was no rebel involvement."

"Are you sure?" I said.

"Positive. This is the first time the Blackcoats have done any sort of real damage, which is exactly why Augusta's spooked."

Maybe Nina had been wrong after all, but the way he hesitated only confused me more. "I've heard rumors—"

"Rumors are rumors because no one can back them up," he said shortly. "I've explained what happened. If you're going to push it, I'm not sticking around."

"You don't want to talk about them, fine," I said. "I get it. I've lost people, too. But you *will* answer my question."

"I already told you—"

"Not that one. The one before. Was I or was I not involved with the Blackcoats?"

Knox eyed me for a long moment, as if deciding whether or not I was worth the truth. "She got involved in that sort of thing about a year ago, and despite what Daxton wants you to think, she didn't trust me. I don't think she trusted anyone, not even her mother. The first time I heard the speeches was when I saw them with you."

I studied him, searching for any signs that he was lying. His expression was maddeningly blank. "Okay. Thanks," I said. If I let him know I suspected him, he would only try that much harder to hide the truth.

"You're welcome." Knox started to enter his room, and I hesitated in the doorway, another question on the tip of my tongue. He stopped, his eyebrows raised. "Was there something else?"

I cleared my throat. "Have you ever been Elsewhere?"

Something changed in his expression, something so tiny that it was gone before I could figure out what it was. "Yes. My father and I take a semiannual trip together. He considers it a bonding experience."

Bonding over hunting innocent people. What could possibly bring a father and son closer together? And the way he said it, as if it were no big deal—as if all the fathers and sons in the ruling class did it. For all I knew, they did.

"Okay." I turned away and headed down the hall, and when I heard footsteps behind me, I stopped.

"Lila," he said, and I refused to look at him. It wasn't his fault, but I was getting really, really sick of everyone calling me Lila. "I'm heading out to a club around ten tonight. Nothing fancy, but I figured you might get a kick out of it. Some of our friends will be there, and I'm sure they'd like to see you."

Friends. Of course Lila had friends, and that would only mean more lying and desperate attempts to get my story straight. The last thing I wanted to do was to see more people who knew Lila well enough to be able to tell the difference between us.

However, it was exactly the opening I needed. A chance to leave this place and find Benjy before it was too late.

"Aren't we on lockdown?" I said.

Knox shrugged. "That's never stopped us before."

If the clubs Lila frequented were anything like the one where Daxton had found me, it would be crowded. That would give me a chance to break away and find Benjy, though if the club was close to Somerset, it would take a while to get back to the Heights.

It didn't matter. Even if I had to walk there in heels, I would do it.

"All right. I'll go," I said.

"Knew you'd come around," said Knox with a wink. "See you at ten o'clock."

Once I was inside my suite, I leaned against the closed door and took a deep, shaky breath. I had less than fifteen hours to not only come up with a way to find Benjy, but also to figure out how I was going to convince him that underneath Lila's face, clothes, and VII, I was really Kitty Doe, and I wasn't nearly as dead as I was supposed to be.

IX

KEY

The more I thought about it, the more impossible my plan felt. With my real face, it would have been easy to slip away and get lost in a crowd, but with Lila's, all eyes would be on me. If by some miracle I did get away, someone else would surely spot me—and once I reached the Heights, I would stick out like a sore thumb. A VII had never had a reason to set foot in our run-down suburb before.

Even if I did make it to Benjy, what would happen after that? There were a million things only the two of us knew that would prove who I was, but where could I take him to guarantee Daxton wouldn't get his hands on him?

I didn't sleep well that morning, tossing and turning in the massive bed that could easily have held five people. Eventually I gave up and dragged myself into the sitting room, where I collapsed onto the sofa in a cocoon of white fur. I picked at the lunch tray the servants brought and tried to think of someplace within the city where Benjy would be safe, but nothing came to mind. The odds were stacked a mile high against us. Then again, they usually were, and that had never stopped me before.

A knock on my door made me jump. Knox wasn't due for

hours, and I scrambled off the sofa and padded over, half expecting him to be waiting with a change of plans.

Instead, Greyson stood outside my suite. His shoulders were hunched and his hands shoved into his pockets, and when he looked at me, the coldness in his eyes made me shiver.

"You didn't come see me."

I frowned, wary of the accusation in his voice. "You didn't come see me, either," I said, silently willing Celia or Knox to appear.

Resignation passed over Greyson's face. "You said you'd come see my inventions, and you didn't."

Right. I shrugged, not sure what Lila would've said or done. No one had told me if she got along with Greyson. "I can come see them now, if you'd like."

"Don't bother." At first I thought he was going to leave, but then he pulled something out of his pocket and thrust it toward me. "I made this for you while you were gone."

I took the necklace. From a distance it looked like a simple silver disk dangling from a chain, but when I examined it, I could see tiny grooves running through it like a labyrinth, breaking it into sections.

"It's beautiful," I said. "Thank you."

Greyson ducked his head, but not before I spotted the hint of a smile. "It's not just a necklace, you know." With nimble fingers he pulled a section of the disk apart, and it unfolded into an instrument I instantly recognized.

"A lock pick?" It put the crude ones Benjy and I made out of paper clips and hairpins to shame.

Greyson nodded. "There are three different ones in there that'll open any lock, and if you put it together and pass it over an electronic security device, it'll open any of those, too. Before you left..." He hesitated. "When you said you felt trapped,

I thought maybe this would help. So no one can make you stay if you don't want to."

He handed the necklace back to me, and I stared at it, speechless. I wanted to tell him that no one had ever given me this kind of gift before, but this wasn't for me. It was for Lila.

It wasn't fair for Greyson to go on thinking that I was his cousin when I wasn't. He and Lila must have been close if he'd made her something like this, and it would only be a matter of time before he found out I wasn't her.

"Greyson," I said, brushing my fingers against the disk. It was warm against my skin, probably from his pocket. Or maybe he'd clutched it all the way here, worried I wouldn't like it. That Lila wouldn't like it. "I need to tell you something."

"There you are."

Augusta's voice stole the confession from my tongue. She set her hand on Greyson's shoulder, but her icy gaze was focused on me.

"I've been looking all over for you, Greyson. Your father wants to see you in his study. Just because we are working from home today does not mean you can skip your lessons."

Greyson made a face. "I decided to take the day off. Someone else can learn how to run the country for once. Like Lila."

Augusta's grip on his shoulder tightened, and she steered him away from me and toward the atrium. "Lila has her own duties to attend to. Besides, she is not the one who will take over for your father."

He twisted around to look at me, and I forced a sympathetic smile. Lila would probably have felt sorry for him, but all I could imagine was Greyson on one of the floating platforms in Elsewhere, cackling as he shot into a sea of innocent faces.

I clutched his gift and pushed the image out of my mind. Just because Daxton was all right with hunting his own people didn't mean Greyson was, and I refused to think that anyone capable of creating such a beautiful gift could be evil. Not until he proved me wrong. In the meantime, I had to tell him who I really was before something I did gave it away. I was short on friends here as it was. The last thing I wanted was to lose any trust he might otherwise have been willing to offer.

I studied the necklace for a moment, and when I looked up, Augusta stood in front of me. Greyson was gone.

"Do not talk to my grandson," she said. "If he initiates a conversation, you will make up an excuse and walk away, do you understand?"

"He knocked on my door. What was I supposed to do, slam it in his face?"

"Yes," she said. "Greyson must not know about this. If you tell him, I will not hesitate to make arrangements for you and your little friend to be reunited Elsewhere."

My little friend. Benjy. "If you hurt him, I'll go straight to the media and tell the entire world what you and Daxton did."

"By all means, go ahead and try. Give me an excuse to have you executed for treason."

She took a step toward me. Even though she was close enough for me to see every line in her face, I refused to back away.

"You may think you have a modicum of control, but I have a dozen stories ready to explain away your presence here. Even if you do live long enough to talk to the media, I control what news is presented to my people, and I assure you, your words will die before anyone else hears them." She touched my jaw, trailing her cold fingertip down to my chin. "You *will* stay away from my grandson. Understood?"

I shook my head. "He has a right to know his cousin's dead."

"He has the rights I decide to give him, as do you and everyone else in this country." She straightened, her stare never leaving mine. "Do not underestimate me, Kitty Doe, not even for a moment. Because if you do, I promise you will spend the rest of your short life regretting it."

Without another word, Augusta turned on her heel and walked away. Clenching my fists, I slammed the door and locked it, not caring if it was something Lila would have done. Whatever it took, I would find Benjy that night, and even if we had to leave the city, I would get him to safety. He'd been protecting me nearly all our lives, and now it was my turn to protect him.

Knox knocked on my door at exactly ten-thirty. When I opened it, he gave me a once-over and raised his eyebrows. "I thought we were going clubbing, not looting the place."

"You're wearing all black, too," I said, grabbing a leather jacket from the closet. I'd dressed in a pair of fitted black pants and a black silk tank top, and at the last minute, I'd crammed a matching hat in my pocket. If I tucked my hair up, no one would be able to see the telltale blond, and the silk scarf in my other pocket would cover the VII on the back of my neck. With any luck, I would have a chance of getting to the Heights without being spotted.

"So I am." He offered me his arm, and when I wrinkled my nose, he chuckled. "Let's go before someone sees us. Wouldn't want to get caught before we even leave the wing."

I trailed after him into the hallway, expecting to head to the atrium. Instead he opened the door to his suite, and I hesitated. No matter how much I trusted him relative to everyone else in Somerset, that didn't mean I wanted to see his bedroom.

"Don't give me that look," he said. "This is how we're getting out."

"I'm not afraid to knee you if I have to," I said as I ducked past him and entered his sitting room.

It was exactly like mine, except decorated in navy blue instead of white. The fireplace crackled, and it had a homey feel to it that my suite didn't. He led me down a short corridor, and I was so pleased his suite was half the size of mine that I almost didn't notice when he opened the closet door.

"In here," he said, and I snorted.

"I am not going in your closet."

He shrugged. "Suit yourself." He stepped inside and shut the door behind him, and I stood there stupidly, trying to decide what to do. I heard a rustle and a soft scraping sound on the other side, and with a huff, I yanked open the door.

He wasn't there. I squinted in the darkness, pushing the jackets aside, but all that was behind them was wall.

"Up here."

I jumped. Above me Knox leaned out of a hole in the ceiling with a flashlight in hand. The opening was too big to be the air vent I'd discovered the day before, and Knox dropped down a rope ladder.

"How did you find this?" I said as I hauled myself up. He reached down to help me, but I pushed his hands away.

"Someone else showed me," he said. "It doesn't see much use, but it'll get us out of Somerset."

I pulled myself up into the ceiling. It was an entire walkway, high enough for me to stand, and I spotted a railing a few feet away. "Are the other rooms connected, too?"

"Just this one," he said, covering the hole with what looked like a piece of ceiling. "C'mon, and keep quiet. If someone's on the other side of the walls, they could hear us."

The layer of dust on everything made my nose itch, but I held in my sneeze. Knox and his flashlight led the way, and we headed down a rickety staircase that creaked underneath my feet. It wasn't until we reached a heavy wooden door several levels below the basement that Knox spoke again.

"The tunnel goes on for about a mile underground, and when it ends, we'll be on the other side of the wall. Think you can manage it?"

I gave him a dirty look and snatched the flashlight from him. As I marched into the tunnel, which was dark and dank and smelled of earth, he chuckled.

There were no turns, so I didn't have to ask Knox for directions. Except for the shuffle of our footsteps, it was eerily silent, and I could hear him breathing behind me. Finally I couldn't take the quiet anymore, and I glanced over my shoulder to look at him.

"What are we going to do?" I said. "Hang around a club for hours and drink ourselves stupid?"

"Something like that. Don't you want to be surprised?"

"I hate surprises."

He smirked. "I don't blame you."

We walked along in silence for a few more seconds. "You said we're meeting friends," I said. "Shouldn't I at least know their names?"

"Lila didn't."

"But they were her friends."

"When you're as famous and powerful as Lila was, you have lots of friends," he said. "Don't worry about it. Lila hated them as much as you will."

I didn't ask. If all went well, I wouldn't have to spend more than a few minutes with them before I had the chance to slip away.

When we reached the other end of the tunnel, Knox took the flashlight back and led me up another old staircase. This time the door was made of metal, and though it looked rusted, the hinges must have been well oiled, because it didn't squeak when he opened it.

As soon as I stepped through the doorway, I understood why. We were in an alleyway somewhere beyond the walls of Somerset, less than ten yards away from a busy and brightly lit street. Knox pulled the door shut behind him, and this time he took my arm without asking. His flashlight was gone.

"Just act natural," he said, leading me to the street. Despite the late hour, there were people everywhere, laughing and chatting as they leaned against the moving walkways. When Knox and I stepped on, heads turned our way, and Knox's grip on my arm tightened.

The walkway made me feel like I was floating. There was a rail to hold on to, but Knox was sturdy, and I'd seen pictures of him and Lila out together. They were always arm in arm, so letting go of him wasn't an option even if I could've wriggled away. With any luck, he wouldn't be as strict about it in the club.

Above us, screens lit up with the same kind of news scrolls that appeared at the bottom of the television. The monitors secured on the sides of buildings loudly advertised different products for things that as a III I could never afford and as Lila I would never need, and I attempted to look as bored as possible. Lila had probably been down this street hundreds of times before.

We passed shop after shop, some with magnificent window displays showing off the latest in fashion or electronics, and others that belonged to the intimate cafés where only the rich could eat. They were the same kind of places I'd mocked before, knowing full well I would never be ranked high enough to get in. Now that I was Lila, every door was open to me.

Across the street stood the smoldering remains of a small building, the only reminder that this wasn't paradise. From the way it still smoked, I was sure it was one of the buildings that had been bombed the night before. Orange barriers blocked the walkway beside it, and at least a dozen Shields lined the perimeter, each holding a rifle.

Panic slithered through me. The Shields in the Heights were always on the lookout for someone to arrest or kill, and we avoided them at all costs. But here, everyone walked right on by as if they weren't even there. Was that what being a V and VI meant? Never having to fear the Shields?

"A testing center," said Knox, so close his breath tickled my skin. "The other two places were ministries."

"Which ones?"

"The Ministry of Ranking—my father's," he said. "And the Ministry of Wealth and Distribution. Neither of them were destroyed, but the bombs took out a nice chunk."

"Did it make any difference?" I said, and Knox shook his head.

When we stepped off the walkway, he led me down a side street. A line of people dressed in outrageously tight and colorful clothes wound around the corner, and as we passed, every eye was on us. I spotted a few more Shields in the distance and tensed, but Knox squeezed my hand, and I forced myself to relax. I wasn't a III anymore. They weren't going to arrest me just for breathing the wrong way.

The doorman lifted a velvet rope blocking the entrance to the club, and Knox ushered me inside a dark hallway. Deafening noise pulsated around us, and even the floor shook in time to the beat. There was no hope of conversation here.

At last the hallway opened up into a large room packed with people writhing to the music. Colored lights flashed green and blue, and half-dressed girls who couldn't have been much older than me danced ten feet in the air, suspended by wires or some magic trick I couldn't see. As Knox led me down a raised walkway that bridged the front of the club with the rear, everyone stared at us.

It was quieter in the back, which was cluttered with tables and couches, but I still had a hard time hearing. Our table was behind another velvet rope, guarded by a man nearly as big as the one at the door. By the time Knox and I sat down, a crowd had gathered, and Knox gestured for them to join us. Within seconds I was squished between Knox and a girl whose eyelids were covered in thick green glitter, and one by one, they leaned over to kiss me on the cheek. When they were done, the urge to wipe it with a napkin overcame me, but too many people were watching.

Talking wasn't necessary, since everyone seemed determined to do it for me. I was told about how much I'd been missed, how D.C. hadn't been the same without me, and next time I went to Aspen, I had to take them with me. Waiters came and went, providing the table with an endless supply of drinks, but I didn't touch any of it. I had to be clearheaded when I snuck out.

It was hard to tell how much time passed with the incessant chatter and pounding music, and after a few songs, my head throbbed along with the beat. I sank lower and lower into my seat until finally Knox touched my arm and leaned in close enough for me to hear him.

"Do you want to dance?"

I would rather have banged my head against the table repeatedly, but when the alternative was listening to a dozen people talk at once, dancing didn't seem so bad after all.

"Yeah," I said, and everyone moved to let us out. Relieved to leave them behind, I allowed Knox to wrap his arm around my shoulders, and we both ignored the catcalls coming from the table.

The music grew to an earsplitting level when we reached

the dance floor. Maybe it was my imagination, but the crowd seemed to part for us, making room in the center of the chaos.

I knew how to dance, but this wasn't dancing. This was writhing and grinding and perspiring bodies pressed together, and a trickle of sweat ran down my spine. By the time this was over, the makeup I had painstakingly applied would be ruined.

Knox faced me, and his mouth moved, but for the life of me I couldn't tell what he was saying. He took my arms and guided them around his shoulders. We were half an inch apart, and even if I'd wanted to move away, the wall of people around us gave me no choice but to stay put.

I locked my hands behind him, and he wrapped his arms loosely around my hips as he started to dance to the rhythm. I clumsily struggled to move with him, making sure that half inch stayed between us, and I was sure I looked like an idiot. Celia had shown me videos of Lila dancing, and at age six, she had been leaps and bounds better than I would ever be.

Knox didn't seem to mind, though, and he gave me an encouraging smile. Something inside me gave way, and I smiled back, enjoying myself for the first time since this whole mess had started. He was a forgiving partner, and as a new song began, he guided my hips in time to the beat.

He was a good dancer, too. A number of the girls around us kept an eye on him, but he didn't seem to notice, instead focusing on me. I held his stare awkwardly at first, unsure whether I was allowed to look away or not, but eventually I relaxed and lost myself in the music. The more I watched him, the more I understood why the other girls were practically green with envy. The way he looked at me, the way we moved, the heat between us—in the low lights of the club, it was intoxicating.

He set his forehead against mine, and for a moment I let myself believe that the way Knox looked at me was real. That he wanted me and not just my face. He brushed his fingertips against my jaw, and before I knew it, his lips touched mine, so light that I could barely feel them.

I kissed back.

I had no idea how long it lasted. Seconds, minutes, an hour—time was lost to the thumping bass and slick bodies around us, and when Knox deepened the kiss, I went along willingly, tangling my fingers in his hair. He tasted like alcohol and sweat, and the way my mouth fit against his—

Not my mouth. Not my lips.

I wasn't the girl he pretended he was kissing. And he wasn't Benjy.

My eyes flew open. How much time had we been dancing? I broke away from Knox and glanced at his watch, too cowardly to look him in the eye.

Dammit. It was nearly midnight already.

Before I could say anything, someone pushed me into Knox, and I landed squarely against his chest. I babbled apologies that were lost in the roar of the music, and he glowered at the person behind me.

The moment was gone. Suddenly all I could feel was the overwhelming heat, and I wiped my forehead with my sleeve. I needed to get out of here.

I stood on my tiptoes and yelled into Knox's ear, "Bathroom?"

He took my arm and led me through the crowd, which once again parted to let us through. The VIP bathrooms were behind a heavy curtain in the back of the club, and on the other side, I squinted against the blinding hallway lights. We were alone now, and I was all too aware I could still taste Knox.

"Is this it?" I said, pointing to the nearest door. He nodded. "Kitty—"

"Don't," I said. "It's fine. People expect that from us. I get it. Right now I really need to go."

He sighed and gestured at another door. "Right. I'll be in here. Wait for me when you're done."

I slipped inside and let the bathroom door close behind me. It didn't matter how nice kissing Knox had been. He wasn't my boyfriend—Benjy was. Or would be again, as soon as I found him.

Benjy might have been my boyfriend, said a small voice in the back of my mind, but Knox was my fiancé. And if I survived the next few months, he would be my husband.

Lila's husband, the same voice corrected. That was who he'd been thinking about, not me. Not some pathetic III who couldn't even read. Besides, Knox had only kissed me because he knew everyone expected it.

Something inside me deflated, and I pushed the thought out of my mind. I was being ridiculous. Right now I had to focus on Benjy. I'd have plenty of time to angst about Knox later.

I cracked open the door and peered into the hallway. It was empty. Creeping into the corridor, I eyed the three exits. The first was the door Knox had gone through, and the second led back into the club, which left the third at the very end.

It was a stairwell that only led up. I glanced back at the curtain. If I tried to leave through the front, too many people would see me. Pulling my hat from my pocket, I tucked my hair underneath and started up the stairs, hoping it led to an exit.

It opened up into another hallway, this one longer and full of doors on either side. Judging by the way the floor trembled, I stood above the club, which meant my chances of finding an exit were slim. But at this point, even a window was better than nothing.

I waited, but only silence came from the corridor. If anyone was up here, they weren't talking. I hurried down the hallway. I'd be trapped if someone appeared, but I also had a greater chance of finding an exit at the far end. Even if someone did see me, no one in their right mind would go after a Hart. I hoped.

Halfway down the hall, I heard voices from behind a door. I ducked down and listened for any signs that someone was about to leave, but all I heard were two men arguing.

"You can't be serious," said the first. "I can't go back to my manufacturer and tell him this is all I got. He'll kill me."

"I'm not in the habit of buying from thieves," said a second, so low I could barely make out the words. I leaned in. "And at the price you're charging, that's exactly what you are."

"With all due respect—"

"If you had an ounce of respect for me, you would offer me a reasonable price," said the second voice. "It's clear you don't, so I will take my business elsewhere."

The door opened without warning. I jumped away, but it was too late. Any chance I had at hiding was gone.

"Lila?"

My mouth went dry. Knox stood in the doorway, but that wasn't what caught my attention.

It was the gun in his hand.

X

LIES THAT BIND

"What the hell do you think you're doing?" said Knox, grabbing my elbow. Behind him the door slammed shut, but not before I caught sight of a portly man surrounded by open suitcases of guns.

"I was trying to find you," I said. A lie, but he had no way of knowing for sure.

"I told you to wait."

"I've never been very good at listening." I jerked my arm away. "What were you doing in there? And what are you doing with *that?*"

Knox tucked the gun into the back of his pants. "None of your business. Let's get you back downstairs before everyone starts to wonder where you went."

I stayed put, and though he was strong enough to drag me, he didn't. "Were you buying those?"

"Not yet. The price was too high, but he'll lower it soon enough. Why are you so curious?"

I shrugged. Guns were illegal for everyone except Shields, but apparently those laws didn't apply to VIs and VIIs, either. "Can you teach me how to use one?"

Knox stared at me. "You want to learn how to shoot?"

"Yes. Can you teach me?"

"No."

"Then I'm sure Augusta would love to know what you do on your nights out."

Several seconds passed. I half expected him to threaten me—or worse, take a swing—but instead he burst out laughing.

"I like you," he said, reminding me so firmly of Daxton that I nearly recoiled. "Sure, I'll teach you. Why do you think you need to learn?"

Instead of answering, I started toward the stairwell. It was a stupid question. He knew how much danger I was in. "This doesn't have anything to do with what happened to Lila, does it?" I said.

He fell into step beside me as we descended the stairs. "Why do you think it does?"

"You like answering questions with another question, don't you?" I said, struggling to come up with a reason that didn't include my knowing he'd been told about Lila's assassination ahead of time. "Guns are for killing people or making them do what you want. You only have two hands, so there's no reason for you to have so many guns. That means you were going to give them to other people, which means either you need money or you're upset about something. Since you're in no danger of starving, Lila's the obvious answer."

He eyed me. "Yes, it has to do with Lila."

"What about her?" I said. "How she died, or—"

"The guns are for the people who supported her," he said. "That's all I'm telling you."

I whirled around in the middle of the stairwell, and he grabbed the railing to stop from plowing into me. "You said you'd never seen the speeches before. Were you lying?"

"What? No." He looked flustered, and a hint of satisfaction

crept through me. "I had an idea of what she was doing, but I kept out of it. Celia filled me in after you were Masked."

"Celia was using her to overthrow Daxton, wasn't she? That's why Lila was killed."

Knox didn't meet my eyes, and that was all the answer I needed.

"Is Daxton going to kill Celia, too?" I said, and Knox shook his head. "Why not?"

"It's—complicated." He frowned. "Daxton, he—"

Below us, the door clanged open, and I froze. Knox pressed me against the wall, and as footsteps thudded up the stairs, he kissed me hard.

"What's going on here?" said a gruff voice, and Knox pulled away, looking annoyed.

"What does it look like?" he said, and the burly security guard below us paled.

"Miss Hart, Mr. Creed—my sincerest apologies. I didn't realize—"

"That much is obvious," said Knox, and he tucked me underneath his arm. "If you don't mind, we'll be going now."

The guard stepped aside as Knox led me down the stairs. Once we were back in the corridor with the bathrooms, I slipped away from him and took a deep breath to clear my head. Pretend or not, he was a great kisser.

"You can't just—*do* that whenever you feel like it," I said, trying to sound angry, but it came out more like a whine.

"Is that so?" said Knox. "I'll try to remember that next time we're seconds away from being caught fifty feet from an illegal arms dealer."

He waited, his eyes on me, and I had to turn away from him so I could refocus. I didn't have time to care about the guns or the way he kissed me. My chances of having another opportunity to sneak away and find Benjy were all but nonexistent now, and making a break for it wouldn't do me any good. Knox was taller than me, and I was sure he could outrun me.

That left the truth. I had no guarantee he wouldn't try to stop me, but I did know about the weapons. If that's what it would take to get him to bring me to Benjy, I would do it.

"I need to get to the Heights."

"Why's that?" he said, leaning against the opposite wall.

"Benjy's taking his test tomorrow, and this is my last chance to find him before he disappears."

Knox raised an eyebrow. "The Heights are fifteen miles away. What do you expect to do, walk the entire way?"

"If I have to." I crossed my arms. "And unless you want everyone finding out about what happened tonight, you're going to help me."

"We're already helping you," he said. "You can't try to take charge like this. It'll derail everything we've been doing."

"What *have* you been doing? You can't just tell me everything's being handled and not expect me to think you're lying."

"And why would I lie to you?"

"To get me to cooperate."

"You're already cooperating," he pointed out. "We know what we're doing, and you're going to have to trust us."

No, I didn't. I could walk right out that door, and short of dragging me kicking and screaming back to Somerset, there was nothing Knox could do about it. Taking a deep breath, I pushed the curtain aside and did exactly that.

Hundreds of people stared at me as I stormed over the bridge and out of the club, but I ignored them. Once I reached the street, I headed back toward the walkway, jumping onto one heading east.

"This is going to end eventually."

I scowled. Knox could follow me all he wanted, but that wasn't going to change a damn thing.

"What are you going to do then? Keep walking until your feet blister?"

He leaned up against the railing and directly into my line of sight. I looked away.

"Tell me, Lila," he said. "How do you plan on finding him? He won't be at the group home anymore. Are you going to walk the streets until you spot him?"

"If I have to," I said through gritted teeth. Benjy would show up at the testing center in the Heights the next morning, and that would be as good a place as any to wait for him.

"And how are you going to explain to him who you are?"

"I'm going to tell him the truth. Despite what you and everyone else seem to think, usually that's the best way to handle things."

"Fair enough." Knox cracked his knuckles. "How are you going to tell him that you're marrying someone else?"

I glared at him. "You bring that up now?"

"He's your boyfriend, isn't he? Won't that bother him?"

Of course it would, and Knox knew it. It didn't matter, though. Benjy would know the only reason I was marrying Knox was to stay alive. He would understand. But I would never forgive myself if something happened to Benjy because I didn't reach him in time.

Eventually the walkway ended, and we set out on foot. The buildings became smaller, more run-down, and there were fewer lights. Knox tried to take my elbow, and even though I shrugged him off, he stayed close.

When the street ended, I stopped at the crossroad. We had to have walked at least three miles by then, and my feet were throbbing, but I couldn't give up. "Which way?"

Knox shrugged. "You're the one leading. You figure it out."

I tried to imagine a map of the city in my head, but while I could picture the squiggly lines that indicated streets, I had no idea which one we were on. I squinted up at the sign, struggling to recognize the letters, but it was hopeless. I couldn't do this without Knox's help.

"Please," I said tightly. "They could kill him."

We were alone on the street now, but Knox kept glancing around nervously. I didn't know why, since he was the one with the gun. "Trust me, okay? We're not going to let anything happen to Benjy." He set his hand on my arm, and when I tried to pull away, he tightened his grip. "Do you want to know a secret?"

"No. I want to find Benjy."

He leaned in closer anyway. "You're the most important person in the family right now. Daxton and Augusta need you to help undo the damage that Lila caused. Once lockdown is over, they're going to ask you to make speeches that denounce everything Lila spent the past year building. They can't do it on their own, and letting the news of Lila's death become public will only prove that what she was saying was right. They can't have that. They're not going to kill Benjy to keep you in line, because as far as they know, he's the only reason you agreed to go along with this in the first place."

I dug my nails into my palms. "They can replace me."

"Not as easily as they want you to think. Your eyes make you special, for one. And being Masked is rare, and it's never used like this. Not replacing someone completely." He grimaced, and for a moment I thought I saw a flicker of pain in his eyes. "All going to the Heights will do is risk our lives—mine, yours, and his. Come back to Somerset with me, and you'll see Benjy again. Celia and I have already arranged it."

I gaped at him. "What? When? How?"

"Patience." He nodded to the left. "If you really have to do this, the Heights are that way. I'll even go with you. But trust me, Kitty—nothing's going to happen to him."

"What if it does? What if something happens that you didn't see coming?"

"Then I'll hand you a loaded gun and close my eyes," he said. "You have my word."

Except I had no idea how much his word was worth. The thought of placing Benjy's life in his hands made me nauseated, but Knox was right. I had no real plan. Even if Benjy were still in the Heights and did show up at the testing center in the morning, it would be next to impossible to convince him to come with me, let alone find a place to keep him safe.

"By the time you find him, Augusta and Daxton will realize you're gone," said Knox, "and they'll know I'm with you. I won't be able to protect you anymore."

Hot tears blurred my vision, and I blinked rapidly. I had a VII and the face of a Hart, but I was still as powerless as I'd been as a III. It wasn't fair.

"Fine," I said, turning away from him and walking back the direction we'd come. "If anything happens to him—"

"It won't." Knox easily kept up with me, and he pulled his tiny phone from his pocket and pressed a button. "Greg, we need a ride."

Seconds later, a voice replied, "I've got your location. I'll be there in ten."

"Got it." Knox hung up and slid his phone back into his pocket. "And before you ask, no, I won't tell him to take us to the Heights, and he's my driver, so he won't listen to you."

I scowled. There went plan B.

Instead of dropping us off near the alleyway that led to the tunnel, Knox's driver brought us straight to the front entrance of Somerset. A dozen guards milled around the sealed gates, and they shined flashlight after flashlight in our eyes. By the time they were finally willing to believe we were who Knox said we were, I was half-blind.

That wasn't the worst part, though. That came when we walked into the drawing room, where every member of the Hart family had gathered despite the late hour. Celia and Daxton stood together in the middle of the room, both with their arms crossed and identical scowls on their faces. Augusta sat next to Greyson, and they talked quietly with their heads bent together as we entered.

"*There* you are," said Celia. "See, Mother? I told you they'd be back soon."

"You should never have left in the first place," said Augusta. "We are in the middle of a national security crisis, and you two thought it would be a good night to go out?"

"It was just to a club," said Knox, sounding much more relaxed than I felt. "Nothing happened."

"You should both consider yourselves lucky," said Augusta. "How did you get out?"

"Through the exit, of course," said Knox.

Augusta narrowed her eyes. "Do not lie to me, Lennox. Guards were posted in the atrium all evening. Not one reported anyone coming or going."

"That's because we snuck out the servants' entrance," I said. All eyes turned on me. I had no idea if there really was a servants' entrance, but in a place this size, there had to be.

"Is that so?" said Augusta slowly. She took a step toward me. "And how was it you managed to sneak off the grounds?"

"It's not that hard, you know. If you're really that determined to keep everyone locked up, you should do a better job of it."

Her lips curled into a sneer. "Very well. You are hereby confined to your suite until the end of lockdown. Argue, and

I shall extend it until further notice. And you—" She focused on Knox. "If I hear of you dragging her out into the streets at all hours of the night again, I will call off the engagement and have you banished Elsewhere. Do you understand?"

I stepped forward. "It was my idea, and if you punish Knox for it, I swear you'll never see me again. I escaped once, and I can do it again."

Augusta and I stared each other down for several seconds. I could see every wrinkle around Augusta's eyes, and her pupils were so small that they looked like pinpricks. No matter how angry she was, though, I refused to be the reason anyone else was sent Elsewhere.

Daxton cleared his throat. "Er, Mother. Lila. If you will—there's no need for this. Lila knows what she's done wrong, and Knox is an adult. If he chose to violate lockdown, that's his risk to take. But Lila's back now, see? Still in one piece."

Augusta took a long, deep breath and finally moved away. I felt Knox's hand on my back, and when I glanced at him, I saw a strange combination of fear and pride on his face.

"My restrictions for Lila still hold," said Augusta. "You are to be confined to your room until the end of lockdown."

I didn't care what she did to me as long as she didn't send Knox to his death. "Fine. Want me to go now, or should I stick around for another lecture?"

She waved her hand dismissively. Celia smirked, and Greyson eyed me with his brow furrowed. I didn't wait to find out what his problem was, and I turned sharply on my heel before storming off.

A guard trailed after us as Knox walked me back to my suite. He said nothing until we reached the door, and when he did, his voice was laced with amusement.

"Impressive," he said, bending down to brush his lips against my cheek. "No one ever stands up to Augusta and lives."

I wasn't entirely sure he was joking. "Yeah, well, guess you were right about how much they need me. See you when she decides my sentence is up."

I wanted to add something about Benjy, to tell him to take care of him, but the guard moved closer. Instead I gave Knox a small smile and slipped inside Lila's suite, closing the door behind me.

Benjy's life was in his hands now, and if he did something to get him killed, Elsewhere would be the least of his problems.

I was locked in my suite for two days straight. Servants brought me my meals on silver platters, and I had an endless amount of movies and music to keep me entertained, but that didn't make it any better. More than once I thought about using the necklace Greyson had given me to pick the lock, but I didn't want to risk letting Augusta know I still had a way to escape.

There was nothing I could do for Benjy anyway. The day of his seventeenth birthday, I spent the morning staring out the window, wondering where he was and if he would get a VI. No matter what Knox and Celia had planned, they couldn't predict every variable, and anything could happen to him. I wanted to believe them badly, but all I could do about it now was hope.

Even though I didn't use the lock pick to escape, I did use the air vent to try to find out what was going on. After my meals, I waited until a servant took my tray away, which guaranteed me at least a little time to spy on Knox before anyone else checked in on me. Augusta never bothered, but Celia knocked a couple of times. We exchanged nothing more than a few words, but it seemed to be enough to reassure her I wasn't going to disappear anytime soon. And even though I knew it was unlikely, I half hoped Greyson would stop by again.

No amount of crawling through the vents told me what was going on with Benjy, though. Knox never mentioned his name, and I began to wonder if he was on Daxton's side after all. Maybe he'd only said those things to keep me from walking all the way to the Heights. I almost dropped into the room and asked him, but my escape route was too precious for me to give up yet. He'd asked me to trust him, and I would until he gave me reason not to.

On the evening of the second day, as I lay flat in the vent listening to Knox mumble to himself, I heard his door open. A second later it shut, and the click of the lock was so loud it echoed up through the vent. I peeked through the grate in time to see Knox remove his reading glasses. "What is it?"

"Lockdown's nearly over." Celia. I let out a silent sigh of relief. At least I wouldn't be cooped up much longer. "We won't have much more time."

Time for what? Did she mean Benjy?

"It can wait," he said. "It doesn't need to be done immediately."

"Yes, it does," she said. "You know what's at stake. As soon as Daxton rallies the country again, we'll lose our window."

"I already told you, the price was too high. We'll have to wait anyway."

I strained to hear every word. The guns he was going to buy—would he finally explain why?

"We have enough for the first wave, if it comes to that," she said. "But we can do this without bloodshed and with the country on our side the moment we tell them Lila's dead."

My mouth dropped open. Augusta and Daxton would kill her for sure. And probably me, as well.

"I know," said Knox. "Believe me, I know. But the moment we release that information, there will be no taking it back. She'll be gone, even if we have Kitty—"

"Kitty isn't a factor in this," said Celia.

"Yes, she is. You said it yourself—she's part of this now. And we have the chance to make the best of it. She can touch thousands, Celia. Millions, if everything goes according to plan. She knows better than any of us what the people go through. She can help us, and you'd be an idiot to waste that."

Something inside me swelled as Knox spoke. I'd never been useful before, and it was an odd feeling to be needed. But most of all, he was sticking up for me when he didn't know I was listening. Any question I had about whether or not I could trust him disappeared.

"Fine," said Celia. "We'll see what Kitty can do. That won't change what's going to happen the moment lockdown's over, though. They've been booking an arena in every big city since they killed my daughter. By the time the tour's over, we'll lose what small advantage we have. He'll convince everyone that everything's fine and we're the enemy. We've worked so hard, Knox—Lila worked so hard. We can't let him win."

"So what?" said Knox. "Are you saying we do this tonight?"

"Yes. It's the only chance we'll have before he leaves." She paused. "I'll need the syringes."

I heard a drawer open, and Knox handed her a small black bag. "Purple's for you. How are you going to give him the other one?"

"You, of course," she said, and Knox snorted.

"No."

"Knox—"

"*No.* I got the product. You figure out how to make it happen. I'll do a lot of things for you, but this isn't one of them."

Before Celia could reply, there was another knock on the door. Knox hastily put his reading glasses back on, and he and Celia exchanged a look.

"Go in the other room with him and close the door," he

said quietly. "I'll fill you in after. Make sure not to bother him. He can't know he's part of this, too."

Celia disappeared, and after a few seconds, Knox called out, "Enter."

I tried to see who it was, but the grate blocked my view of the door. "Sir," said a booming voice that could only have belonged to a guard. "Lockdown is over."

"Thank you," he said, shuffling a few papers. "When you tell Lila, will you inform her that I would like to see her?"

I didn't wait around to hear the guard's answer. I slid backward through the vent as fast as I could, dropping into Lila's suite right as he knocked. I hastily pushed the end table back, wincing as it scraped against the floor. Wiping the sweat off my forehead, I called for the guard to come in.

A key turned in the lock, and the door opened. "Miss Hart," he said. "Lockdown is over. Mr. Creed also asked for your company as soon as you are willing."

I lay curled up on the couch, trying my hardest to keep my breathing steady. "Thanks. I'll be right there."

I splashed some cold water on my face, but I was too curious to bother changing out of my pajamas. Once I'd dried off, I shuffled down the hallway to Knox's room and knocked.

"Enter," he called, and I slipped inside. Just like before, he sat behind the desk, his reading glasses perched on his nose.

"If you're going to tell me lockdown's over, I already know," I said. Knox shook his head and gestured for me to close the door. I frowned, but obeyed. "I can't go with you anywhere. I'm still in my pajamas."

"Yes, Lila, I realize that." He removed his glasses and rubbed his face. "Would you please allow me to speak?"

He'd called me Lila. Someone else must have been listening. I crossed my arms, annoyed but silent.

"Thank you," he said. "Now, I am pleased you were told

lockdown is over, but that was not my purpose in inviting you here tonight. Instead, I would like to introduce you to my new assistant. Mr. Doe," he called. "If you would join me."

A tall boy with red hair stepped through a door on the other side of the suite, and the room seemed to close in on me until I could barely breathe.

Benjy.

XI

BENJY

He'd cut his hair. It had always hung past his ears, but now it was cropped close, making his jaw look stronger. Benjy was also cleaner than I'd ever seen him before, and the clothes he wore could easily have come straight from Knox's closet.

I had thought they would find him a job far away from here, or assign a guard to watch his back. But Benjy, here in Somerset, in the same house as Daxton and Augusta, who would happily kill him to get me to cooperate—

This was Knox's idea of protecting him?

I was halfway across the room before I stopped myself. He didn't know it was me. I was a stranger to him, but he was the same Benjy I'd known all my life. Even the way he walked was the same, his steps full of purpose and direction. But there was something in his expression I didn't recognize. Exhaustion, maybe, or resignation.

"Benjamin," said Knox. "This is my fiancée, Lila. Lila, this is Mr. Benjamin Doe."

My tongue felt heavy in my mouth, and it took me a moment to speak. "Hi, Benjamin."

He offered me a smile and a polite nod, but there was no happiness behind it. "Miss Hart. It's an honor to meet you."

"You, too," I said faintly, unable to tear my eyes away from him. He took a stack of books from Knox's desk and set them down on the coffee table. "How—uh, how long have you worked for Knox?"

"Benjamin started today," said Knox. "I thought since he and I will be working so closely together from here on out, you two should be introduced."

I itched to walk to the couch and sit beside him. "Did you just take your test?" I said, trying hard to keep my voice even.

Benjy nodded, but he didn't offer any information other than that. I looked at Knox, and he finally met my eyes.

"Mr. Doe is a VI," he said. "Quite admirable for someone with his background."

I blinked rapidly. No matter what happened to me, he would have a chance. He wasn't stuck in the life I would have had if I'd stayed a III.

"If you'll excuse me, I need to talk to Celia," said Knox. "I will return shortly."

As he passed me on his way out the door, he leaned in toward me. To my horror I thought he was going to kiss me in front of Benjy, but instead he whispered, "Tell him."

And then Benjy and I were alone. My hands shook, and I had to cross my arms to hide them. I knew I had to say something, but with the way Benjy was hunched over his work, he didn't seem the least bit interested in me.

He had to know, though. I couldn't let him go on thinking I was really dead, especially not with the danger he was in by being here. He'd have a better chance of protecting himself if he knew. Daxton and Augusta had stolen my entire life out from under me; I wasn't going to let them take Benjy's, too.

Stepping toward the couch, I cleared my throat, but he still didn't look up. That didn't make any sense. No matter how moody Benjy felt, he was always friendly.

"So." My voice sounded hoarse. "How do you like it here so far?"

There were probably a thousand other things I could have said—including spitting out the truth—but I didn't know how to tell him. I needed him to look at me, even if all he saw was Lila.

"It's nice, thank you," he said. When it became obvious he wasn't going to say anything else, I gathered my courage and sat on the couch near him. I was tempted to reach out and touch him, but I clasped my hands together in my lap.

"Benjy?" I said, dropping Lila's uppity accent so I sounded like myself. He froze. "Could you please look at me?"

When he did, his eyes were rimmed with red. "I'm sorry, Miss Hart. I don't mean to be rude. You remind me of someone I used to know."

I hesitated. The longer I waited to tell him, the more I would risk him being angry with me when I finally confessed. He was obviously upset, and this wasn't a game. "I remind you of Kitty Doe, don't I?" I said. "She was your girlfriend, and she disappeared on her seventeenth birthday."

Benjy looked away. "She didn't disappear. She was killed."

I set my hand on his arm. "No, she wasn't."

"Yes, she was," he said, but he didn't move away from me.

"No," I repeated softly. "I wasn't."

My heart hammered as I waited for him to react. He was still for several seconds, and the silence overwhelmed me, threatening to destroy everything if we both stayed quiet. Maybe he hadn't heard me right.

"Benjy, please. I know I look like Lila, but it's me."

He jerked away as if I'd burned him. "Don't," he said sharply. "I don't know how you know about her, but if this is some sick joke—"

"It's not." I faced him, this time keeping my hands to myself. "Listen to me—I don't know how much time we'll have before Knox comes back or someone else shows up, so please let me tell you what happened."

He said nothing, his body rigid and his expression guarded. Taking his silence as permission to continue, I took a breath and told him everything that had happened since the night of my seventeenth birthday. How Daxton had bought me and offered me a VII, how they'd killed Tabs and Masked me to look like Lila, the lessons Celia and Knox had given me, what Elsewhere was and how Daxton had forced me to watch Nina die—everything except the deal I'd made with Celia and what had happened at the club with Knox.

By the time I finished, Benjy was staring at his hands. It took him several moments to speak, and when he did, it was in a shaky voice, as if he was struggling to keep himself under control.

"How do I know you're telling the truth?" he said. "How do I know this isn't some prank?"

I bit my lip. The dozen different ways I'd come up with to prove who I was vanished, and all I could think about was that day at the market after I'd been marked with a III.

"On my birthday, you gave me a present," I said. "It was a purple flower from a vendor selling perfumes. A violet. You said—you said they never gave up, like me."

I saw a spark of recognition in his eyes, and I pushed on.

"The first time you kissed me, it was the middle of January, and you were trying to teach me how to read for the zillionth time. It was a kid's book about a spider, and you were trying to show me how the patterns in the letters formed words. You were so excited when I read it back to you that you kissed me." I smiled faintly at the memory. "It wasn't until you tried to show me with another book that you realized all I'd done was memorize the first one when you read it to me."

To my relief, Benjy smiled as well, but it wasn't his usual boyish grin. Instead, like everything else about him, it was pained. "That wasn't the first time we kissed," he said.

"No, but it was the first time you kissed me instead of the other way around."

He turned away and wiped his eyes with his sleeve. I heard a strange choking sound, and when he finally faced me, I realized he was crying.

"Kitty," he whispered. "This isn't possible."

Everything in me wanted to move closer to him, to pull him into a hug and never let go, but I didn't. Not yet. "I'm sorry—I tried to get to you, but they're watching everything I do, and—and I knew you'd see Lila instead of me and—"

"Don't apologize," he said, and he brushed his fingers against my cheekbone, an inch from my eye. "I see you now."

I let out a soft sob. "I've missed you."

Benjy wrapped his arms around me, and I buried my face in his chest. No one had held me like this since I'd become Lila, and everything bad that had happened in the past month faded away. For a few golden moments, everything was all right again.

I don't know who kissed who first, but even though they weren't my lips anymore, it was like I'd never disappeared. There was a hunger to his kiss that was new, but everything else about it was distinctly Benjy. That moment of pretend in the club with Knox had been hot, but this—I was home.

Someone cleared their throat, and I jumped guiltily. Expecting Knox, I looked over Benjy's shoulder, but when I saw who was standing there, I paled.

Celia.

"I see you've told him," she said, her smooth voice sending a chill down my spine. Benjy gripped my hand, and I squeezed back, trying to reassure him.

"Knox said I could. If you have a problem with it, take it up with him."

"I have no problem with it," she said, stepping inside and closing the door. "In fact, I'm delighted to meet you, Benjy. I've heard quite a lot about you from Kitty."

Benjy nodded respectfully, but his shoulders tightened. "It's a pleasure, ma'am. I hope you've only heard good things."

"Of course," said Celia. "I'm sure there are only good things to tell. I also hear you're quite trustworthy—is that true?"

"Yes," I said flatly. "He knows how dangerous it'll be if anyone finds out he knows."

"Good. I'm pleased you both understand what's at stake." She focused on me. "Kitty, darling, why don't I give you two another moment, and once you're finished, you come see me in my suite? I've got something I'd like to discuss with you."

I nodded weakly. A discussion with Celia right now couldn't be a good thing.

She slipped back through the door, leaving me and Benjy alone again. He laced his fingers in mine. "I don't trust her."

"She's up to something," I said, and with a sigh, I told him about the deal we'd made. About how I'd agreed to continue Lila's work.

Benjy stood and started to pace in front of the couch. "Do you realize what could happen? I'm not going to let you do this to yourself."

"You don't have a choice," I said. "I don't, either. They know how much you matter to me. When the Shields went to the group home to find me on my birthday—"

Benjy stopped. "I told them where you'd gone when they came back. I thought if they caught up with you in time, you wouldn't have to—you know, and they had no proof you were stealing..."

He trailed off, but he didn't have to finish. "I know," I

said. "I'm glad you did. If you hadn't told them, you and Nina would have both—"

I couldn't make myself say it. Benjy blinked hard. "She's really gone?"

"I'm sorry," I said, my voice breaking. "I didn't know. If they find out I told you everything, they'll send you there, too." I paused. "We have to pretend we don't know each other. You can't be—happy around me or even hint that you suspect. I don't want anything to happen to you, okay?"

"I don't want anything to happen to you, either." The seconds ticked by, but finally he nodded. "All right. We can do this, but I swear if they hurt you—"

"They won't, and if they do, then we'll figure something out. We'll run away if we have to." I glanced toward Knox's closet. "Benjy, if you ever need to leave—"

A knock echoed through the room, and a moment later Knox entered. "I see you two have become better acquainted," he said, heading back to his desk. "Celia wanted me to remind you that she'd like to see you."

"Right." I stood, and without warning, Benjy caught me in a giant bear hug and kissed me deeply. Unless Knox gave us another moment alone, it would likely be our last for a long time.

"Hey," said Knox. "That's my fiancée you're kissing."

I could have killed him for that. Benjy immediately let go of me, and my insides twisted as I watched him return to the other room without once looking back.

I glowered at Knox. "Thanks for that."

"You'd better get used to it," he said. "No one else is going to be so forgiving if they find you kissing my assistant."

"Yeah, we know." I stormed toward the door. Before I yanked it open, I added, "Why did you even bring him here?"

"Because I thought you would be glad to see him again."

"Yeah, but Daxton and Augusta know he's here, don't they?"

He sighed and removed his glasses. "They won't hurt him."

"As long as I behave," I said. "Except you and Celia are asking me to do the exact opposite."

"You will be protected," he promised. "As will Benjy."

"Just like you protected Lila?" I said. He was quiet for a long moment.

"If Daxton and Augusta wanted to kill him, no bunker in the world would keep him safe forever," he said. "This way, he gets to live his life—a charmed life at that, as a VI and the future minister of ranking's most trusted adviser. If we all survive this, he will have more opportunities than he ever dreamed of before today."

"And if we don't?" I said tightly.

"Then he would have died no matter where he was. At least now he knows the stakes. He knows you survived. And you will both have each other for however long circumstances allow."

I remained still as a silent war raged within me. I would never be with Benjy like I'd planned, not anymore. But he was here now. He knew I wasn't dead, and I would get to see him as often as I liked. And despite my anger, I knew Knox had a point. No one could hide from the government, not forever. Benjy deserved the chance to live the life he'd earned with his VI, and no matter what happened, I would do everything I could to make sure Daxton never got to him like he'd gotten to Tabs and Nina.

"Thanks," I said, forcing the words out through my clenched jaw. "For letting me see him. You're *sure* he'll be safe here?"

"Safer here than someplace where no one's watching his back," said Knox. "And you're welcome."

At last I left. Before heading to Celia's suite, I returned to mine and changed out of my nightclothes. My mind raced with the possibilities of how Daxton and Augusta might use Benjy against me, and by the time I knocked on Celia's door, I had to take a deep breath to calm myself down. I would tell him about the secret passageway the first chance I got. At least then we'd both have a way out.

"There you are," said Celia. "Come on in."

Just like my suite, hers was luxuriously decorated. Everything from the couches to the carpet was a rich purple, and framed pictures of her, Lila, and a man I didn't recognize were everywhere. I sat down on the sofa and tried not to look nervous.

"I don't need to tell you the danger Benjy is in," she said, sitting across from me and pouring herself a cup of tea. She offered me one, and I shook my head. "When Knox approached my brother about taking him on as his assistant, Daxton was thrilled with the idea."

My blood ran cold. "Knox said he was safe here."

"Knox is an idealist. I'm a realist." She took a sip of her tea. "You won't be useful to them forever, you know, and when the time comes, no amount of protest is going to save Benjy, either."

"I won't let them hurt him," I said.

"Is that so? How do you plan on stopping them?"

I looked at my hands. Once I told Benjy about the passageway, he might have a chance to escape when the time came. With Lila's face, I would never be able to hide in a crowd, but Benjy—he could do it.

"Why are you telling me this?" I said.

"Because I have a solution for you." Setting her teacup down, she fished a cloth bag from her pocket. It was the same bag Knox had handed her earlier. Reaching inside, she pulled out two small syringes. One was filled with purple liquid, and the other clear. "Have you ever used one of these before?"

I leaned back into the sofa, as far away from her as possible. I remembered all too well the night Daxton had knocked me out with a needle. "I'm not taking that."

"I'm not asking you to." She held up the purple one. "This is a nonfatal dose. This—" She held up the clear syringe. "This combination will stop the heart almost instantly once it's administered in full."

My hands shook, and I shoved them underneath my legs to keep Celia from noticing. "Is that your solution? You're going to kill Daxton?"

"No," she said calmly. "You are."

XII

BLOODBATH

According to Celia, the plan was foolproof.

She would take the purple dose near Daxton's suite and toss the syringe into the small fountain nearby. The evidence would dissolve, she claimed, and no one would be any wiser.

After that, she would stumble around the corner and distract Daxton's guards. Thirty seconds—that's all she would have before she passed out, and that was where I came in. While the guards were busy attending to her, I would sneak into Daxton's room and find a way to give him the fatal dose. Someone had disabled the security cameras, she assured me, and no one would be able to pinpoint it on me. Once I was done, I would sneak back out, get rid of the syringe, and return to my suite to wait for the news of Daxton's death.

It would look like someone had attempted to poison them both, Celia said. It would take the blame off her, and Knox would vouch for me if it came to it. Augusta would blame some unknown assassin, likely associated with the Blackcoats, and there would be chaos for days. But Daxton would be dead, and Augusta didn't have Greyson on a tight leash like she did her son.

"What if I don't want to?" I said, and Celia gave me a look that could have melted diamonds.

"Whose life do you value more? Daxton's or Benjy's?"

And that was the end of the argument.

I still wasn't convinced it was the best thing to do, though. There had to be another way, one that didn't involve taking so many chances, but Celia was adamant. Daxton was due to travel across the country the next day now that lockdown was over, and if I wanted to do this, it had to be now.

"The first time you do something wrong, he'll murder Benjy," said Celia. "You know that."

I did, but that didn't mean I was ready to kill someone with my bare hands.

I hid behind a corner a few yards from the entrance to Daxton's suite, which took up two levels of an entire wing on the opposite side of the mansion. As I waited, I clutched the syringe and tried to remember that this was for Tabs and Nina and everyone else who had died because of Daxton. This was nothing more than justice, and if anyone deserved to die for his crimes, it was him. No matter how passionately he claimed he was making the world a better place, when the most I could have hoped for as a III was an early death, I couldn't see how it was benefiting anyone but those who were lucky enough to be born into a position of power. Or like Benjy, smart enough to earn it. And while I knew better than to think Celia was doing this to help me protect him, I also knew that Daxton had killed her daughter. So far she'd shown remarkable restraint, but it must have been easier to face him knowing this was her plan all along.

Celia's strangled cry echoed down the corridor, and they were soon joined by shouts from the guards. When I peeked around the corner, I saw two uniformed men hunched over Celia, who lay on the floor shaking violently. Horrified, I stared, forgetting for a moment that my time was limited. What if she wasn't okay?

No. I had a job to do. Celia would be fine, and even if she wasn't, she was willing to risk it in order to give me a chance to kill Daxton.

I shook myself out of it and snuck toward Daxton's door, opening it as silently as I could. Once I slipped into the dark living room, I noticed the light was on underneath an adjacent door. Taking a breath, I knocked.

"Come in," said Daxton distractedly. If he had any idea about the commotion in the hallway, he wasn't letting on.

Stepping inside, I glanced around, my grip tightening around the syringe. Daxton sat behind a massive black desk that spanned nearly the entire width of the room. Bookcases as high as the ceiling surrounded us, each shelf packed tightly with volumes that looked like they hadn't been touched in decades. A pair of fountains trickled on either side of the door, but what caught my eye was the portrait of the entire Hart family hanging on the wall behind Daxton. In the painting, he sat on what could only be called a throne, his wife posed beside him and her hand resting on his. Celia and Augusta stood behind her, and I could almost feel Celia's hatred through the canvas.

Jameson, Daxton's elder son, stood at his other side, his chin raised with pride. He was handsome—much more handsome than Greyson, who lingered nearby, smaller than he was now. But the most surprising part of the portrait was Lila, who stood on the fringes of the frame, her blond hair perfectly curled and her expression matching her mother's. She hated the family as much as Celia did, and I still didn't understand why. Was she parroting her mother? Following in her footsteps? Or was there a reason no one had explained to me—a reason Lila had risked her life for the people beneath her?

I opened my mouth to greet Daxton, but he held up a finger and looked down into a screen on his desk.

"Yes, I realize that, Creed," he said. "Do remind the other ministers that even though they outnumber me, I outrank them, and their privilege is granted at my pleasure. If they do not like the allocation of funds for the next quarter, there are dozens of others who would be happy to sign their name in exchange for the title of minister."

"Of course," said a man—Knox's father. "I will let the council know. Thank you for your time, Prime Minister."

Daxton waved his hand over the monitor, and it went dark. He straightened, and a poisonous smile spread across his face. "Ah, Kitty. I see you've been released."

"Yeah, they told me lockdown was over."

"Did you see the present I left you?" he said, and I hesitated.

"You mean Benjy?"

"Indeed. And how is your little friend?"

I pressed my lips together. Talking to Daxton about him seemed wrong, like I was somehow tainting Benjy. "He's good, I think. And don't worry," I added. "I'm not going to tell him who I am."

"Of course you won't. You're far too smart for that." Daxton slipped around the desk and stopped in front of me, his expression a mockery of sympathy. "It's such a terrible thing, being separated from the one you love. After my wife died..." He sighed and cupped my cheek. "Well, I'm afraid I've never been the same."

I glanced up at the portrait. "I'm sorry. That must have been hard."

"It was," he murmured, closing the distance between us. "I would have done anything to get her back, but that isn't how the world works, now, is it?"

It seemed to me that that was exactly how the Harts' world worked, but I didn't dare say it. I clutched the syringe. He was close now, and all it would take was one stab.

"Tell me, Kitty," he said, his mouth inches from mine. I could smell garlic on his breath. "Now that you have what you want so badly, how do you intend to thank me for it?"

"With words," I said. "I'm your *niece,* Daxton."

"You're not my niece," he said, running a hand down my arm. I shrugged it off, and he set it on my waist instead. "Lila was always so beautiful. When Mother told me her plan, I was so certain we would never find someone who could pull her off, but here you are. So like her in every way. She refused me, too, you know."

He traced my lips with his fingertip, and I had to clench my jaw to stop myself from biting him. "Is that why you killed her, you sick bastard?"

Daxton chuckled. "Of course not. I would hardly go to all this trouble for something I could have any time I wanted."

His hand slipped under my shirt, brushing against Lila's butterfly tattoo. My resolve hardened, and before I could second-guess myself, I kneed him hard between the legs.

Daxton doubled over, grunting in pain. "You stupid bitch," he wheezed. "You just earned your boyfriend a death sentence."

I uncapped the syringe. "The only person dying today is you," I said, and I jammed the needle in the side of his neck and pressed the plunger.

What are you doing?

Benjy's voice echoed through my mind, and for a split second, I couldn't breathe.

I wasn't a killer. Doing this made me no better than Daxton, and I hated him too much to want to be anything like him.

He went rigid in my arms. I grabbed his neck to hold him steady as I yanked the needle out and threw it aside, but it was too late. Half the dose was gone.

There was something else, too. Underneath my hand, where his VII tattoo faded into his tan skin, I felt ridges—

But not a VII.

Instead they were in the shape of a single V.

I stumbled backward. Daxton touched the spot on his neck where I'd injected the poison, and when he pulled away, a bead of blood stained his finger. "What did you—"

He hit the floor with a thud, and panic seized me. Half a dose. Would it be enough? I had no idea, but I couldn't bring myself to finish him off.

My heart pounded. He wasn't Daxton Hart. He'd been Masked, like me, and all this time, he wasn't the real prime minister.

Was he dead? A second passed, and his chest rose and fell. Not yet. Half a dose wasn't enough, and no matter who he was, when he woke up, they wouldn't bother sending me Elsewhere. They would finally have a reason to execute Lila. Would they kill Celia, too, and Knox? And what about—

A bead of sweat trickled down my forehead. If Daxton woke up, he would kill Benjy. I needed to give him the rest of the dose.

I glanced around, searching for the syringe. Where was it? I dropped to my hands and knees, searching the lush carpet, but it wasn't there. It wasn't anywhere.

The fountains. I rushed to the nearest one. The syringe lay inside, already half dissolved. I scooped the remains out, but it was too late. The poison was gone.

No. No, no, no. I rushed to Daxton's side. His breaths came slowly and laboriously, but he was still alive. My eyes fell on a throw pillow on a couch nearby. I could smother him. It would only take a minute, and then he wouldn't be a threat anymore. It was my only option.

I tried to cross the room, but my feet were glued to the floor. I couldn't do it. I couldn't be like him. They'd taken everything from me already—I couldn't let them take this last piece of my humanity, as well. III or not, I was better than that. I was better than him, whoever he was.

Shouts from the hallway echoed through the room. I'd waited too long. The guards who were dealing with Celia would undoubtedly have called in reinforcements by now, and I was trapped.

Frantically I searched the ceiling. In the corner I spotted an air vent the size of the one in my suite, and I didn't waste any time. Hopping over the impostor's body, I scrambled onto the massive desk, knocking over a stack of books in the process. With any luck, they'd blame the mess on him.

Using one of the sturdy bookcases, I climbed to the ceiling and knocked the cover out of place. I had just enough room to squeeze through it, and with so much adrenaline pumping through my veins, I had no trouble at all lifting myself up into the ceiling. After covering the vent once more, I collapsed in the tunnel, breathing heavily. I was safe.

But not for long.

I slipped back into my suite as I silently berated myself for ever trusting Celia. Her plan hadn't been foolproof; a million things could've gone wrong, and at least two did. The guards arrived faster than she'd anticipated, and I hadn't had the courage to kill him—whoever he really was. I'd backed out, and for that, my life might be forfeit.

Less than a minute after I'd thrown what was left of the

syringe into the toilet and sank onto the sofa, I heard shouts coming from the hallway. A pair of guards burst into the room, but unlike my first night in Somerset, they didn't try to drag me off to the safe room.

"What's going on?" I said, but neither of them answered. Moments later Knox strode in, his mouth set in a thin line.

"Knox?" I said. He offered me his hands. I took them, and I couldn't hide how badly mine trembled.

"It's your mother," he said. "The doctors think she's been poisoned. She's been taken to the infirmary."

That was all? Nothing about Daxton? "Is she okay?"

"I don't know. But there's something else."

I held my breath. If he was dead, I would be directly responsible for it. But if he wasn't...

"It's the prime minister." Something in his eyes flashed. "He's also been poisoned."

I opened and shut my mouth. Did Knox know that Daxton had been Masked, too? Did Celia know? Did Greyson?

"Is he—is he still...?" I said shakily.

Knox nodded, and I clutched his hands to keep from swaying. The guards stepped closer, but Knox shook his head, and they moved back. They were here to protect me now, but the moment Daxton woke up and revealed I was the one who'd tried to kill him, they would come for me and Benjy.

I must have looked as hysterical as I felt, because Knox guided me back onto the sofa and knelt next to me. "Lila," he said, and even though I was dizzy with fear, I made myself look at him. "It's all right. Your mother's going to be okay. And Daxton..." He paused, and his expression hardened. "I promise you that everything will work out."

He knew something had gone wrong. He had to, because Daxton wasn't dead. And no matter how stupid I'd been letting Celia talk me into this mess to begin with, I wasn't about to tell Knox what had happened. If he knew Daxton was Masked and discovered I'd found out—

"Think you can make it to the infirmary?" said Knox, and I nodded. Lila would be expected to visit her mother even though I wanted to stay as far away from Daxton as possible.

He and Celia had been brought to an underground level on the other side of the mansion. The infirmary took up the entire floor of the wing, and even though the walls were painted the same color as the summer sky, the corridors were so narrow that I couldn't shake the feeling of being caged.

The infirmary had no waiting room packed with the sick and dying, like the public hospital I'd visited after breaking my arm when I was ten. Instead a doctor dressed in a white uniform led me and Knox into Celia's room, where she was hooked up to the machine that beeped in time with her pulse.

I stepped forward, and tears stung my eyes. They weren't as fake as I wanted to convince myself they were. As nice as it was to know that nothing had gone wrong with Celia's part of the plan, I needed to know what had happened with Daxton.

Thankfully Knox seemed to understand, and as I took Celia's hand, he spoke to the doctor. "How is the prime minister?"

"Alive," she said, flipping through papers she held in the crook of her arm. "We don't know much more than that. He hasn't woken up yet, but his vitals are much weaker than Celia's."

"Do you know how this happened?" said Knox, and from across the room I saw him set his hand on her arm.

She scowled and shifted away. "We're not sure. Both of them have needle marks on their skin, but in different places, and we haven't found any syringes."

"Someone did this?" said Knox, unfazed by her rejection.

When she nodded, I squeezed Celia's hand, wishing she were conscious so she could help figure this out. She was the one who'd gotten me into this mess, but I was the idiot who hadn't thought it through before going along with it.

"Thank you," said Knox, and the doctor left the room. He closed the door behind her, and I looked down at Celia, not letting go of her yet. "Did anyone see you leave?" he said quietly.

"No. I went through the air vents."

His eyebrows shot up. "You went through the *what?*"

I pointed at the ceiling. "See that one up there? It's a little smaller than the one in Daxton's office, but it's the same idea."

While he squinted up at the grate, I studied Celia. Her chest rose steadily, her heartbeat was strong, and she looked peaceful as she slept. Not like the woman who'd lost her daughter and was willing to do whatever it took to get revenge. She couldn't have known her brother was Masked, I decided. If she had, there would be no need to try to kill him. All she would have to do was tell the media that the prime minister was a fake. But if I spilled his secret, there was no telling what would happen to me and Benjy. For now, I had to keep my mouth shut and hope it didn't matter anymore.

"How the hell do you fit through that?" said Knox, still staring at the vent. I shrugged.

"It's not exactly hard."

"Speak for yourself." He shook his head incredulously. "But if no one saw you, good. What about going in?"

"Celia distracted them like she said she would." He nodded, and I wished he had been the one to sneak into Daxton's office instead of me. He wouldn't have lost his nerve. "What happens now?"

"I don't know." He leaned against the wall and shoved his

hands in his pockets. “We hope Daxton doesn’t pull through, and in the meantime we try to stay alive.”

“And if someone finds out what really happened?”

He sighed. “Then the bloodbath begins.”

XIII

FINE LINE

I stayed with Celia for the rest of the evening, waiting for her to wake up. Knox disappeared after an hour, and once the adrenaline faded, I leaned my head against the wall and allowed myself to drift off.

"Ahem."

My eyes flew open. Augusta stood in the doorway, her face as smooth as ever despite the fact that both of her children—no, her only remaining child and the man pretending to be her son—were unconscious in the infirmary.

"Augusta," I said. Her name stuck in my throat. "Sorry, I didn't hear you come in."

"Has she woken up?" said Augusta, looking pointedly at Celia.

I shook my head. "The doctor said she'll be okay, though. She's just sleeping it off. How—how's Daxton?" She had to know he'd been Masked. Maybe she was the only one who did.

Augusta sniffed. "That is none of your business. You will have the nurses alert me the moment she wakes, do you understand?"

I nodded.

"And, Kitty," she said, taking a step toward me. "If I find out you had anything to do with this..."

The blood drained from my face. "I would never—I would never hurt them," I said, barely keeping the panic out of my voice. If she thought for a moment that I was really behind it, I wouldn't have a chance to explain. "And I was in my room the whole time. Knox left right before the guards arrived. He'll tell you."

"Yes," she said coolly. "I am sure he will."

She turned on her heel and started to glide out of the room. She wasn't convinced, and there was nothing I could do to change her mind. However, like the day we'd met in the Stronghold, my mouth opened and words came out before I could stop them.

"Why do you hate me?"

Augusta stopped, and she slowly turned to face me once more.

"You didn't need to have me Masked," I said. "You're the one who decided to do it—you're the one who decided to get rid of Lila in the first place, so it isn't that. I don't understand—"

"I do not hate you," said Augusta crisply. "You are simply not one of us, nor will you ever be, and I do not appreciate your insubordination. I loved my granddaughter, but she made her decisions knowing full well what the consequences would be."

"So you just killed her for it?" I said. "What if it were Greyson?"

"Do not talk about my grandson," she snapped, and I flinched in spite of myself. After a tense moment passed, she took a breath and said in a steadier voice, "Being a Hart means more than having the name. It means upholding the foundation that has seen this country through its darkest hour. Without it—without *us*—the country would crumble, and all of the strides we have taken would be for nothing. Lila was dangerous. She had the ear of the nation, and she was telling them half-truths and lies that suited her agenda rather than their best interests. She thought she was untouchable."

"So you proved her wrong?" I said, my voice shaking.

"I did what I had to do to ensure the country's stability. Every citizen in this nation depends on my family, and we cannot go back to the way things were."

She paused, and her expression grew distant, as if she were seeing something that wasn't really there.

"You and I are not so different," said Augusta at last. "I was three years old when the economy collapsed. Both of my parents were killed in the resulting riots. My mother was shot trying to get us to safety, and she died in front of me."

I stilled. I'd never heard about Augusta's life before she married into the Hart family. As far as I knew, no one had.

"I grew up in an orphanage as well, though it was nothing like the ones we have now." Her eyes reddened, and she took a deep, shuddering breath. I'd never seen her so undone before. "I had to fight for every morsel of food. Half of us slept on the floor because there were not enough beds. My education was limited, and what passed for school was an insult, so I stole books to teach myself instead. I did not have anything handed to me, but I made something of myself anyway. And after I met my late husband, I finally realized that everything I had gone through happened for a reason. It gave me the strength to survive, and it turned me into the person I needed to be in order to live the life I deserved."

She stared straight at me, and I couldn't look away. "So you see, Kitty, I understand you better than you think I do. I also remember what the country was like before the Harts worked miracles to stabilize it. I am the only one who does anymore, and for the sake of the country—for the sake of the people—we cannot go back to the way it was.

"I love each and every member of my family with all that I am," she added. "I never wanted to hurt Lila. I agonized over the decision, but in the end, we must expect from ourselves what we expect from our people. We must set the example. She knew the consequences, and though I begged her not to, she chose to go through with it anyway. She is the one who pulled the trigger on her life, not me. I loved her, but I have a duty to my country. We all do. And I will not allow us to return to that dark time. My grandson will not go through what I did. No one ever will again."

As I watched Augusta, weariness and heartache passed over her face, and for a fraction of a second, she looked her age. I would never like her, but in that moment, I thought I understood her. Celia and Greyson were all she had left. If Augusta really did feel she had to sacrifice her granddaughter to keep the country stable—

What sort of person could do that?

Someone who loved control more than her own family. As quickly as it had come, my sympathy for Augusta vanished. Still, as much as I wanted to hate her for doing this to Lila—for doing this to me—she loved Greyson. So much so that she was willing to destroy anything that threatened to taint the world she'd created for him. So much so that she'd turned a stranger into the most powerful man in the country so Greyson wouldn't be an orphan, too.

Just like everything I did was for Benjy, everything she did was for Greyson, and now I finally understood.

"I'm sorry for bringing it up," I said, choosing my words carefully. "And I'm sorry Lila put you in that impossible position. You should never have had to go through that." I faltered, and a moment passed before I could force the rest out.

"Thank you—thank you for telling me. I know you'll never like me, but I hope—eventually you'll trust me. I want what's best for the country, too."

The seconds ticked by. I half expected her to hurl more insults and justifications at me, but to my surprise, her expression softened. "Very well. I accept your apology. Now, if you'll excuse me."

I said nothing as she left, and once the door closed behind her, my entire body felt like it was folding in on itself. I curled up in the chair, staring at Celia and willing her to wake up. She would know what to do about this whole mess. Knox was gone, and who knew how long it would be before he came back? I didn't know how to handle any of this alone with Augusta breathing down my neck, whether or not there was uneasy peace between us for the time being. Chances were, it wouldn't last the night.

Twenty minutes later, I heard a timid knock, and I straightened. "Come in."

Benjy entered, pale and disheveled. I started to rise, but he stopped cold, staring at the bed. "Is that—"

"Celia. She'll live." I settled back in my chair. I ached to feel his arms around me, but it was too risky. "Does Knox know you're down here?"

He sat across from me, careful to keep his distance. "He's the one who told me where you were, but then the guards came and asked me all these questions about the prime minister."

"Like what?" I said, lowering my voice.

"They asked me where I was this evening, what I was doing, what Knox was doing—" He rubbed his face and focused on Celia. "You're sure she's going to be okay?"

I nodded, and even though a doctor or nurse could walk in at any time, I took his hand. "I think so. Someone tried to kill them," I said, and shame washed over me. I wasn't used to lying to Benjy, but I couldn't tell him, not if they suspected him. The more he knew, the more danger he would be in. Besides, it wasn't really a lie, was it? Just an omission.

I bit my lip. That was exactly how a Hart would justify it. They had taken away my face and name, but I'd thought there was no way they could take away who I really was. Then I'd kissed Knox, and now this. Seemed they were winning after all.

"Are you okay?" he said, squeezing my hand.

"I'm fine. Whatever it is that got to them—" I stopped and watched the rise and fall of Celia's chest. If Daxton pulled through... "Benjy, you can't be around me, okay? I love you, but if someone sees us together like this, we'll both pay the price."

He scowled. "Someone needs to watch your back. I'm not going to sit here and let them hurt you."

"They're not hurting me. They wouldn't, not after all the effort they put into making me look like Lila. But Augusta is watching me like a hawk, and if she sees us together, she'll make sure we both regret it. Please, Benjy," I begged. "For me."

At last he nodded. He didn't look happy about it, but he didn't have to be. He only had to agree. "All right. Just—don't die, okay? I couldn't take losing you again."

"I won't. You're not allowed to die, either." Remembering what Celia had said the morning I'd gone hunting with Daxton, I added, "Keep your head down and do what they tell you, and everything will be okay."

Benjy stood and kissed me on the cheek. "You, too. I'm here if you need me."

He tucked a folded piece of paper into my hand and left.

I waited until he shut the door before I opened his note, and for the first time in what felt like forever, I smiled.

He'd drawn two stick figures standing on a beach, with waves and a sand castle nearby. Their little fingers were interlocked, and between them was a sideways figure eight—the symbol for eternity.

"Love you, too," I whispered. I refolded the note and tucked it safely in my pocket. As long as we were both alive, I had to believe that everything would be okay.

Celia awoke shortly after midnight, just long enough for me to tell her Daxton was still alive. She was furious, but as each day passed and he remained in a coma, I breathed a little easier as it seemed less and less likely that he would regain consciousness.

Greyson spent hours every day at the impostor's bedside, and when Celia demanded I leave her alone, I stayed with him. Augusta was so busy running the country in Daxton's place that I was all but forgotten in the aftermath. That was exactly how I wanted it.

"You're lucky," said Greyson two days into his bedside vigil. We barely spoke, and even when we did, I was usually the one doing the talking, chatting about anything other than the V-shaped ridges I knew lay on the back of that man's neck. Getting Greyson to speak to me was about as effective as moving the walls with my bare hands, though, so when he did, I looked at him, surprised.

"How?" I said.

"You don't have to rule if you don't want to," he said. "My father—I know he isn't the god he wants the world to think he is. I know he's not perfect, and I've seen the things he's done just like everyone else in this family. But he's still my father."

He hesitated, and I had to bite my tongue to stay silent. "If I tell you something, will you promise to never tell anyone?"

"I can keep a secret." If only he knew just how well.

Greyson ducked his head. "I don't want to be the prime minister," he said so quietly that I had to strain to hear him. "It was always supposed to be my brother, not me. He's the one who trained for it, and as horrible as it sounds, the worst part about this is now there's no one standing between me and that title. It'll be me next, and Grandmother would rather choke on acid than let Celia have it instead of me."

"Maybe it won't happen," I said uncertainly. "Maybe he'll wake up."

When Greyson looked at me, his eyes were rimmed with red and he wore a twisted mockery of a smile. "I'm not that lucky."

I didn't know what to say. The silence built up around us, and finally Greyson sighed and leaned back in his chair.

"My mother and brother were killed by the Blackcoats," he said. "I knew it was only a matter of time before they came for me and my father. I was hoping I'd be first, though."

"No one should hope for that kind of thing," I said quietly.

He shook his head. "I should have died with them anyway. The four of us were supposed to go to the theater for a performance, but I didn't..." He paused. "Something came up with China, and my father wanted Jameson to stay behind and help. He refused, though, and not even my father could make him do something he didn't want to. So I stayed instead. We were supposed to be right behind them, no more than a few minutes late, except—"

He stopped. The seconds ticked by, and I wanted to comfort him, but I had no idea how. None of my friends in the group home had parents or siblings to lose. *Family* was almost a dirty word, since they'd been the ones to give us away to begin with. But the devastated look on Greyson's face made it clear how much he'd loved his.

"There was a bomb planted in the car," he said. "The officials who investigated the case, they said whoever put it there probably didn't realize my mother and brother would be in it. It was my father's car, and he used it to drive all over town. We always used a separate one, but because it was supposed to be all four of us..."

His voice broke, and I studied the floor to avoid looking at him. "I'm sorry," I said. "I can't imagine what that must feel like."

"Of course you can. You know exactly what it's like to lose a parent."

I had no idea what had happened to Lila's father, who must have died when I was very young. I couldn't even remember any article Benjy read ever mentioning Celia being married. I'd seen the pictures on her wall of the three of them, though, so they must have been happy once. And now Celia was the only one left.

Greyson watched me, and I squirmed underneath the intensity of his stare. "It was a public execution," he said. "My father accused him of treason, claiming he had planned to kill us so Celia could become prime minister. You were seven years old, and my father made you and Celia watch. Death by firing squad. You screamed—" Greyson winced as if he could still hear it. "Celia had to hold on to you so you wouldn't get in the way. She covered your eyes, but you still heard it. After that, you sneaked into my room almost every night and slept at the foot of my bed. Said you could hear the guns going off when you tried to sleep by yourself. When the servants found out, they had another mattress moved into my bedroom for you."

I shivered. No wonder Lila had hated Daxton so much. Being forced to watch her father's execution—I didn't need to know what having a father felt like in order to imagine it. If Daxton had done that to me, I would have strangled him with my bare hands. Though he had in a way, hadn't he? By murdering Nina in front of me. I'd wanted to kill him then, and if he hadn't cuffed me to the railing, I would have.

Lila was smart enough to know that it wouldn't have changed anything, though. Even if the title was passed down to Greyson, Augusta still ruled, and Greyson would have been risking his own life to go against whatever she said. Before Daxton died, there had to be a plan in place to stop her. But Celia, sick with desire for revenge, hadn't thought it through. She'd only seen an opportunity and taken it.

"The night you got here was the first time in ten years that Lila was in Somerset and didn't sneak into my room," said Greyson. "I thought I'd done something to make you mad, but everything you say, the way you talk to me and look at me—it's all wrong. You look like her, but you're not her, are you?" He swallowed. "They Masked you, didn't they?"

Augusta's warning echoed through my mind, but there was no hiding it now. If he knew, there was nothing I could do to convince him I was her. So I nodded.

"Please don't tell Augusta you know," I whispered. "She'll kill me."

"So will my father." Greyson grimaced as he looked at Daxton's still form between us. "Is that what happened to Lila? Did they—did they kill her?"

"They did," I said gently. "I'm sorry."

He didn't say anything for several minutes. My hand twitched as the desire to take his overwhelmed me, but I resisted. The last thing he probably wanted was for me, some screwed-up version of his best friend, to touch him. Instead I focused on the rise and fall of Daxton's chest, wishing with everything I had that it would stop.

"Celia did this to him," said Greyson suddenly, breaking the silence. I opened my mouth to protest, but he kept going. "Don't bother denying it. I know my own family, no matter how many secrets they try to keep from me. I understand why she did it, too. If I'd had any idea they killed Lila..." He paused again, and at last he looked me in the eye. "How long have you been her?"

"About a month. Daxton bought me at a club on my seventeenth birthday. I was a III." I searched his face for any sign of shock or disgust, but his expression was blank, and he held my stare without flinching. "He offered me a VII for helping him out, and he didn't say how, but—he's the prime minister. I couldn't say no." I tugged on a lock of Lila's hair. "They took me to a car and knocked me out. When I woke up, I looked like Lila. I had no idea it was going to happen until it was already over."

"That sounds like him," said Greyson. "Who else knows?"

"Celia," I said. "Knox. Augusta."

His Adam's apple bobbed. "So everyone. And none of them thought I should know that my best friend was dead."

"I'm sorry. I wanted to tell you, but Augusta..."

He rubbed his eyes. "I know. You're the last person who should apologize, and I'm sorry they put you through this. No one deserves to lose their identity like that. What's your name?"

My name. It was such a small thing, but I'd thought no one would ever ask me again. "Kitty. My name's Kitty."

Greyson offered me a watery smile. "Kitty. It's nice to meet you. I'm Greyson." He stuck out his hand, and I took it. His grip was warm and firm. "Friends?"

Another thing I thought I'd never have again. I smiled back, and for a few precious seconds I allowed myself to push my nagging worries aside. Even if I was dead tomorrow, at least I would have this.

"Yeah," I said. "Friends."

After nearly a week in the infirmary, Celia was finally released. That night, someone knocked on the door, and I opened it, expecting to see Greyson. Ever since our conversation over Daxton's bedside, we'd been spending more and more time together. We played card games and chess to pass the time, ate our meals separate from Augusta, and he told me everything he knew about Lila, things even Celia hadn't known.

"She talked about running away all the time," he said. "That's why I made her that necklace. She felt trapped here, and I thought if she had a way out, maybe...maybe she wouldn't leave me."

"I can't imagine her wanting to leave you," I said, and it was the truth. I'd never met anyone like Greyson. Even though darkness permeated every corner of Somerset, he made me smile. He was no Benjy and I was no Lila, but he seemed to need a friend as badly as I did.

When I opened the door, however, Celia stared back at me, not Greyson. She was pale and unsteady on her feet, and I stepped aside to let her in, not wanting her to collapse in the doorway. She made her way slowly to the sofa and sat down with none of her usual grace.

Her dark hair was lank and dirty, and the circles under her eyes made her look like she hadn't slept in days. Considering all she'd been doing was resting, I had no idea how she could still look so tired. The poison, I assumed. Maybe this was what it did to someone who survived.

"I hear you and Greyson have been talking," she said. Her voice was hoarse.

"Yeah." I tried to keep the wariness out of my tone. "He's nice."

"You're lucky my mother's been too busy to notice." Celia stretched out across the couch and closed her eyes, leaving me no place to sit beside her. Instead I perched on the edge of an armchair and nervously picked at my nails. As the seconds passed and she said nothing, I scowled.

"What do you want?"

Celia cracked open an eye. "World peace. A hot bath. My real daughter and not a spineless replacement. You didn't give him the full dose, did you?"

"I didn't have time," I lied. "The guards were coming, and Daxton was struggling. It was a miracle I got that much in him."

"So you say," she said mildly. "My fault for trusting you with it. If Daxton ever wakes up, I won't make that mistake again."

Infuriated, I clenched my fists so tightly that my nails cut into my palms. Any chance she had of finding out about Daxton from me vanished. "Did you just come here to insult me, or was there a point?"

"Of course there's a point." With a groan, Celia sat up. "Mother dropped by my suite and reminded me that before this whole mess started, Daxton scheduled a speech for you in New York tomorrow afternoon. Since I'm ill and he's half-dead, Knox will escort you."

I crossed my arms. Knox had made himself scarce since that night, leaving me to fend for myself. "What's the speech about?"

"An apology for making them believe that there was ever a reason for revolution. I've given Knox your real speech, though. It's about Daxton," she added. "The media isn't going to report on what happened, so it's up to us to get the word out, starting in New York."

"Why?" I said. If I went off script, there was no telling what Augusta might do to Benjy. "He's not dead. What's the point in telling everyone he's in a coma?"

"Hope," said Celia. "To show your supporters that there's a light at the end of the tunnel. No matter what he wants the people to think, Daxton isn't immortal."

No, the dead certainly weren't. I bit the inside of my cheek. "What if Augusta decides to have someone Masked in his place?"

"That's exactly why we have to do this," said Celia. "To make sure Augusta doesn't have the chance. Having someone Masked is a risk, but she'll do it if she has to. She's already proven that."

More than Celia knew. It would be so easy to stand on a podium and tell the world that Daxton wasn't really Daxton after all; it would give Celia the opening she needed to snatch the country from her mother, but I would also be signing my own death warrant. Along with Benjy's. "What will Augusta do to me?"

"Nothing. She'll threaten and posture, but in the end, with Daxton in such bad condition, she needs you more than ever. Tell the world she's lying about Daxton's health, and they'll flock to you. Lila's supporters have more power than Daxton and Augusta want to admit," she added. "That's why you were Masked, and that's why Augusta will still need you even if you go off script. Without Daxton, she won't be able to charm the country into believing whatever she wants. Lila has that power. Do what I tell you, and I swear nothing will happen to you—or your boyfriend."

I stared out the dark window, and I could feel her eyes boring into me. Celia would only accept one answer, and as long as Knox was going along with this, I had to believe that she was telling the truth. Knowing someone had been Masked as Daxton didn't give me the upper hand; it painted an even bigger target on my back. If I didn't gain some leverage I could use, my days after he died would be numbered. And if he woke up, I could very well be looking at the last hours of my life. Gaining the public's trust after proving everyone else was lying to them could be the insurance I needed to buy more time. "Fine. Send Benjy with us, and I'll do it."

Celia's smile was about as welcoming as broken glass. "Good girl."

That night I crawled through the air vent toward Knox's room again. Celia had left shortly after giving me a recording of a twenty-minute speech to memorize, and after listening to it twice, I needed a break. Walking over to Knox's room would have been much easier, but I hoped Benjy would be there, and if Knox left, I didn't want anyone wondering why I spent so much time alone with him.

I didn't want to run into Celia again, either. When she'd handed me the earpiece with the recording of my speech, her hand had lingered, and even though I couldn't be sure, I thought I saw her eyes watering. I didn't know what that meant, but I knew it couldn't be good.

Just as I reached the opening that would drop me into Knox's suite, I heard the murmur of voices rise to meet me. I stopped, careful not to make a sound. The first person was Knox, but the second voice didn't belong to Benjy.

"I know it isn't ideal, but my mother has him under her thumb, and we can't leave it like this. If we do, it will have all been for nothing."

Celia. I inched closer to the opening, straining to catch

her every word. They were going to finish Daxton off after all. Good.

"There has to be a better way," said Knox, his voice tense with anger. "You can't just get rid of him."

"Of course I can. I have a responsibility to do whatever it takes."

"Maybe it won't come to that," said Knox. "How do you know for sure he'll do whatever Augusta wants? Have you considered talking to him about it instead of jumping to conclusions?"

I frowned. Knox had been fine with it before. Why had he suddenly changed his mind?

"And risk the entire operation?" Celia paused, and when she spoke again, her voice was much more sympathetic. "I know how much you care about him, Knox. I love him, too. But I'm not asking for your permission. I'm telling you as a courtesy, so you can say goodbye."

"I'm not going to say goodbye to him, because you're not going to do a damn thing," said Knox. "And if you do, so help me, I will destroy you."

"No, you won't. You have just as much at stake as I do, and if I go down for it, so will you."

"Then I'll go down for it, too. But I'm not going to leave without warning him."

"Go ahead, but don't expect it to change things. Daxton killed my daughter, Knox, and I'm not going to let him get away with it."

"So this is your solution?"

"Do you have a better one?"

"I can think of a dozen."

Celia sighed. "You only think you can. Sometimes sacrifices have to be made for the greater good. Lila understood that, and so do you."

"This isn't for the greater good," said Knox. "It's revenge. They killed Lila, and your plan for Daxton didn't work, so now you're going to go after him."

My eyes widened, and I covered my mouth to stay silent. She wasn't talking about Daxton.

"Revenge or not, having Greyson in power will still give Augusta a direct line to the pulse of the country," she said. "I'll do whatever it takes to stop her."

"Then stop her. Leave Greyson out of it."

"You don't think I've tried? Mother is too well protected. She won't let her guard down like Daxton."

"Then find another way."

"I'm sorry, Knox," she said. "But there is none."

I slid back through the vent, not waiting to hear the rest. Whether or not Knox warned Greyson, I would. He'd done nothing to deserve this, and no matter what it took, I wasn't going to let Celia kill him.

XIV

EQUALS

I burst into Greyson's suite, not bothering to knock. He stood behind a table, wearing goggles that made his eyes look twice as big as they were supposed to be. His living room had been converted into a workshop, with long counters covered with bits and pieces of things I couldn't identify.

Looking up at my unannounced entrance, he set down whatever new thing he was working on. "Everything all right?"

I shook my head, grateful he wasn't wasting time with pleasantries. "Celia wants to kill you."

Greyson blinked owlishly. "Nothing new there. She's had it in for all of us for ages."

"This time she means it. I overheard her and Knox talking, and—"

"Kitty." His voice cut through mine. "It's all right. Even if she does try something, I have guards, and I can take care of myself. I appreciate the worry, but I know my aunt, and I know that no matter how fast she talks, she'd never hurt me."

I balled my hands into fists. He didn't get it. "No matter what you think she's capable of doing, this time she's going through with it. She has a plan."

"What is it?" he said with the air of someone who had better things to do but knew the conversation wouldn't be over until he heard it all.

I hesitated. "I don't know. I overheard her and Knox talking, and I think he knows, but—"

"So you broke down the door to tell me that Celia's going to kill me, and that's it?" he said, not unkindly. "Do you know when?"

"Tomorrow. Knox and I are going to New York, and she's going to do it then so we aren't here to help you."

"Then I'll make sure to keep an eye out for her," he said. I started to protest, but he cut me off. "Kitty, really. This is my family, and I know how they operate. Nothing's going to happen."

"Please," I said, bursting with frustration. "Just *listen* to me. Celia's crazy. She's determined to get revenge on Daxton for what happened to Lila, and she said she'd do whatever it takes, even if it means hurting you."

"She talks a lot, that's all. She was blowing off steam. I'm flattered you came to warn me, but—"

"I'm the one who tried to kill Daxton."

He stilled. "What?"

A knot of panic formed in my stomach. "Not because—I didn't do it on my own, I mean. Celia, she told me to—"

"And you just do whatever Celia wants?" said Greyson softly.

"You have to understand. Daxton killed my friend, he killed the only parent I've ever had, he took away who I was—"

Without saying a word, Greyson headed into another part of his suite. I trailed after him, refusing to let the conversation end like this.

"He attacked me," I said, stopping short of his bedroom. He

stood with his back facing me, and his arms hung loosely at his sides. "He talked about how Lila was so pretty, and he—he—"

"Did he hurt you?" said Greyson quietly, and I shook my head.

"No. I kneed him and—used the syringe Celia gave me. I know it was wrong, but—"

"If you poisoned him, then why isn't he dead?" said Greyson, finally turning to face me. He was pale, but other than that, he looked as if we were having a normal conversation. Not discussing how I'd nearly managed to assassinate the man he thought was his father.

"I couldn't do it. I tried, and only half of it..." I swallowed tightly. "That isn't the point. Celia arranged it. I stupidly went along with her, and I'm sorry—not because Daxton didn't deserve it, but because it hurt you. Celia's unhinged. She—"

Greyson raised his hand, and I fell silent. "My family has been fighting each other for longer than I've been alive. It's how they keep themselves entertained. I stay out of it. They know that, and none of them come after me."

"It's different now that Lila's dead," I said. "Celia really wants to hurt Daxton, and she'll do it through you if she has to."

"I won't let it happen," he said. "Can you try to believe me for now? If I'm wrong, you'll be the first to get to say I told you so."

A dozen reasons why he was being absurd ran through my mind, but if he refused to help himself, there wasn't much I could do about it. "Fine," I said. "And if you do wind up dead, I'll be mad at you."

"I'll be mad at me, too," he said with a rare smile. "So let's hope I'm right."

Benjy wasn't with Knox when he arrived at the airport the next morning, and I said nothing as we boarded. If they weren't willing to let Benjy come, then I wouldn't be their puppet anymore. Maybe once I opened my mouth and they realized I wasn't saying the words they wanted me to say, they would start treating me like a person instead of a weapon.

Greyson weighed heavily on my mind as the jet tore down the runway. I was exhausted; I'd spent all night going over ways Celia could get to him, even with the guards he'd promised to keep with him. If she could get to the prime minister, Greyson would be a cinch. But I didn't know how everything worked well enough to begin to guess how she might do it, especially in her frail state.

"I need to talk to you," I said once we were gliding through the air and my ears no longer popped. Knox had his nose stuck in a book, and he didn't even glance at me when I sat down across from him. I was supposed to be memorizing Celia's speech, but since I wasn't going to say it, there was no point.

"Knox," I said, sharper this time. "We need to talk."

"I'm sorry I couldn't bring Benjy, but he had to stay behind to take care of some things. I assure you he's well guarded."

"That's not what this is about," I said. "I know what Celia has planned."

Knox raised an eyebrow, and finally he set his book down. "Oh? And what's that?"

"She's going to kill Greyson, and you're going to let her."

"You must not have heard our conversation correctly," he said. "I made it perfectly clear that I'm not."

"Then what are you going to do about it?"

"None of your business," he said, opening up his book again. "Now, if you don't mind, I have work to do."

I glared at him, but he didn't seem to notice. "I'm not giving Celia's speech."

Knox's eyes stopped moving across the page. Now I had his attention. "Why's that?"

"I said I would if Benjy came along. Benjy isn't here, so I won't. I would have considered it if you were nice, but you're being a jerk, so—"

He snapped his book shut. "You do realize the world doesn't revolve around you, yes?"

"I grew up with forty other kids and one adult to watch over us," I said. "Yeah, I realize the world doesn't revolve around me, thanks."

"If you can't accept that this is all bigger than you, then fine, say whatever you want. But the audience doesn't want to hear about how the pain they feel every day of their lives isn't real. They aren't there to listen to you tell them that everything they've hoped for is a joke. If you want to take that away from them just to piss me and Celia off, then do it. Right now I have more on my mind than how to keep you happy so you'll do the right thing."

I glowered at him. This was another trick, another way to manipulate me, and I hated him for it, but that didn't make him any less right. The people in the audience—they were me, but their marks would never magically turn into VIIs. The frustration I'd felt that had pushed me toward theft and following Tabs to a brothel—they lived with that every single day. I hated that Daxton hadn't asked me whether or not I wanted to be Masked, but if he had, I would have said yes. I didn't want to live my life miserable and desperate for something eternally out of reach. These people had never had a choice.

They didn't need me to tell them that, though, not if their lives were anything like mine had been. And I couldn't keep living under Celia's thumb.

"I warned Greyson," I said. "I told him that I was the one to go after Daxton."

Knox exhaled, and for a moment I thought he was going to yell at me, but instead he closed his eyes. "It doesn't matter. Greyson probably already knew. Augusta treats him like a child, but he's smarter than the rest of us combined."

Smart enough to know his father wasn't really his father? "Are you sure Celia won't hurt him?"

"She knows Greyson's security has been beefed up since the attack. If she wants to get to him, she's going to have to be a lot smarter than she has been."

"And what if she is?"

When Knox looked at me, I saw a hint of fear, and it scared me more than anything he could possibly have said. "Then she'll spend the rest of her life regretting it."

New York City was unlike D.C. in so many ways that at first I wondered if we were still in the same country. Buildings as tall as the sky rose around us, and there were so many people that the sidewalks seemed to overflow. The streets were blocked off to other traffic, and as we passed by in a limousine with tinted windows, everyone stared at us.

"How big is this place?" I said as we turned yet another corner. I craned my neck to try to see the top of the skyscrapers, but it was impossible. I'd never known anything that tall existed.

"It's the biggest city in the country," said Knox. We'd barely spoken for the rest of the flight, but once we stepped off the plane, I hadn't been able to contain my excitement. Other than my brief stay at the Stronghold, I'd never been outside the District of Columbia before. Was this what the rest of the country looked like?

"How many people live here?" I said, my eyes glued to the skyline.

"Now? Ten million. Before the population laws were put into effect, there were over twelve million people living here."

"And they have the rank system, too?"

"The entire country uses it."

"Oh. Right." My cheeks grew warm. I tried to distract myself by figuring out how many floors there were in one of the buildings, but we drove by too quickly.

"You're pretty when you blush," he said, which only made my face grow hotter. "Lila rarely ever got embarrassed." He shifted closer to me, and the leather squeaked underneath him. "I have to admit, I'm curious what you're going to do about Benjy. Seems he's quite in love with you."

"What do you mean?" I said, fighting the urge to move away. There wasn't anywhere to go anyway.

Knox's lips twisted into an amused smirk. "I mean, how do you expect to still be his girlfriend when you're sleeping in my bed?"

I dug my nails into the gauzy fabric of my dress. "Benjy knows what's at stake," I muttered, turning away from him to stare out the window again. "Unlike some people, he doesn't get jealous."

"Are you sure?"

Knox's lips were so close to my ear that I felt his warm breath on my cheek, and his fingertips danced across the back of my neck, tracing the three ridges underneath my skin. From anyone else, it would've been a warning, but from Knox it felt like a promise.

I shivered. If it weren't for the fact that I needed him to get back to D.C., I would've murdered him right then and there.

Seconds passed like hours, and by the time I found the words to tell him off, he was halfway back to his seat, looking bored and distant, not tempting and warm and—

I really was going to kill him.

"Do you have your earpiece?" said Knox, and I nodded, forcing myself to focus on the passing buildings. If he was going to play these kinds of games, I'd play them, too.

"I don't need it, though."

"Oh?" he said. "Do you have the entire thing memorized?"

"Yes," I said flatly, silently daring him to challenge me.

"Which speech will we have the privilege of hearing this afternoon?"

"I already told you, Celia and I had a deal. She didn't hold up her end, so I won't hold up mine. I'm not your puppet."

"Yes, I realize that," said Knox, and out of the corner of my eye, I saw his jaw twitch. Good.

Ten minutes later, the car pulled to a stop in front of a huge stadium, and through the door I heard a strange murmur. I pressed my ear against the window, and my eyes widened.

Lila, Lila, Lila—

The audience was chanting her name.

"Take your earpiece out so you don't get confused," said Knox, not seeming the least bit fazed. "Wouldn't want you to start rattling off both speeches, would we?"

My mouth went dry. "How many people are going to be there?"

As the chauffer opened the door for us, Knox slid out first and offered me his hand. I didn't take it. "It's an open event, so anyone who wanted to come and could afford to take a day off will be there. Mostly IVs and above, but I suspect there will be some IIs and IIIs in the audience, too. Many of them are Blackcoat supporters, but the majority will be everyday citizens who've come to see you, and every last one of them already loves you. Trust me, you have nothing to worry about."

I wiped my sweaty palms on my dress. Easy for him to say.

Together we walked into the building, where we were met by a guide who bowed but said little else. As he led us through the maze of concrete hallways, the sound of Lila's name grew louder, and the very walls seemed to shake. The audience began to stomp their feet, and by the time we reached the platform that would lift me up onto the stage, I could barely hear myself think.

"You can do this," shouted Knox. He set his hands on my shoulders and looked me straight in the eye, dead serious now. Whatever he'd tried to do in the car, those thoughts were gone now. "Those people are here for you. Remember who you are and what you're here to do. If you want to give Augusta's speech, I won't stop you, but do me and all twenty thousand people out there a favor and remember what it was like when you were a III. Then decide what you're going to say."

My heart nearly stopped. "Twenty *thousand* people?"

"If I'd told you ahead of time, you would never have left the car."

Now I had no choice. I yanked my earpiece out. "Here." I closed his fist around it and stepped backward onto the platform. "This isn't a game, and I'm not your damn pawn."

"I know. Everything's in your hands, Kitty. You're in control. This is your chance to prove what kind of person you really are underneath that face."

The platform began to rise, and Knox and I locked eyes until the lights onstage blinded me. The cheering turned into a wall of sound, and the bright lights wound up being a good thing—because even though I could hear them, I couldn't see how large a crowd of twenty thousand people really was.

All of them had come to see Lila, not me. To hear her words, to cheer as she encouraged them to keep fighting. I wasn't her, though. I was a nobody trapped in the body of a Hart, and if they knew the truth—

I inhaled sharply. Lila would never have won me over because she hadn't known what it was like to be a III. She'd lived with her cushy mansions and private jets, and even though being a Hart couldn't have been easy, especially after what Daxton had done to her father, she'd never known what it was like to want for basic human rights and necessities. The entire world laid itself out before her, ripe for the picking. These people didn't know what that was like, and she had no idea what it was like to be them.

I did. And I knew what I was going to say.

Pushing my worries about Greyson from my mind, I took a breath, opened my mouth, and began.

The applause was deafening. The stage shook underneath me, and security guards fought to keep the audience from spilling onto it. Even if they did, I didn't care.

Lila had always spoken about the founding fathers of the country and wars none of us had ever heard of. She treated everyone in the audience like an equal, and that was her charm, but she had access to information that we would never have the chance to learn.

So instead I spoke about things everyone who wasn't privileged lived with day in and day out. Hunger, discrimination, looking in the eyes of our so-called betters and knowing their lives were worth more than ours simply because of the tattoo on the back of their necks. Having to give up children they loved because they couldn't afford the fines, and what those children went through—what I'd gone through, abandoned and growing up never knowing who I really was. I couldn't tell them I knew firsthand what it was like, but I could paint a picture so vivid that they all understood exactly what kind of shame and worthlessness Extras experienced every single day.

I talked about change; real change, not just returning to what the United States had been like before the ranking system. Lila thought a complete overhaul of the country's political structure would lead to utopia. I thought a world where I could walk into a market and buy an orange without risking my life would be a good start. And as I relayed the news of the attempt on Daxton's life and how he lay in the infirmary in a coma, I dared to hope that it was time for our country to be placed in the hands of someone who valued every life, not simply the ones who could make his better. Someone like Greyson, if he wanted the job. And if he didn't, then someone who had everyone's best interests at heart, not just the Vs and VIs.

The platform lowered me beneath the stage amid the roaring applause, and I could barely breathe. For the first time, having Lila's face felt right. If this was the kind of work I could do as her, then losing my identity was worth it. I was just one person, but there were thousands counting on her to spread the word—counting on *me*. I'd never been needed before, not like this, and it was exhilarating.

Beneath the stage, Knox met me with a warm embrace and congratulations, and I hugged him back. "Did I do all right?" I said once we were winding through the hallways underneath the stadium. His arm was still around my shoulders, and for once I didn't mind.

"More than all right. That was the best speech Lila has ever given." Despite his enthusiasm, there was something behind his smile that I didn't understand.

"What?" I said, but he shook his head.

"Later."

My mood dampened, but I still felt like I was glowing. As we wound our way through the corridors, the crowd's cheers didn't fade, and I clung to them as if they were my lifeline. These were people who knew what it felt like to be considered less than someone else. They understood, and they wanted change as badly as I did.

It wasn't until we were safely tucked back inside the limousine that Knox's good mood seemed to deflate, and when I looked at him, he refused to meet my eye.

"What is it?" I said. "Did something happen?"

Knox grimaced. "I got a message from Somerset while you were talking. Greyson's gone missing."

XV

UNDERGROUND

The sun hung low in the sky by the time we returned to Somerset, but within the brick walls the day showed no signs of ending. Guards flocked to me and Knox when we stepped out of the car, and we were ushered inside, where Augusta stood rigidly in the center of the sitting room. A servant was sweeping up the remnants of a shattered vase.

"Celia did this," I said the moment we entered the room. I half expected Knox to elbow me, but he didn't say a word in her defense.

"Yes, I realize that," snapped Augusta, and she sat down stiffly in an armchair. Knox set his hand on my back and led me to the nearest couch. "Do tell me how *you* can be so certain."

"I—" I stopped, and instead of looking at Knox and giving him away, I focused on the intricately patterned carpet. "I overheard her talking to someone about hurting him last night."

"And you didn't think to come to me about it?" said Augusta, her voice like venom. I winced.

"I told Greyson. He said that Celia wouldn't hurt him or try to take him or anything crazy like that."

"Greyson has always thought the best of his family, despite significant evidence to the contrary," said Augusta. "The Shields are investigating, but she has already fled the city."

"So now what?" I said. "How are we going to get him back?"

"*We* are not going to do a thing. I will find my grandson, and in the meantime, you will remain here in Somerset. Until Greyson is found, you are the heir apparent, and I will not have anything happening to you, as well."

My mouth dropped open, and I turned to Knox for confirmation. His mouth was set in a frown, and he nodded.

With Daxton incapacitated, it was Greyson. After Greyson, it would have been Celia. And after Celia—Lila.

Me.

"I can't do that," I blurted. "I can't—"

"You won't," said Augusta sharply. "Greyson will be found, and Daxton will wake up. Now, I have no more time for this. Go to your suite and stay there. There will be guards posted outside, and if you need to go somewhere, they will accompany you. You are not to go anywhere without them, do you understand?"

Her entire body trembled, as if she were moments away from exploding, and I nodded numbly. Even if I wanted to, I had no idea where Celia and Greyson could possibly be. And it would only be a matter of time before Augusta discovered I hadn't given her speech in New York. When that happened, I needed as much goodwill as I could get.

Knox led me out of the room, and we were joined by half a dozen guards. We walked silently to my suite, and when we reached it, Knox bent down to kiss me on the cheek. As he did, he whispered, "Come see me." Before I could ask why, he shut the door, and I was alone.

I scurried into the vent so fast that I almost beat him to

his room. As soon as he sat on the couch, I dropped from the ceiling, and his eyebrows shot up.

"You weren't kidding," he said. "You really fit up there?"

"I'm here, aren't I?" I crossed my arms. "Why did you want to see me?"

Before he answered, Benjy came out of the room adjacent, and relief washed over his face. "Oh God, you're all right. I heard about Greyson." He pulled me into a tight hug and buried his face in my hair. I wrapped my arms around him, too scared and worried and a dozen other emotions to speak. Benjy was warm and real and solid, and I needed that. I needed him to remind me that this wasn't all some crazy nightmare I couldn't wake up from.

A few moments later, Knox cleared his throat. "As I was saying, I asked you here because I think I have a way of getting Celia to give Greyson back with as little bloodshed as possible."

I tucked myself underneath Benjy's arm. "How? She's irrational, and we have no idea where she is."

"You're going to have to trust me on this. If I'm wrong..." He hesitated. "It's better you don't know the details."

"If you'd just listened to me on the plane, we could have warned Augusta before this happened," I said. "I'm not stupid, you know."

"Yes, I realize that. You can say 'I told you so' as much as you want later on. Right now we have bigger issues to tackle." He looked at Benjy. "Can you cover for us for a few hours?"

Benjy blinked. "I, uh—"

"The correct answer is yes." He looked at me. "Go put on a pair of boots and something that isn't a dress. And a hat. Benjy, while she's changing, I'll fill you in on what you need to do."

"Do I get a choice?" I said.

"I thought you wanted to help Greyson."

"Of course, but—"

"Then put on a pair of boots," he said. "Now. We don't have any time to waste."

I stood on my tiptoes to give Benjy a long, lingering kiss so Knox couldn't miss it. With one final glare in his direction, I climbed on his desk to reach the vent, making a point of stepping on his embedded monitor and leaving shoe prints behind.

The trip through the underground tunnel was as dark and dank as last time, but now Knox and I hurried. We didn't talk, and the only sounds we made were our muffled footsteps on the dirt floor.

It was dark outside when we exited into the alleyway, and Knox led me away from the crowded streets. "Where are we going?" I said as we ducked around a trash bin that smelled worse than the sewers.

"We can't take the main streets," he said. "Someone might see us."

I followed him through the winding alleyways, noting each turn in case we got separated. Knox was careful to make sure I was with him, though, and we hadn't gone more than a mile when we reached a lone metal door. As Knox punched in a nine-digit code, faint music caught my attention. I glanced around the corner, and across the street was the club we'd visited the night I'd caught Knox with the gun.

"In here," he said, pushing open the door. I followed him into a narrow hallway with only a few bulbs lighting the way. The ceiling was so high that it was obscured by darkness, but I heard a faint rustling above us.

"What is this place?" I said.

He didn't answer. As we passed underneath a light, I looked up again, hoping to catch sight of whatever was making that noise, but all I saw was the glint of something metal.

At the second light, I tried again. Squinting upward, I could just make out the shape of another metal object, but this one looked like—

A rifle.

Blocking the light with my hand, I stopped, giving my eyes a few seconds to adjust. As they did, the silhouette of a man standing against a rail came into focus, and he was pointing his weapon directly at me.

"Knox," I said. He set his hand on my shoulder to keep me moving forward, but I planted my feet on the floor. "There's someone up there."

"There are a dozen people up there," he said. "They make sure no one comes in who shouldn't be here. Now come on. We don't have much time."

A dozen, undoubtedly all armed. I was so dizzy I could barely see straight, and Knox guided me forward through the seemingly endless hallway. The urge to turn around and bolt was overwhelming, but even if I did, Knox would catch me, and this was important. This was for Greyson. If they hadn't shot us yet, chances were they wouldn't unless I did something stupid. Like run.

Finally we reached the end of the corridor. It was another door, and this time there was a twelve-digit password. Knox punched it in effortlessly, and I purposely looked away, not wanting to risk the wrath of the guards above us.

Once we were inside, the hallway was much wider and brighter than the first. Doors lined the corridor, and when we passed a few that were open, I noticed that there was a bed, desk, and chair inside each room. Individual living quarters.

"Am I allowed to know what this place is now?" I said, but he smiled wanly and pressed on. The floor was concrete and the bedrooms weren't fancy, but many of them looked lived in. As we passed another open door, however, there was no bed inside. Only rows and rows of weapons, bullets, helmets, and other things I couldn't name.

We turned the corner, and I stopped when I saw a large common room area with a brightly lit kitchen that reminded me of my group home. A few people lounged on shabby chairs, and they all waved hello to Knox. None of them gave me a second look.

"Colonel Sampson," said Knox to an official sitting behind a desk. On the screen in front of him was a map I didn't recognize, but I was sure I'd seen him somewhere before. "Is she still here?"

Sampson stood hastily and saluted. "Yes, sir."

I stared. The black uniform, the silver lining—

My eyes widened. He was the official who'd come to the group home with the Shield to arrest me.

No, not arrest me. They'd wanted to take me to Daxton.

"And no one leaked it?" he said. Sampson shook his head. "Good work, Colonel. Thank you."

Knox took my arm and led me down another corridor, this one with the doors spread farther apart.

"Am I the only person in D.C. who didn't know about this place?" I grumbled, and Knox ignored me. We turned again, and I began to figure out the pattern of the rooms. Even though the corridors were long, we were only walking the length of the building over and over again as the hallway snaked around itself.

"Who's still here? Celia?" I said, but once again, Knox didn't answer. Instead he stopped in front of a door that blended in with the others. When he knocked, I held my breath. Would Celia have taken Greyson someplace only a mile from Somerset when the entire country was looking for him?

The door opened a fraction of an inch, and no matter how

I craned my neck, I couldn't see around Knox. "I need to talk to you," he said.

"I figured as much," said a soft female voice on the other side. Celia. I narrowed my eyes. "What's it about this time?"

"Can we please talk about this inside?" said Knox. "I don't want anyone to overhear."

"Did I not make myself clear when I said I didn't want to be bothered?"

"This is important."

"It's always important." She sighed. "What is it this time?"

"Greyson's been kidnapped," said Knox. "I need your help getting him back."

The door opened immediately, and he stepped inside, motioning for me to follow. The room was bigger than I expected, with a dresser and a few colorful accents, and it felt much homier than the others we'd passed.

"God, Knox, you brought *her?*"

I whirled around, fully prepared to tell Celia that I hadn't exactly wanted to come, but my retort died on my lips when I saw who it was. Her blond hair was cropped to her shoulders, and she wore the kind of shabby clothes only IIs and IIIs were given, but her eyes were still the same ocean-blue as mine.

"Of course I brought her," said Knox, and he made a vague gesture toward me. "This is Kitty. Kitty, this is—"

"I know who she is," I said. "She's Lila Hart."

XVI

LILA

I stood still as Lila circled me. She studied every detail in my face, my hands, even going so far as to make me show her the tattoo on my hip. When she brushed my hair from the back of my neck to see my VII, I tensed.

"They did a remarkable job," she said. She sounded exactly like her mother.

"Celia was there to make sure they got every detail right," said Knox. He leaned against the closed door, his arms folded across his chest. "Kitty gave a speech this afternoon in New York in front of thousands. No one suspected a thing."

"That's incredible," said Lila, touching the three ridges on the back of my neck. "Where did they find her?"

"They found *her* at an auction," I snapped. "And they lied in order to get *her* to do this."

"Doesn't surprise me. They lie about everything. You didn't tell my mother I was here, did you, Knox?"

He shook his head, and I gaped at them. "Wait—Celia doesn't know you're alive?"

"Of course not." Lila made a face. "She's half the reason I did this. She made me give her speeches because she thought everyone would like me better than her. The attention was nice, and of course it's terrible what some of those people go through, but it wasn't worth my life, you know?"

The *attention* was nice? I stared at her, speechless. Everything I'd done, all the risks I'd taken to live up to her ghost, and she hadn't even wanted to do it in the first place.

"But—" I sputtered. "How could you say those things to all those people and not believe it?"

"Of course I believe it," she said. "I wouldn't have gone along with it if I didn't, you know? But it was all Mom's idea. And if she wants to be prime minister, she can go ahead and give her speeches herself."

"*Her* speeches?" I said. "But you're the one—"

"They were all written by her," said Lila, and she sighed, as if she'd explained this a dozen times before. "You have to understand—I love my mother, you know? But she ignored Grandmother's warnings and insisted I stay and keep giving speeches. She said the rebellion was more important than any one life, even if it was mine. So—I mean, what would you do? Stick around? No, thank you."

If Celia blamed herself for her daughter's death, no wonder she'd become so unhinged. "So, what?" I said, deeply unimpressed. "You decided to run away and let your own mother think you were dead?"

"Yes," she said. "Because I'd rather be on the run for the rest of my life than be eaten by worms."

"Augusta suggested a trip to Aspen," said Knox. "My father tipped us off about her plans, and Lila's bodyguard volunteered to take her place."

"Madison," said Lila fiercely. "Her name was Madison, and she was my friend."

"She wasn't your friend. She was your double, and she had a sworn duty to protect you."

"Double?" I said. I wasn't the first to be Masked as Lila?

But both of them ignored me. "There were better ways to do it," spat Lila.

"None that kept you alive," said Knox.

"I don't care. You should have warned me, and we could have come up with something else."

"There *was* nothing else," said Knox. "Madison knew what she was sacrificing, and she was happy to do it."

"No one should have had to die for me," she said viciously.

"No, she shouldn't have, but it was our only choice. Your life was more important."

"Only because you decided it was."

"Stop it, both of you," I said. "I'm sorry Madison died, and I'm sorry this had to happen, but none of it is going to help us find Greyson. And every second you spend arguing is a second we lose."

Knox had the decency to look guilty, but all Lila did was glare at him and sit stiffly on the edge of the bed. "Fine. What's your master plan for getting him back?"

"We go public with everything that's happened with you and Kitty," said Knox. "We don't know where Celia is, but you can bet she's glued to the news for any sign of what's going on with Daxton. So we use the media to send her a message, offer her a trade. You for Greyson."

Lila's mouth dropped open in unison with mine. "Are you kidding?" she said. "How on earth did you come up with that gem?"

"I've been thinking about it since Celia first told me her plans." Knox glanced between us. "She's only doing this because she thinks you're dead."

"Yeah, and we worked long and hard to convince everyone. Now you want to undo it?"

"Yes," he said. "For Greyson's sake. She kidnapped him because he is what Augusta values the most, and she thinks Augusta did the same to her. Once she understands that you're alive, she won't harm him. She isn't a monster. Besides, Kitty's proven to be more controllable than you were." I opened my mouth to protest, but he cut me off, still focused on Lila. "There's a chance Augusta will let you go once she has Greyson back."

"Yeah, and then she's going to sprout wings and a halo and be declared a saint," said Lila. "I'm not that stupid."

"Do you have a better idea?" he said, and then he glanced at me. "Or you?"

"Yeah," I said. "How about we do something that doesn't involve Augusta having me killed the first chance she gets? I'm only alive because everyone thinks Lila's dead."

"And I'd like to keep it that way," she said. "Come up with another plan, because I'm not playing along with this one, either."

"We do have another option," said Knox, and we both looked at him expectantly. "We could let this play out. Celia will kill Greyson if she hasn't already, and then Kitty can become prime minister after Augusta bites the dust in another twenty years." He drummed his fingertips against the wall. "I like it."

I bit my lip. He was being sarcastic, but that was exactly what would happen if Lila didn't help us. Greyson would die, and this time it really would be my fault. If I'd told Augusta ahead of time, or if I'd done more to convince Greyson to stay safe, this would never have happened. I could take the coward's way out and keep myself safe, or I could do this and risk Augusta's wrath.

And as much as I hated to admit it, Knox had a point. I might not have been cooperative all the time, but I was more willing to listen than Lila was. If Augusta had me killed, things would go back to the way they'd been before this whole mess had started, and she couldn't afford that right now, not with Daxton's life hanging in the balance.

"Maybe we should do it," I said quietly. "Greyson did nothing to deserve this."

Lila rolled her eyes. "You can try to guilt me all you want, but I'm not going to die for my mother's dream."

"No," I said. "You'd rather have Greyson die for yours."

Lila glared at me, and I returned the look. Running her fingers through her hair, she sighed heavily. "You're both going to make me do this, aren't you?"

"No, we're not," said Knox. "But I'm hoping that you will for Greyson. Once it's over, I'll do everything I can to help you get away from them. If we did it once, we can do it again."

She closed her eyes, and suddenly I felt like an intruder on a private conversation. I glanced at the door, wishing Knox wasn't leaning up against it so I could slip out, but he probably wouldn't let me anyhow.

"All right," she said. "I'll do it—for Greyson, not for either of you."

I breathed a sigh of relief. "Thank you," I said, and she gave me a strange look.

"Why do you care?"

"Because he's my friend," I said. "And I really don't want to be prime minister."

"No one does except Daxton." She looked at Knox. "He doesn't know you know, does he?"

Knox shook his head, and I frowned. "He doesn't know you know what?" I said.

To my surprise, Lila grinned viciously. "You want to know the real reason why Daxton wanted me dead?"

"Because he tried to sleep with you and you didn't want to?" I said, and that wiped the smile right off her face.

"How do you know about that?"

"He tried the same thing on me. Said you refused him, too."

Her mouth twisted into a dangerous smirk. "Yeah, well, turns out that Daxton isn't really Daxton after all."

She watched me, as if she expected me to faint at what she clearly thought was an earth-shattering revelation, but I shrugged. "Yeah, he's a V. I know that already."

Her mouth dropped open. "*Knox!* You *told* her?"

"Of course not," he said, uncrossing his arms and straightening. "How the hell did you find out?"

"I felt it on the back of his neck," I said. "You know, too?"

"I felt it when he went after me," said Lila. "I mean, my uncle was rotten, but he'd never do *that,* you know? The next day, Knox told me Daxton's replacement was going to have me killed. If you know, too, then how are you still alive?"

I shrugged. "Because I stuck a syringe in his neck and tried to kill him."

"Ah, so you're the reason he's in a coma instead of a coffin."

I bristled. "Does anyone else know who he really is? Celia? Greyson?"

"Just Augusta, as far as we can tell," said Knox.

"Why not let them know?" I said.

"Because Greyson's lost enough family already, and Celia's too much of a loose cannon right now. There's no telling what she would do if she knew." Knox set his hand on the door. "Come on, both of you. If we're going to do this, we need to do it quickly."

Lila slipped on a pair of shoes and snatched a leather jacket hanging from a hook. "It's Kitty, right? He's going to kill you when he wakes up."

"Then I guess I should make sure he never does," I said.

Lila smirked. "I like her," she said, and as she skipped out the door, Knox and I followed.

★ ★ ★

Lila led the way back to Somerset. She knew every twist and turn through the alleyways, and once we were deep inside the dirt tunnel, I asked how she knew the route as well as Knox did.

"Who do you think showed him?" she said cheekily, nudging Knox in the side. He grimaced and shrank back. I didn't blame him.

Once we returned to Knox's room, he disappeared out the door, leaving me and Lila alone. I was too nervous to sit down. Instead, as Lila stretched across the sofa like she owned it, I stood in the corner, insignificant and afraid. I tried to reassure myself that Augusta still needed me, but I didn't know for sure. Now that they had the real Lila, they could do whatever they wanted with her, and chances were good that I would be dead within hours if I stayed. I couldn't run away and let Celia kill Greyson, though, despite what it could cost me.

No, I thought as Benjy entered the room. He was the one price I wasn't willing to pay. No matter what Augusta did to me, I trusted Knox to watch his back. Benjy was a VI in his own right. With me dead, there would be no reason for Augusta to threaten him anymore.

"You're back," he said, not yet spotting Lila lying down on the couch.

"Yeah, it didn't take long." I walked over to Benjy and tucked myself underneath his arm. He turned to give me a kiss, but before his lips met mine, he stopped.

"Is that—" he said, staring at Lila. She grinned and waggled her fingers at him.

"It is. Turns out she's alive," I said, forcing a small smile. "She's not exactly what I expected."

"Can you leave now?" he said, and the hope in his voice nearly killed me. I gave him a quick kiss.

“Not yet. Knox is trying to get Greyson back by using Lila as bait. Augusta is going to need one of us to stay, and Lila doesn’t want to.”

“Oh.” Benjy frowned, worry clear in his eyes. I rubbed his back.

“Aren’t you going to introduce me?” said Lila, flashing him a coy smile, and I scowled.

“Lila, this is Benjy, my boyfriend,” I said, and her eyebrows shot up the same way Knox’s did when he was surprised.

“Boyfriend? Is this a recent thing? Did Daxton let you break up with Knox? Lucky.” She sighed. “Not that I don’t adore him, but we’re, you know. Just friends.”

I shook my head. “You and Knox are still engaged, but Benjy and I’ve been together for a few years. We grew up in the same group home.”

“And he followed you here?” she said.

“I earned a VI,” said Benjy. “I’m Knox’s assistant.”

Lila let out a low whistle. “Congratulations. That makes you the smartest person in Somerset. Only two percent of the population gets a VI, you know.”

Benjy cracked a smile. “I know.”

He stayed with me as we waited for Knox to return, neither of us bothering to make ourselves comfortable. He must have known what was coming, but at least he didn’t try to reassure me that everything would be all right. I held on to him tightly, not willing to let go. Especially not with Lila looking at him the way she was.

After what felt like hours, Knox returned. By then Lila was dozing on the sofa, but the moment the door opened, she sat up, suddenly wide-awake. When I saw who entered behind Knox, I understood why.

“I see you’re not dead after all,” said Augusta. “Pity. We paid all that money for your empty crypt.”

"I'm sure you'll find use for it eventually," said Lila, all traces of playfulness gone. "Did Knox fill you in?"

"Yes. It is a horrendous idea with more holes in it than I care to count." Augusta glanced in my direction. "The servants will help you both clean up and even out your appearances before we do this. Cooperate." She looked at Knox. "Make sure they're both ready in an hour."

"Of course," he said, and without another word, Augusta left.

"Does this mean I have to bathe?" said Lila, and she was lucky Benjy had a grip on me, because I itched to wrap my hands around her throat and squeeze. Greyson could have been dying at that very moment.

"Yes," said Knox. "And it's about damn time. You're disgusting."

"No worse than you on an average day."

She stood and flashed him an impish smile, and then she skipped into his bathroom like it was her own. Knox exhaled and turned his attention to me. "I'm sorry about this."

"Don't apologize," I said. "It's not your fault."

"Yes, it is," said Benjy, and I squeezed his hand.

"He's right," said Knox. "And I promise I'll do everything humanly possible to make sure you both remain safe."

So I wasn't imagining the risks after all. The game had changed, and my time was limited. "If—" I swallowed, unable to look at Benjy. "If they decide to get rid of me, don't let them send me Elsewhere, okay? Even if you have to pull the trigger yourself."

Beside me, Benjy stiffened, but I tightened my grip on his hand. I would rather have died here than be hunted like an animal.

Pain clouded Knox's expression. "Kitty, I can't—"

"Yes, you can," I said. "You can and you will. Say it."

He closed his eyes, and after a long moment, he nodded. "I won't let them send you Elsewhere," he said. "Even if I have to pull the trigger myself."

Benjy made a strange choking noise, and before I realized what he was doing, he let go of me and stormed into the hallway. I stood paralyzed, wanting to follow, but I couldn't. As much as it hurt, letting him go now was the kindest thing I could do for him. At least then he would have time to prepare.

"Thank you," I said to Knox. "Really."

"Don't thank me for promising to kill you. Thank me for doing everything I can to make sure it doesn't come to that."

I forced a small smile. "I will when all of this is over."

Any hope I had left was fading fast, though, and I needed to start preparing myself for the inevitable as well, no matter how many promises Knox made. He couldn't control the outcome, and neither could I. But we could both control the way I died.

Sometime during the month she'd been away, Lila had cut her hair above her shoulders, and the woman Augusta sent to even out our appearances cut mine to match. I'd never had it that short before, and my head felt strangely weightless. I could barely stop touching it long enough for her to put on what little makeup was supposedly necessary to hide any other differences between us. I couldn't see them, and I doubted the public would, either, but Augusta was adamant. We had to look identical.

By the time a guard led us to the drawing room, Augusta was there with a small camera crew. As we entered side by side, dressed in the same soft gray sweaters and black pants, the reporters gawked at us. I kept my head down, too worried about everything else that was going on to bother with them. Would Augusta get rid of me as soon as the cameras stopped rolling, or would she make sure Greyson was safe first? Or did she know she could never control Lila and I was her only shot?

Was I going to die today or not?

I swallowed my questions as a member of the crew positioned Lila and me on either side of Augusta. The same crew member told me to cross my legs, and Augusta agreed. There had to be some differences between us so Celia didn't think it was some kind of camera trick.

Once we were settled, Augusta handed us both cue cards to read. I stared at mine blankly, unable to sort out the words, but Knox knelt down next to me before the cameras started rolling.

"It says, 'My name is Madison, and I have been working as Lila's body double for the past three years,'" he said. "That's all. Got it?"

I nodded, and he patted me on the shoulder. A cameraman called for him to get out of the way, and he moved to the side, still within my range of vision. He gave me a small smile, but I couldn't return it.

Bright light flooded the room, and I flinched. The same cameraman counted down, and I threaded my fingers together and struggled to keep from fidgeting. Beside me, Augusta sat up straighter and lifted her chin, and as the countdown reached one, she took a breath.

And then we were live to the entire nation, and there was no going back.

XVII

STANDOFF

The plea lasted less than two minutes. Augusta didn't say a word about Lila's supposed death, nor the fact that I'd been masquerading as her for weeks. I awkwardly said my only line when the cameraman pointed at me, and that was that. No member of the public had enough pieces of the puzzle to figure out why I had to be there, but it wouldn't save me. They knew now that there was someone out there who looked exactly like Lila, and she would be scrutinized for months until they were sure it was her.

Once it was over, Lila and I returned to her suite to wait for Celia to respond, and Knox trailed after us.

"This better work," said Lila.

"It will," said Knox, and he set his hand on my back. "You did a good job."

I started to reply, but Lila beat me to it. "It wasn't exactly hard."

He squeezed my shoulder, and I said nothing. Whether or not half the country was convinced Lila was some kind of divine savior, she was still a Hart.

Once we entered the suite, the guards shut the door behind us, and Lila stretched and cracked her back. "I claim the big bed," she said, heading toward her bedroom. She tugged on the knob, but it didn't budge. "Please tell me someone has the key."

Right. I'd locked it to make the guards think I was asleep while Knox and I had sneaked out. I slipped past her, and using the necklace Greyson had given me, I unlocked it for her. As soon as it opened, she waltzed inside and closed the door behind her, and I heard the click of the lock once more.

"Is she always like this?" I said when I returned to the living room.

"This is one of her good days," said Knox. "Try to get some sleep while you can."

I curled up on the couch instead of heading into her second bedroom, but after a few fitful attempts to nap, I gave up. Knox sat nearby, staring into the crackling fire. Occasionally he stood and tended to it with one of the pokers, but we spent several hours in silence.

Whatever happened, there was nothing I could do to stop it now. I'd agreed to this, and I had no choice but to see it through. I clung to the hope that everything would go according to plan and in the end, they would still need me, but I knew hope alone wouldn't do it. Augusta had to see that I was more easily controlled than Lila. She had to recognize that this short life was better than the long one that waited for me on the streets as a fugitive III, and because of that, I would stay. But Lila wouldn't, not for long. Not when she still had a choice.

However, Augusta had also lost all of her family in one fell swoop, and I was sure that when she was given the choice between a real Hart and a fake, I would lose every time.

"Can you make sure Lila gets this when it's over?" I said to Knox, touching my necklace. It was rightfully Lila's, but I couldn't bring myself to give it up. Not yet. "Greyson gave it to me thinking I was her, and—she should have it."

"Of course," he said. It was well past midnight, and the flames were dying. I glanced up at the air vent in the corner of the room. It would be easy to escape now, but without knowing where Benjy was or that Greyson was all right, I couldn't bring myself to leave.

"Knox?" I said softly. "I'm scared."

His jaw tensed, and his Adam's apple bobbed. "Yeah, me, too."

"What if Celia isn't willing to make the trade? What if she decides Lila isn't worth it?"

"She will," he said. "She loves Lila more than her own life. She made mistakes, manipulating Lila into being the face of her rebellion—"

"Lila really didn't believe in what she was saying?" I said. "Even after seeing what Elsewhere was really like?"

"She did," he said slowly. "But when you live the life of a Hart, it's hard to see past your own privilege. After what happened to her father, Lila wanted to help her mother, and Celia is persuasive. It wasn't worth dying for, though. The idea is to stop the murders, not to get more people killed."

"And you helped her fake her death?"

He rubbed his face wearily. "I should have told Celia. I know that now, but Lila was so damn scared, and Celia would have gone after her if I'd told her the truth."

"It's not your fault," I said. "Lila shouldn't have run away in the first place."

"What should I have done instead?" said a voice behind me. Dressed in pajamas, Lila moved into the space between us, blocking Knox from my view. "Tell me, Kitty, since you seem to have it all figured out—what else was I supposed to do?"

I sat up. "You should have stayed. If you didn't want to talk to all those people, then you should have told your mother no. Then no one would have wanted you dead, and you wouldn't have had to run away."

"And you wouldn't have my face," she said. "And Greyson wouldn't be kidnapped."

"Exactly."

She took a step closer to me, and behind her, Knox stood, but he made no move to pull her away. "I love my people," she said in a trembling voice. "Maybe I didn't want to risk my life, but I wanted to help them. I just thought there were better ways to do it."

"How can you help them now?" I said. "What good are you holed up in a bunker?"

Her jaw tightened, and anyone in their right mind would've backed off with that wild look in her eyes, but I didn't care anymore. I was as good as dead anyway, and when that happened, I couldn't think of anything worse than Lila running away again and abandoning all of the people who counted on her.

"You're no better than my mother," she said, her eyes watering. "Not everyone's prepared to die for the greater good, all right? We can't all be heroes. I do my part down there, and no one has to know. I had no idea they were going to have someone Masked, and I'm sorry they put you through that, but that isn't my fault. I thought if everyone believed I was dead, it would have made me a martyr. I thought it would fuel the rebellion. They know I'm alive now, though—the entire world does, and they also know their leader abandoned them and kidnapped Greyson. Some of them love him as much as they love me, you know. Do you really think they're going to be happy about this?"

"Wait," I cut in, my head spinning with everything she wasn't saying. "Who do you mean by *they?*"

Lila rolled her eyes. "They had you giving speeches and everything, and they didn't *tell* you?"

"Didn't tell me what?" I said, looking at Knox over Lila's shoulder. He focused on the carpet, not meeting my eye. "Knox?"

"Celia thought it best if we kept you in the dark as much as possible," he said. "We didn't know you, and this isn't something you shout from the rooftops."

Lila snorted and rubbed her cheeks with her sleeves. "What he's trying to tell you is that my mother is the head of the Blackcoats, and he's her first lieutenant."

Silence filled the room, and I stood there dumbly, my mind racing. It made sense, didn't it? With how much Celia hated her family, what they'd done to her, her attempt to kill Daxton—I didn't know enough about the Blackcoats to decide if I'd been an idiot for missing it or not, but with the way Lila stared at me, I felt like one.

This went way beyond sibling rivalry between Celia and Daxton.

I took a deep breath, trying to make sense of the knot of words on the tip of my tongue. "So those bombings—all those people dying—"

"I didn't mean it, okay?" said Lila, her eyes overflowing again. "My mother never goes into the bunkers, so Knox decided he could hide me in one close by. He told the other lieutenants to keep their mouths shut, and I didn't know that this would happen." She sniffed and looked at Knox. "Mother won't be happy when she finds out you hid me, you know."

He ran his fingers through his hair. "Do you really have to tell her, Lila? Everyone has enough to worry about already. I'd rather not have to worry about Celia killing me, as well."

"You make sure I get to crawl back under my rock, and you won't have to worry about it."

"He already promised he'd help you," I said. "You don't need to blackmail him into it."

She smiled ruefully. "Haven't you heard? It's our family's way of saying 'I love you.'"

"Lila," said Knox sharply, and she gave him a withering look. He turned back to me. "Kitty, I'm sorry we didn't tell you, but—"

"You lied to me," I said. "You told me you had nothing to do with this before Lila died."

"You did?" said Lila, eyebrow raised.

Knox opened and shut his mouth. "I—"

Without warning, the door burst open, and Augusta marched into the suite. I paled. Had she been listening?

If she had, her expression didn't show it. Instead she clasped her hands together and looked down her nose at the three of us. "Good, you're all up. Get dressed. We've received word from Celia, and we're making the trade at dawn."

Lila swore under her breath and stormed back into the bedroom. I stood motionless, and Augusta raised one perfectly arched eyebrow.

"You, too, Kitty."

My insides clenched uncomfortably. "I thought you were trading Lila for Greyson," I said, my throat like sandpaper.

"We are."

"Then I'm not going," I said. "You have Lila. You don't need me."

Augusta took a step toward me, and with monumental effort, I stood my ground. "I thought you might be difficult, which is why I have another deal for you. You can take it or leave it, but know that I do not bluff."

"What, going to offer me my freedom if I do this one last thing for you? I know what *freedom* means, and I'm not interested in being sent Elsewhere."

"What about your dear friend?" said Augusta. "Benjy, is it?"

My blood turned to ice. "You can't."

"I already have. Benjy has been taken to a secure location, and he will be released following the exchange. Whether he continues to work for Lennox or is sent Elsewhere all depends on your willingness to participate."

Cold rage spilled through me, spreading from the tips of my fingers to my toes until I was numb with fury. I'd let them get away with destroying my life and stripping me of my identity, but if Augusta sent Benjy Elsewhere—

No. It wasn't going to happen. Even if it meant stepping in front of whatever bullet was coming my way and smiling when it hit me, if it gave Benjy the life he deserved, I would do it.

"Do we have an accord?" said Augusta, and I nodded, not trusting myself to speak. "Very good. Now do as I say and meet us downstairs in five minutes. Knox, I trust you will see they make it on time."

"Of course," he said, and with that Augusta left. As soon as the door closed behind her, Knox touched my arm. "Whatever this is, Kitty, I won't let anything happen to him."

I shrugged his hand off and walked away. "You already have."

Knox wasn't allowed to come with us. The helicopter waiting behind the mansion only seated five passengers: Augusta, Lila, me, and two guards. As we lifted off the ground, I pressed my forehead against the window and watched Knox grow smaller as he raised his hand in a silent goodbye.

I didn't return it. It wasn't his fault that Benjy was in danger, but he was the one who'd come up with this stupid plan in the first place, and if anything happened to Benjy, I would never forgive him.

The helicopter soared over the city, and I stared down at

the unfamiliar buildings. From the street I was sure I would have recognized them, but from the sky, they looked foreign. For a moment I closed my eyes and tried to imagine what my life would have been like if I'd gotten a IV. I wouldn't have stolen that orange or had to leave the city and Benjy behind; I would never have followed Tabs to the brothel; and Daxton would never have gotten his slimy hands on me. If only I'd done better on the test, my life would have been unrecognizable, and Benjy would have been safe as a VI in a government building somewhere far away from Augusta.

I spent most of the trip trying to figure out what she was planning. Five passengers meant one of us wouldn't be returning, and somehow I didn't think it would be a guard. Maybe she intended to keep her bargain with Celia, and I would be the one sitting next to Greyson on the way back. Or maybe she was going to kill me and blame it on Celia so Lila would be on the flight home. I bit my lip and pictured a reporter talking about the heroic death of Lila's body double, protecting her from harm. Maybe they would make up an elaborate story about how I'd jumped in front of Celia's bullet. Maybe I would even get a funeral.

The helicopter touched down in a clearing surrounded by mountains. The sky was the kind of gray that announced the approaching dawn, and this high up, there was already a swirl of snow in the wind. I drew my coat tighter around my body, but it didn't help keep out the biting cold.

"You're sure this is it?" said Lila as we stood together beside the helicopter. It blocked out the wind from one side, but it was still freezing. I shivered and slipped my hands inside my sleeves, but when I glanced at Lila, the cold didn't seem to bother her.

"Yes, I am sure," said Augusta, checking her watch. "It is not quite dawn. Give them a moment."

I searched for any sign of Celia or Greyson, but I only saw bare trees and frozen ground. "How could they survive out here?" I said, trying to keep my teeth from chattering.

"The family has a cabin a few miles from here," said Lila. "There are hiking trails all along the mountain. I don't get why you didn't send guards to flush them out, Grandmother."

"Because I don't trust your mother not to kill Greyson," said Augusta. "Now hush."

My feet grew numb while we waited, and I had to stamp them against the ground to get the blood flowing again. It smelled like winter up here, crisp and cold and dry, and I breathed deeply in an effort to keep myself from panicking.

At last, when we'd waited so long I thought my fingers would fall off, one of the guards pointed to something in the distance. "There," he said. "I see them."

Augusta motioned toward us. "Girls, on either side of me."

I moved next to her, and this time the numbness that washed over me had nothing to do with the cold. I squinted at the tree line, and finally I saw them: two figures arm in arm trudging over the hard ground, one with dark hair and the other with a knit cap. Celia and Greyson.

"Hello, Mother," called Celia. She and Greyson stopped twenty feet away from us, both wearing thick winter coats, scarves, and gloves. At least Celia hadn't made him freeze to death getting here. A gun holster hung at Celia's hip. "I see you brought both of them."

"So I did," said Augusta frigidly. "And now you have a choice, my darling. You get to pick the one you keep. Isn't that exciting?"

Celia's expression hardened. "I want my daughter."

"I know that, dear," said Augusta. "But which one is she?"

I frowned. The only differences between us were so minor that there was no possible way Celia could see them from a distance. I couldn't even see them when Lila and I were both looking into the same mirror.

The solution was simple. I glanced at Lila, hoping she would tell Celia the truth, but she was strangely silent. I opened my mouth to do it for her, but before I could make a sound, Augusta cut me off.

"Choose wisely," she said, her voice echoing as it carried through the clearing. "Because whichever one you leave behind will die."

XVIII

PASSWORD

My confession that I wasn't Lila died on my lips.

The moment Augusta announced one of us wouldn't be leaving the clearing alive, I understood why Lila had chosen to run rather than risk death. No matter how much I'd prepared myself for dying at the hands of this twisted family, the thought of it happening now made the world spin and the edge of my vision go dark.

With Augusta between us, I couldn't see Lila's reaction, but I did feel Augusta's hand wrap tightly around my shoulder.

"Not a word, girls," she said. "Else I promise you both a slow and painful death."

Engulfed in mind-numbing fear, I could barely breathe, but that was nothing compared to the look on Celia's face. Her mouth hung open, and she looked between us wildly.

"Grandmother, you can't do this," called Greyson. "Celia will let me go, and there's no reason for anyone to die. Think about what you're doing. She's your daughter."

"Celia is no longer any daughter of mine," said Augusta, her voice rising. "She tried to kill my son, and she kidnapped my grandson."

"Only because she thought you'd killed her entire family,"

shouted Greyson. "If you do this, Grandmother, you won't just lose her. You'll lose me, too."

Her grip tightened on my shoulder, and I winced. If I survived this, I'd have a nasty bruise. "You don't understand now, but you will in time," she said. "Now, Celia—you have ten seconds to make your choice, or I will make it for you."

The guards drew their weapons. When the one beside me pressed the barrel of his gun against my neck, all I could think of was Benjy and how he'd stormed off before we'd had the chance to say goodbye. Would he hate himself for it, or would he eventually forgive himself? Would my death save his life? Or would he be sent Elsewhere so Augusta wouldn't have to worry about him, either?

"Five," said Augusta. "Four. Three. Two—"

"The one on the left," cried Celia.

The crack of a gun echoed off the mountainsides around us, and I instinctively ducked, covering my ears with my trembling hands.

I was still standing.

My eyes flew open, and Augusta smiled cruelly down at me. She set her hand on the back of my neck and traced the three ridges underneath my VII. "Go, Lila," she said. "Go to your mother."

On the other side of her, crumpled in a heap, was Lila. My stomach twisted violently, and it took everything I had to put one foot in front of the other. But as I walked away, I noticed a tiny blue plume sticking out of her neck, and her chest rose and fell with shallow breaths.

She was still alive. Would that have been me if Celia had chosen Lila? Had Augusta known which of us was which?

As I crossed the clearing, Greyson knelt on the snowy ground and gathered up Celia, who had collapsed. She'd kidnapped him and threatened to kill him, and he was *hugging* her.

“Greyson,” said Augusta sharply. “Come.”

The look he gave her could have melted steel. He helped Celia to her feet, and without wasting any time, she reached for me. As she wrapped her arms around me, I looked at Greyson, and he touched the middle of his chest—right in the place where the silver necklace rested against mine.

As the guard led him away, I gave him a small smile, and he returned it. Even if I never saw him again, at least he was safe.

Celia held me so tightly that she nearly broke my ribs. “Lila?” she whispered.

“I’m sorry,” I said. “But she’s still alive. It was some kind of dart—”

Celia swore and pushed me away as if I’d burned her. She stumbled forward and desperately searched the group across the clearing, where Augusta ushered Greyson into the helicopter, but Lila was already gone.

“Come on,” said Celia, grabbing my wrist. “We have to get out of here.”

I didn’t question her. Just as the roar of the helicopter started again, another gunshot echoed off the side of the mountain, and a clump of dirt exploded in front of me. I ducked.

“What—”

“What do you think?” she growled.

I kept my head down as Celia pulled me into the forest. The earth around us took bullet after bullet, and I ran blindly, my lungs burning. Even after we reached the trees, we kept going.

Celia led me down a winding trail, and we didn’t stop until we reached a vehicle parked on the edge of another clearing. Without saying a word, Celia opened the door and pushed me inside, slamming it shut behind me.

She jumped into the driver’s seat and ran her thumb over a sensor. The engine purred to life, and she stomped on the accelerator. "You're sure she's still alive?" she said, steering the car expertly around curves I didn't see coming.

"I saw her breathing," I said as I wrestled with my seat belt. "I don't think Augusta knew who was who until after you chose."

Celia breathed a sigh of relief. "Thank God."

Once I managed to slide the buckle together, I squeezed my eyes shut and willed my stomach to settle. The twisting path did nothing to help. The heat was on full blast, and soon a trickle of sweat ran down my forehead. My heart raced from the adrenaline rush, and I knew taking off my jacket wouldn't cool me off much. Besides, I'd have to put it back on later, and if we really were being chased, it would waste precious seconds.

"Why did you kidnap Greyson?" I said as she sped down the side of the mountain. "You must have known this kind of thing was going to happen."

"How could I?" she said. "I had no idea she was still alive. It's really Lila? How did you find her?"

"It's her," I said, and I launched into everything that had happened since she'd taken Greyson. She demanded details, especially about where Lila had been hiding. I made a point not to mention Knox's role.

"Christ." She turned the wheel sharply again, and the car emerged from the trees onto an open road. Celia sped up, and the forest became a blur. "None of them told me. She was with them the whole time, and not a single one of them said a word."

"They love her. You said so yourself."

"I can't believe she let me think she was dead." Celia shook her head in disbelief. "Where did I go wrong?"

It wasn't my place to tell her, so I didn't answer. Instead I stared out the window and kept my eyes peeled for any signs of a helicopter in the morning sky.

Suddenly a great boom rattled the car, and I twisted around to look out the back window. Several miles away, a cloud of black smoke rose into the clouds, and orange flames flickered up from the trees.

"What was that?" I said, panicked, but Celia was silent. Her grip on the wheel tightened, and when it became obvious she wasn't going to answer me, I added, "Where are we going?"

"To the city," she said. "I'm getting my daughter back."

By the time we passed through the outskirts of D.C., it was nearly noon. I tried to nap, but I couldn't find a comfortable position, and I was too worried about Benjy to fall asleep anyway. I'd fulfilled my side of the bargain, but I knew better than to think Augusta would do the same.

We ditched the car a few miles from Somerset and started out on foot. Avoiding the crowded main roads, we took back streets and alleyways, which muted the buzz of the city. The sky rumbled above us, threatening a storm, and on the side of a building I noticed a screen with a picture of Celia's face on it. Words scrolled underneath it, but I had no idea what they said.

"Celia," I said, pointing to the picture. The blood drained from her face. "What is it?"

She stared wordlessly at the screen for a good half a minute. When she spoke, her voice was rough. "They're saying—they're saying I'm dead. And that Lila and Greyson are safe, but in the middle of the rescue attempt, you—Lila's double—valiantly gave your life to protect her." Celia swore. "I can't believe she'd do this to me."

I could. It was exactly like I'd predicted, except the part where Celia had died, too. "It's not a bad thing." Before she could snap at me, I added, "If everyone thinks you're dead, you'll have an easier time of disappearing."

"I've never had a problem before," she muttered, and we continued forward in silence.

I didn't recognize where we were until we reached the metal door. Now that I knew it was the Blackcoats' bunker, a shiver ran down my spine as we stepped into the dark hallway.

"Why are we here?" I said.

"Because we need weapons," said Celia. "Now stop asking questions."

Before we could take another step, however, light flooded the corridor, and I could clearly see dozens of guards pointing their rifles directly at us. My heart pounded. Celia froze, her hand flying to her holstered gun, but even I knew it was suicide to pull it out.

"What's going on?" said Celia in a loud and authoritative voice. "I know the media's reporting I'm dead, but surely you all know better than to believe what they tell you by now."

No one spoke. Seconds ticked by, and I shook as badly as I had on the side of the mountain. None of the guards lowered their weapons. One step and I would be dead. We both would be.

"Stay calm," said Celia softly. "They won't shoot us unless we make the first move."

"How do you know?" I whispered, struggling to keep the rising hysteria from my voice.

"Because I trained them."

At last, when I was so dizzy with fear that I thought I'd pass out, the door on the far side of the corridor opened. "Let them through."

The guards relaxed, and my knees buckled with relief. I stumbled down the rest of the hallway, so dazed that I didn't see Knox standing in the doorway until I was nearly on top of him.

"Steady," he said, taking my arm. While his tone was friendly enough, when he looked at Celia, his expression was anything but. "It's about time you showed up. What the hell happened?"

"I don't know," she snapped. "Exactly how long have you known my daughter was still alive?"

Knox scowled, and instead of answering, he led us through the maze of hallways, his arm wrapped around my shoulders. When we reached the common area, he jerked his head, and everyone cleared out. He led me to the nearest chair, and at last I shook myself from his grip.

"I can seat myself," I said. Now that I'd calmed down, I could feel pain in the side of my cheek from where I must have bit it. When I probed the ragged flesh with my tongue, I tasted blood.

Knox backed away, and behind him, Celia paced, her hand still on her holster.

"I'm sorry for not telling you about Lila," he said. "We tried to include you when I heard about the threats, and when you dismissed them, Lila got scared. I tried to get her to tell you after she was safe, but she was afraid you would make her come back."

Celia looked away, but not before I noticed a shadow of guilt cast across her face. Knox must have seen it, too, because when he spoke again, his voice was gentler. "Tell me what happened."

"I didn't take Greyson to hurt him," said Celia tightly. "You know that. I love him, but I knew it would scare the hell out of Augusta, and—"

"And what?" he said. "You really thought she would hand the country over to you?"

Celia was silent for a long moment, and when she spoke, her eyes glistened with unshed tears. "Dammit, Knox, I thought they'd killed my daughter. I wanted them to hurt, but that didn't mean I was going to hurt Greyson. All I did was drive him out to the cabin. He agreed to come with me, and he was never in any danger."

He'd gone with her willingly? I looked at Knox for any sign he'd suspected Greyson might've done that, but all he did was grimace.

"We had no way of knowing that," he said. "And with the way you've been acting lately—"

"It doesn't matter," she said. "I was acting that way because I thought Lila was gone, but she's not. Is she?" She glanced at me. "They shot her, but Kitty said it was a tranquilizer—"

"Kitty was right." Knox looked at me, and for a split second I saw the ghost of a smile. "Augusta has her locked in her suite now, and she's fine. She and Greyson both are. He's seen the reports that you and Kitty are dead, and he's so angry that if I didn't know him any better, I would guess he'd take care of Augusta himself."

The thought of Greyson killing his own grandmother made my stomach roll. "What about Benjy? Did Augusta let him go?"

Knox shook his head. "He's locked in the safe room. I tried to get her to release him, but she refuses until your body shows up."

I bit my lip. Of course she hadn't kept her word. I'd been stupid to hope she would.

"Does she really think we're dead?" said Celia. "The spray of bullets—"

"They blew up the cabin," said Knox. "She was sure you were in it."

Celia let out a string of curses that made the hair on the

back of my neck stand up. "So now what? I have no way of getting back into Somerset, and the best we can do with Kitty is hope the guards think she's Lila—"

"Actually, there is a way," said Knox. "Kitty, you're staying here."

I snorted. "Yeah, right."

"It's too dangerous, and you have no idea how to handle a weapon."

"Then teach me. You said you would anyway."

He scowled. "If you get yourself killed—"

"Then I promise not to blame you." I stood. "Let's go."

I'd never held a gun before, and the cold metal felt foreign in my hand. Knox ran through the basics, and my quick lesson boiled down to the number of bullets I had, the safety, and the trigger.

"Don't be afraid to use it if you have to," said Knox as he strapped the holster onto me. I slid the gun inside and pulled the hem of my sweater over it, hoping it wouldn't come to that. I'd chickened out injecting Daxton with poison; I had no idea how I would ever work up the courage to shoot someone, but there was no way in hell I was letting them leave me behind.

Celia and Knox took so many different weapons and bullets that it was a miracle they could carry them all. Knox assured me he didn't plan on using his, but Celia made no such promises.

The plan was simple: we would find Lila and Benjy and get out of Somerset. Knox was determined to find Greyson as well and offer him the chance to leave, but his life wasn't at risk if he stayed. I wanted him to come with us as badly as Knox did, but my priority was finding Benjy.

It was freezing in the underground tunnel, and I shivered as I followed the glow from Knox's flashlight. Celia was fuming, and she had been ever since Knox opened the door to show her the entrance into the passageway.

"This has been here the whole time, and no one ever bothered to tell me?" she'd said. She was carrying too many weapons for me to have any desire to answer her, and Knox also stayed quiet.

None of us spoke again until we stood in the empty space directly above Knox's suite. He and Celia started to sort through the arsenal they'd brought, silently exchanging clips and holsters and guns. Without an explanation, Knox handed me a plastic thing that felt like a toy, and he unlatched the hole in the ceiling once they both looked satisfied with their choices.

"We meet back here as soon as we can," he said. "No detours. Celia, you grab Lila. Kitty, you know where the safe room is?"

I nodded. I remembered how to get there from my first night at Somerset.

"Good. You have the password?"

"Yeah." I touched my hip, where the piece of paper Knox had given me was safely tucked in my pocket. I couldn't read it, but if I had time, I could find the right letters.

"All right," said Knox. "I'll find Greyson. Don't hurt anyone unless you absolutely have to. Kitty, the plastic pistol—it's loaded with extremely strong tranquilizer darts. Your other one has bullets. Don't mix the two up, and only use the real one if it's a choice between you and the other guy. Got it?"

I nodded again, and we slipped down the ladder into his empty suite. While Celia immediately headed for the door, Knox watched me climb into the vent.

"I'm sorry for misleading you," he said as I hauled myself up. "Before, when I said I hadn't seen Lila give her speeches—I handle information for the Blackcoats. That's my job. Not public relations. But I knew she was giving them, and there's no excuse for me not trusting you with that."

Right, because now was the perfect time to have this conversation. I wiggled onto my stomach and scooted around until I could see him through the opening in the ceiling. "It doesn't matter."

"It does," he said firmly. "I should have told you, but we barely knew each other. No one can touch Celia and Lila, but I'm a VI. If anyone found out—"

"I get it," I said. "You don't have to explain it to me."

"Yes, I do, because I want you to know that I'm on your side. I want you to trust me."

I hesitated. "I do," I finally said. "And we can talk about it when this is over, but right now I need to go."

"Be safe," he said, and as I pulled the grate back into place, he held his hand up in a silent goodbye. This time I returned it.

I couldn't move from floor to floor in the vents, which made things tricky. By the time I reached the opening closest to a rarely used set of stairs, I was panting from the effort of slithering through the tight enclosure. I dropped out of the vent and ducked into the luxurious stairwell. So far, so good. The corridors were patrolled, but with all that had happened, I held out hope that Augusta had the security team clustered and guarding the family. Knox and Celia were much more likely to run into trouble than I was.

I crept down the stairs, careful not to make a sound. The basement was four floors down, and I slipped through the door, searching the ceiling for an air vent. There had to be one around here somewhere.

But there wasn't. With sinking horror, I even ducked around the nearest corner to see if one was hidden there. Nothing. I backed up toward the stairwell. The only way to get to the safe room was the hallway, where anyone could see me.

My mind was made up before I even considered it. I took a shaky breath and checked my reflection in the shine of the doorknob. After I wiped a smudge of dirt from my cheek, I still looked exactly like Lila. It was a gamble, banking on Augusta not telling the servants that Lila was on lockdown, but I wouldn't leave Benjy behind.

With my head held high, I strode down the hallway. I had Lila's face, and with her attitude, no one would be any wiser. The reports that I was dead helped boost my confidence, but I still held my breath as I passed a group of servants.

Some stared, but I'd grown used to that by now. Visiting Daxton was my only excuse if someone stopped me, even though the infirmary was in another wing and I was heading in the wrong direction. Luck must have been on my side for once, however, because no one said a word.

When I turned the corner and spotted the entrance to the safe room, I froze. A guard stood straight and unmoving in front of the metal door. His gun was bigger than mine, and he likely had some experience using it, which put me at a distinct disadvantage. Had Augusta warned him? And even if she had, would he really threaten to shoot Lila?

It was a risk I had to take. I hid my holster with my long sweater and walked up to him, oozing fake confidence. He didn't step aside when he saw me coming, and for one horrible second I thought I saw the hand next to his gun twitch.

"I want to see him," I said, slipping easily into Lila's prim accent.

He didn't answer right away. Instead he studied my face, apparently looking for any sign that I wasn't Lila. No one could tell the difference, though, not even her own mother, and the guard didn't stand a chance. I forced myself to stare back.

"Did you hear me?" I said in Lila's snooty voice. "Open the door and let me see him."

"I am sorry, Miss Hart," he said stiffly. "I am under direct orders not to open the door for anyone but your grandmother."

I fixed him with the most sinister look I could manage. "Don't make this difficult. *I've* given you a direct order now, you know."

The guard looked pained, and he glanced down the hallway. "I am sorry, Miss Hart, but there is nothing I can do—"

Pop.

The tranquilizer dart hit his thigh, and he collapsed. I tucked the gun back in the waistband of my jeans, and using every bit of strength I could muster, I dragged him away from the door. We were alone, but I knew that wouldn't last long, especially if someone had overheard us.

Pulling out the password Knox had given me, I held it in one trembling hand, and with the other I searched for the right letters on the screen. They weren't in alphabetical order, and it took me twice as long to find each letter. By the time I hit the last one, a bead of sweat trickled down my spine.

The screen turned red with words I couldn't read, and after a moment, it switched back to the keyboard. Confused, I turned the door handle, but it was still locked. Was there something else? A card I had to swipe, a sensor I had to touch for it to read my thumbprint? I looked around the door, but nothing else stuck out. There wasn't even a keyhole. Just the screen with its out-of-order letters.

My hands shook as I tried again. Had I skipped a letter? Had I mistaken one for the other?

Another red screen, and I growled in frustration. Time was running out. It wouldn't be long before someone noticed what was going on, or worse, spotted Celia or Knox trying to escape. I had to do this.

I moved my hand over the letters to try again, but I stopped before I hit the first one. What was it Knox had said when we'd been down there the night of the bombings? Three wrong tries would set off the alarm. I'd already used up two. If I tried again and didn't get it right...

What choice did I have, though? I studied the password again, tracing each letter with my finger and finding the corresponding one on the screen, but I didn't press them. Not yet. I had to be sure.

But I'd been sure the other two times as well, and no matter how I turned the paper, I couldn't make sense of why it wasn't working.

I chewed on my lower lip nervously, and just as I was about to throw caution to the wind and try a third time, it hit me.

Greyson's lock pick.

My hand flew to my neck, and I fumbled with the clasp. Even if it did set the alarm off, it was worth a shot, and it was a better option than using Knox's password again.

Unsure of how it worked, I placed the silver disk on the screen and crossed my fingers. A heart-wrenching moment later, the monitor flashed green and the metal door opened. I swallowed a cry of relief. Finally.

I stuck my head inside the room. Benjy sat on one of the couches, his eyes closed and his arms folded over his chest. The room was ransacked, with every cabinet ajar and every drawer overturned. Apparently he'd tried to find a way out. "Benjy?"

His eyes flew open, and he stared at me in disbelief. "Kitty?"

At least someone still recognized me. "Yeah, it's me. Come on, we don't have any time."

He dashed to my side and hugged me, and his strong arms felt like home. I gave him a brief kiss and took his hand, and together we hurried down the hallway.

"What happened?" he said. "The guards put me in that room—I don't know how many hours it's been—"

"Twelve, give or take." As we made our way through the

maze of corridors, I recounted everything that had happened since the press conference the night before. How Augusta had threatened to send him Elsewhere if I didn't cooperate, everything that had happened with Celia and Greyson, sneaking back into Somerset—

"Wait." Benjy pulled me back as we were about to turn a corner, and we flattened ourselves against the wall. I heard the shuffle of footsteps approaching and held my breath. Beside me, Benjy tensed.

Another servant with a load of laundry. I exhaled. It wasn't them I was worried about.

We reached the stairwell without any trouble. Once again it was abandoned, and a sense of unease overtook me. This was almost too easy. Together we dashed up the stairs, and when we reached the fourth floor, I glanced around the corner. Benjy was too big to fit in the air vent, but it didn't matter. The hallway was empty. Seizing the opportunity, I led him down the corridor toward Knox's suite, listening for any sign we were being followed. All I heard was our own footsteps.

"Get in," I whispered, shoving Benjy through the doorway. Just as I was about to step inside, a shout echoed down the hallway, and I stopped cold.

Bang.

A pair of hands pulled me inside the room, and another covered my mouth, muffling my protest. The door closed, and I fought against them until they dropped away.

"What the—" I stopped. Knox and Greyson stood in front of me, both pale and shaken. Benjy stood off to the side, and I looked around the suite nervously. We were alone.

"Did you hear that?" I said. "Where are Celia and Lila?"

"They haven't come back yet," said Knox as he paced across the room.

"But her suite's right next door," I said. "She should've been back first."

"There's a chance Lila wasn't in there," he said. "If Celia had to go looking for her, or if there were guards—"

I didn't need to hear more. I scrambled onto his desk, knocked the grate out of place, and tried to climb into the air vent. After all the crawling I'd done earlier, however, my arms shook too badly for me to pull myself up. "Someone give me a boost."

Greyson stared at me as if I had two heads, but at least Knox and Benjy seemed to understand. Benjy reached me first, and I tried to step on his shoulder, but he locked his arms around my legs. I couldn't move.

"Benjy—" I began, and he lifted me off the desk. "Let me *go*."

"No." He set me down on the floor and grabbed my wrists so I couldn't climb back on the desk. "There's no reason to go after either of them. You've put yourself in enough danger."

"We can't leave them to die," I said, turning to Knox and Greyson for support, but neither of them looked at me. Greyson dabbed the corners of his eyes with his sleeve, and Knox just stared at the door. "Come on—Greyson, Lila's your best friend. Knox, she's your fiancée."

"She's not going to die," said Knox. "Augusta will make sure of it now that she's the only one left. If we try to help, we'll put all our lives at risk, including hers. None of this is your fault, but Lila—"

"You love her," I said furiously. "Don't tell me it's all for show. You're just going to leave her here?"

"This isn't easy, all right?" he burst out. "If they're able to make it out of here, they both know how. We're no good to them dead, so let's go."

I stood my ground and turned toward Greyson instead.

"Lila came back for you. She did this to help rescue you. And she did this because you, Knox, promised to help her escape again."

"I promised Lila a lot of things," said Knox. "Sometimes you make promises you can't keep. I also promised you I'd watch your back and protect Benjy. That I *can* do. If we don't leave now—"

"So leave," I said. "Get out of here. Especially you, Benjy. But you can't make me go with you."

"I'm not going to let you march to your death again," said Benjy fiercely, tightening his grip on me. "I won't do it."

"You have to." I stood on my tiptoes and gave him a kiss. He refused to return it, but when I pulled away, I noticed some of the anger in his eyes had melted. "Knox, you said so yourself—Augusta won't risk killing Lila, and she can't tell the difference between us on sight."

All three of them were silent. Frustrated, I wrenched my wrists away from Benjy. Caught off guard, he let go, and I raced toward the desk once more.

"Kitty!" protested Benjy, but I was already too far for him to catch me. My fingertips caught the edge of the opening, and using every ounce of strength I had left, I finally managed to lift myself into the vent. Benjy jumped on the desk and snatched my ankle, but I shook him off and crawled far enough inside that he couldn't reach me.

"I'm sorry," I said. "If we leave without her, I'll never forgive myself, and neither will any of you."

"Please don't do this," said Benjy desperately, groping inside the vent. I stayed out of his reach. "Give us some time, and we'll figure something out."

"We don't have any more time. I'll be back soon. And in case something happens..." I hesitated. I didn't want to tell him, but I needed something to distract Benjy, even if it was only for a moment. "Knox kissed me. Twice."

Benjy's hand froze. "You kissed my girlfriend?"

I heard Knox clear his throat. "This isn't the time to discuss it, Benjy—"

"Technically they're engaged," said Greyson timidly, and Benjy growled.

Satisfied they would all have something to focus on other than following me, I started the agonizing crawl through the vent, and this time I didn't bother setting the grate back into place. Either I'd return or I wouldn't, and the secret of how I traveled around Somerset undetected wouldn't matter anymore.

XIX

CRIMSON AND WHITE

Lila sat alone in her suite, her arms crossed and expression sour, and she didn't look the least bit surprised to see me as I dropped from the vent.

"It's about time. Do you know how long I've been waiting?" she said as she stood.

I blinked. "Uh, I'm sorry?"

"Whatever. What was that shot about?"

"You mean you don't know?" I said. "It sounded like it was coming from your room."

"Right outside," she said, gesturing to the door. "It's locked, so I can't check and see."

"We don't need the door." I pointed to the ceiling. "We can get out that way."

Lila looked up at the open grate and made a face. "You're joking, right? I'm not crawling through that. It's tiny. I'll get stuck."

"Doesn't me being Masked mean we have the same body now?" I said impatiently. "If I can do it, so can you. Unless you'd rather go out through the locked door and face whoever's out there."

Lila sighed dramatically. "So I'm just as stuck as I was before you got here. Great."

"You're not stuck. I told you, we're the same size—"

Without warning, the door opened, and I jumped.

Augusta.

She stared at the pair of us, standing side by side and as identical as ever. Shutting the door calmly, she said, "I see you survived. Pity. It does explain why I am hearing reports of Celia running through the manor, though."

She glanced between us, and I saw the confusion in her eyes. She didn't know which of us was which.

"If you're going to kill me," said Lila, "you're going to have to do a better job of it."

My brow furrowed a fraction of an inch before I could control myself, but it didn't matter. Augusta wasn't looking at me anymore. She focused on Lila, who glared back defiantly.

"Is that so?" said Augusta, stepping toward her. She reached out, but Lila slapped her hand away.

"Don't touch me," snapped Lila in the same accent I spoke with when I wasn't imitating her. "You had your chance, and you failed."

"Not yet I haven't," said Augusta, advancing on Lila, who shuffled back. "With one word, I will have a dozen guards in here to arrest you."

"Then do it," she said viciously. "Arrest me, send me Elsewhere, do whatever you want. But when you do, the whole world's going to know that Augusta Hart destroyed her entire family. Your son's dead, your daughter wants to kill you, and you had a stranger Masked as your granddaughter, who wasn't nearly as dead as you thought." This time Lila was the one to step forward. "Tell me, Augusta, how does it feel to know you've let your family fall apart? How does it feel to know Greyson will never, ever love you because of the monster you really are? How does it feel to fail?"

My blood ran cold. For all her bravado, Lila was still a Hart, and she didn't know when to keep her mouth shut.

"I haven't failed, not yet," said Augusta. "Guards!"

Two guards burst into the room, and I shrank back against the wall. Lila stepped forward and held out her wrists, as if she expected them to be cuffed, but I knew better. When the guards looked to Augusta for direction, she gestured toward me.

"Arrest her."

They advanced, and I glanced up at the ceiling. I could try to escape through the vent, but the guards stood between me and the end table I'd always used before. I was trapped.

"What?" said Lila, stunned. "But I'm Kitty. Why are you arresting her?"

"I'm not the idiot you seem to think I am," said Augusta. "That's why."

Bang.

The shot echoed through the room, and I ducked and covered my head as a second one followed. Lila screamed, and I peeked between my arms.

The guards slumped to the floor, and I saw the telltale blue plumes sticking out of their necks. Tranquilizers.

Knox stood in the doorway, and this time the gun he pointed at Augusta was real. "Let her go."

Augusta pulled Lila against her, using her as a shield, and she wielded a glowing poker from the fire. "I don't think so," she said, holding the poker an inch from Lila's chin. "Put down the gun and kick it over, Lennox, or I'll burn her pretty eyes right out of her head. Then we won't have any trouble telling these two apart, will we?"

Lila shrieked and struggled against her, but Augusta held

on tighter. My heart pounded. She had to be bluffing. She wouldn't hurt her own granddaughter like that, would she?

Knox hesitated. At last he slowly set his gun down and stepped away, holding up his hands in surrender. "All right. You win. Now let her go."

Augusta shoved Lila away and crossed to the center of the room. Picking up the gun between her finger and thumb, she wrinkled her nose as if it were some kind of dead animal. "So unpleasant, guns. Far too violent and bloody for my taste. Now, you're going to leave, Lennox, and you're not going to interfere again. If you do, I won't bother sending you Elsewhere. I will have you and your entire family publicly executed for treason. Do you understand me?"

I touched the metal handle of my own gun underneath my sweater. Augusta didn't know I had it, but Knox did. I watched him for any signs of what I should do, but he stared straight ahead and nodded. "Of course, Augusta. You win."

Augusta smirked and started to turn. "Of course I win. I always do. Are you listening, Lila, or do you need another lesson in how to respect—"

A second poker sliced through the air, heading straight for Augusta's chest. Lila cried out, and for one terrible second, I thought she was going to run Augusta through. At the last moment, Augusta pivoted, and Lila missed.

And the next thing I knew, Augusta's glowing poker cut through Lila's stomach until it was sticking out her back.

Lila stared down at the piece of metal that speared her abdomen, her expression frozen in shock. Even Augusta looked stunned, and though it only lasted a moment, she dropped her poker as if she'd also been burned. Lila sank to the floor, and Augusta's expression smoothed.

"I'm so sorry, dear, but you gave me no choice. You're just like your mother."

Knox flew across the room and knelt beside Lila. "Christ, Augusta, what did you do?"

"No matter," she said, and despite her cold facade, her voice broke. "We have a spare."

Knox touched the bleeding wound in Lila's belly, and she moaned. "We have to get her to the infirmary. She's going to die—"

"Kitty?"

Cold terror poured through me, and hoping to hell I'd imagined it, I glanced at the entrance.

Benjy stood in the doorway, and he stared at Lila, his face ashen.

"Benjy, please, it's not me," I said. "You have to get out of here."

Augusta tried to smile, but it wavered. "You're just in time, young man. Why don't you join us?"

Benjy stepped inside, looking between Lila and me. "Is she—"

"She gave me no choice," said Augusta, and for a moment her eyes watered before she blinked and regained her composure. Still holding Knox's gun, she gestured toward Benjy. "You'll cooperate, though, won't you, Kitty? You'll do the right thing, and you and your friend will both get to live."

I stood there, choking on my own fear. Lila was dying because she'd fought back, and I couldn't even find the courage to spit in Augusta's face. I deserved my III. I deserved everything that had happened to me if I couldn't do the one thing I had to do in order to stop this. It was Daxton all over again.

"She needs a doctor," said Knox. He ripped off his shirt and pressed it against Lila's wound, the poker still inside her belly. "You can't do this, Augusta. Think about your family."

She didn't care about her family, though. The only person she did care about was—

"Think about Greyson," I blurted. "They're best friends. If you let her die, he'll hate you, and you'll have no one. You can't hurt him like this, not if you want him to love you anymore."

Augusta stiffened, and for a fraction of a second, I thought I saw her expression waver. "Very well," she said. "I'll give you a choice, Lennox."

I had a clear shot now, and if I unloaded the clip, I would have a chance of hitting her. Knox was close enough that he could wrestle her gun away from her—

But if I missed, she could kill Benjy. I didn't move.

"What choice?" said Knox hoarsely. Lila lay by his side, growing paler and paler as the blood drained out of her. His shirt was soaked now, and his hands were covered in it.

"Do not think for a moment I am not aware of the role you have played in this mess," said Augusta. "You will remain alive because it would pain Daxton to have to tell your father you are dead, and I do not wish to hurt him. So you have a choice—things stay as they are, and Lila dies, or I kill Kitty's little friend, and Lila gets to take a trip to the infirmary to see if she can be saved."

My mouth dropped open. Benjy? But why—

It hit me, and I finally understood.

Augusta knew everything. She knew Celia was the leader of the Blackcoats. She knew Knox had been playing both sides, and she knew how much I trusted him. I would never have gone along with Celia if he hadn't been there, too.

And Augusta knew I would have nothing to do with him or the Blackcoats ever again if he let Benjy die.

For a split second, Knox's eyes met mine, and when his shoulders slumped, I knew what he was going to say.

"No!" I started to stand, but Augusta pointed her gun at me, and I stopped cold. "Please, Knox—"

"Me," said Lila weakly. "Knox, let her kill me. He—doesn't deserve—"

"I'm sorry," he whispered to Lila, and he kissed her forehead before addressing Augusta. "I need Benjy's help carrying Lila down to the infirmary. Then do it."

"I'm afraid that isn't an option," said Augusta. "However, since you've made your decision, I will happily oblige."

All the air left my lungs. Benjy stood still as a statue, and I silently willed him to run. "Please," I begged Augusta, desperation clawing at me. "You can't."

"Oh yes, my darling, I can," said Augusta. "Perhaps now you will understand just how powerless you truly are."

Suddenly the world around me seemed to move in slow motion. Augusta aimed, and Benjy flinched, but everything was sluggish, as if time had slowed down to give me a moment to decide what to do.

My mind was made up. All I needed was that extra second. I pulled the gun from my holster and raised it. I didn't need to know how to aim properly in order to line up the barrel with her body and pull the trigger.

And I did.

Over and over and over again, until only a faint click remained.

In the back of my mind, I heard shouts and the thunder of footsteps. I felt hands on me and tried to shake them off, but when Benjy wrapped his arms around me, I stopped, limp in his embrace, and I dropped the gun.

Out of the corner of my eye I saw Knox and Greyson carry Lila toward the door, and I heard more shouts as a dozen guards rushed in. The sound of Knox's voice filled the room as he issued orders, and the guards went from outraged to determined as they produced a stretcher seemingly out of nowhere and carried Lila away.

But the only thing I understood was Augusta's bullet-riddled body lying in a pool of blood that slowly expanded, staining the white carpet crimson.

XX

TRUST

Benjy refused to let go of me as Knox led us down to the infirmary. Greyson stayed with the handful of guards that remained in the room to deal with Augusta's body, but there was still no sign of Celia. I couldn't find it in me to care. Everything seemed fuzzy, and the only things anchoring me to reality were the feel of Benjy's arms around me and the sound of Knox's footsteps beside me.

I'd killed her. One moment she was alive and talking, and the next she was dead, all because of me. I knew I'd had no real choice. If I hadn't, Benjy and Lila would both be dead, but that didn't stop the guilt from hemorrhaging through me.

When we reached the infirmary, Benjy set me down in a chair and pulled up another so he could sit beside me. By the time I looked up, Knox was gone. I didn't see where he went, but there was only one place to go: Lila's bedside.

Benjy didn't say a word, and I was grateful for the silence. He rubbed slow circles on my back, and I struggled to forget the image of Augusta lying dead on the carpet. Instead I tried to remember what Benjy's face had looked like when she'd been moments away from killing him.

It didn't help.

“I’m sorry,” I whispered. He stroked my hair rhythmically, and for a moment I pretended we were back in the group home and none of this had ever happened. It was just him and me, and the Harts were in a completely different universe.

“You have nothing to be sorry for,” he said. “You did what you had to do. Just—in the future, don’t risk your life doing it, all right?”

I tried to smile, but my chin trembled. “I should—I should never have left you and gone with Tabs. I only went to the club because I wanted to stay with you.”

My voice cracked, and Benjy nuzzled the top of my head. “I know,” he murmured. “You did the best you could with what you had.”

I didn’t deserve him. Burying my face in his chest, I let his shirt soak up the tears leaking from my eyes. “I’m sorry for everything with Knox, too.”

Benjy snorted. “I told him if he touched you again, I’d—”

He stopped, and I knew what he was going to say. He’d kill him. It wasn’t a joke anymore, though.

“Listen, Kitty,” he said, pulling back enough to look me in the eye. “I won’t pretend to be all right with everything that’s been done to you, but I know you didn’t ask for any of it. Lila’s engaged to Knox, and you can’t—you can’t still be her and not be. So—I get that. But you don’t have to be her anymore. We’ll get to leave now, and everything will be okay. We can go someplace where no one will find us.”

My fingers tightened around his. I’d been preparing to die ever since I’d injected that drug into Daxton’s veins, and the possibility of surviving this—I’d given up hope. But in that moment, after everything that had happened that day, I let myself believe Benjy. Celia and Knox and Greyson would allow me to walk away from this, and no one would ever know that Kitty Doe hadn’t died after all. Benjy and I would find a place by the beach, and we would be happy. And neither of us would ever have to see another Hart again.

"That would be nice," I whispered, and Benjy smiled and wrapped his arms around me once more.

A faint sound caught my attention. Four guards rolled a stretcher down the hallway, and I frowned. Who else was hurt?

As they came closer, however, I saw the black body bag lying across it, and I couldn't tear my eyes away. The points of her shoes formed a tent at the end of the bag, and even though it hid her features, I knew exactly what was underneath the thick plastic.

Augusta, dead and full of bullets I'd put in her.

Greyson followed the stretcher, looking as pale as I felt. His hands were stained with blood.

"Greyson?" I said. Instead of answering, he winced and looked away.

Something inside me snapped. I couldn't breathe, and what little I'd eaten in the past day threatened to come up. I pushed myself away from Benjy and stumbled down the corridor. I couldn't take Greyson's anger, too. Not on top of everything else.

"Kitty!" called Benjy, his shoes squeaking against the tiled floor as he darted after me. I didn't stop. Instead I ducked through the nearest door and slammed it shut, enclosing myself in darkness.

In the background, machines beeped and colorful lights blinked, but everything else was black. I took a deep breath. It wasn't my fault. Greyson had to know that. Everyone had to know that. Augusta had forced my hand. If I could go back—

If I could go back, I would have done the exact same thing. Augusta had made her choice, and so had I. As much as the consequences hurt, at least I could live with them. I would have died in more ways than one tonight if I'd let Augusta lay a finger on Benjy. Greyson was grieving for his family, and he needed time. Even if he never came around, even if he never wanted to see me again, I could only be thankful I wasn't grieving for mine.

Slowly I calmed myself down, one breath at a time. Once my head stopped spinning, I groped around the wall and flipped on the lights, blinking against the brightness.

As soon as my eyes adjusted, my stomach dropped to my knees. This was Daxton's room. He lay on the bed, and Celia sat in the chair beside him, her gun dangling from the tips of her fingers.

"Celia?" I said, her name catching in my throat. She didn't acknowledge me. Instead she stared at Daxton blankly, as if she didn't even see him. But I did.

His eyes were open.

"Daxton?" I said. He was watching Celia, but when I spoke, he focused on me.

"Lila?" he said weakly, his voice hoarse with disuse.

Lila. He thought I was Lila. But he'd been in a coma since before Lila had returned, and if he thought I was her, then—

Did he remember she was dead? Did he remember I'd been Masked? Or had he been awake longer, and did he know about Lila returning?

At last Celia stirred. "Is that you?" she said, her eyes bloodshot as they searched my face. "I saw them carrying you into the trauma ward, but I thought it might not be you, and I didn't know for sure—"

"Can I talk to you outside?" I said shakily.

She rose and followed me out the door. The cramped hallway seemed to press down on me and make it impossible to take a deep breath. Benjy waited nearby, but when he saw Celia and me, he moved a respectful distance away. Still within earshot, but at least we would have the illusion of privacy.

"What are you doing here?" I whispered. "You were supposed to find Lila and—"

"I couldn't." Her lower lip trembled, and she looked seconds away from falling to pieces. "I stood there for ages trying to get a clear shot at the guards, but I couldn't. When I stormed them, at first they didn't shoot, but when I hit the first one with the tranquilizer, they fought back, and I had to get away."

The gunshot. The shouting. It had been Celia after all.

"You came down here?" I said, glancing over my shoulder. Other than Benjy, we were alone in the hallway, but that wouldn't last long.

Her face crumpled. "I was going to kill him, but he opened his eyes and said my name, and then I heard shouting, and I saw Lila and all that blood..."

"Augusta tried to kill her," I said. "Lila was trying to protect me or get away or— I don't know."

Celia moaned and sank down against the wall, pulling her knees to her chest. "I thought I could take out Daxton and be back up there in time to help her. I don't know what I was thinking. I don't know why I went to Daxton instead."

I did. Everything Celia had done since I'd met her was angled to get revenge on her family. She had the opportunity to kill the man she thought was her brother, and thinking Lila was safe, she'd taken it. Or at least tried. Just like me, she hadn't been able to do it, either. I found a strange sort of comfort in that.

"Augusta's dead," I said. "You don't have to worry about her anymore. You should go see Lila. They're working on her now, and—and if I were her, I'd want you there."

I offered my hand to Celia. She hesitated, but she took it, and with effort I helped her back to her feet. When I tried to let go, she held on to me, her fingers cool against mine.

"You *are* her," she said, her face inches from mine. "Whatever happens, if Lila survives or—or doesn't, you're her now."

She let go of me. Confused, I watched her hurry past Benjy and disappear around the corner. He gave me a questioning look, and I shrugged. I had no idea what she meant, either.

I still had to deal with Daxton. I reentered his room cautiously, unsure what would be waiting for me. Had he really forgotten I'd been Masked as Lila?

He lay prone on the bed, and around him various machines beeped and hummed. When I entered, his eyes widened, and he struggled to sit up.

"Lila?" he said in the same cracked voice. "Where did your mother go?"

"She went to deal with something," I said, looking for any signs that he knew what was happening. "She'll be back. Do you remember what happened?"

"I was in my office," he said, and my pulse quickened. But before I could make any excuses, his eyes clouded with confusion, and he squinted at me. "You were going on your skiing trip with Knox, weren't you? Do tell me you didn't put that off for me."

Skiing. The fist wrapped around my heart relaxed. Was it possible? Did Daxton really not remember any of it?

"Knox—" I cleared my throat. "Knox and I decided to put it off until you're better."

"You shouldn't have done that," he said in a kind voice that caught me off guard. "I'm just fine."

And so, it seemed, was I. At least for now.

The doctors confirmed it: Daxton didn't remember a thing that had happened in the past six weeks. He didn't remember who I was or how he'd come to be in the coma in the first place. He easily accepted a story about poisoned food, and when I left his room, I breathed a little easier. This changed nothing about what had happened that day, but at least it meant as long as I was careful, my neck wouldn't be fitted with a noose anytime soon.

Midnight came and went before Knox emerged from the area where doctors were still treating Lila. He'd been covered with Lila's blood earlier, but he wore a clean pair of white scrubs now.

"She'll survive," he said. "It was close, but she'll be okay."

"Good," I said, my voice rough from the nap I'd managed to catch curled up against Benjy. His chest was warm, and I could hear his heart beating as I rested my head against him. I didn't want to move.

"Kitty," said Knox. "About what happened in the room..."

I tensed. I wanted to tell him it was all right, that I understood why he'd chosen Lila's life over Benjy's, but I couldn't. Because to me, there was no contest between them. Then again, there likely wasn't any contest between them for Knox, either.

"She would have killed Benjy no matter what I'd decided," said Knox. "You have to understand that. I thought you were going to go after Augusta, but when it became clear you weren't—"

"You decided to give me some incentive?" I said, too drained to put much bite behind it. "If he'd died—"

"But I didn't," said Benjy, holding me tighter. "I'm fine."

Knox cleared his throat. "I'm sorry. That's all I wanted to say. I don't expect you to understand, but Lila..."

I looked away. If our positions had been reversed, if it had been Benjy bleeding to death and Lila whom Augusta threatened to kill, I would have done the same. That didn't mean I would forgive Knox anytime soon though.

I took a deep breath. "Did Celia tell you—"

"About Daxton?" Knox nodded. "She's having Lila moved

to the bunker. We have doctors there, and once she's healed..." He managed a self-deprecating smile. "It wasn't exactly how I'd planned on keeping my word, but at least she'll be free to do what she wants. So will Celia."

"So they're really disappearing?" I said. My insides constricted. "I mean, that's good for Lila. She'll get to be happy. But Celia—"

"It's the perfect opportunity for her to disappear and lead the Blackcoats full-time," he said. "She hates this life, and she wants to spend more time with Lila now that she has her back. It's for the best."

You're her now. Suddenly Celia's words made sense. I hugged Benjy. "No. I'm not staying. I did my part, and Lila's still alive. You don't need me anymore."

Knox grimaced. "I'm sorry, Kitty. I wish you could go, too, but for now, we have a fantastic opportunity. Everyone in Lila's hospital room thought she was you. Everyone thinks you're her. Lila doesn't want to do this, but you—"

"You're going to make me stay." It wasn't a question, and I felt Benjy tense beside me. "Knox—"

"I promise you—I promise both of you that I will fix this." He crouched in front of us. "It kills me to do this when we've asked so much of you already, but we need you. The Blackcoats need you. The people need you. Once it's done, you have my word that you'll be Kitty Doe again, and you'll be free to do whatever you want on the Harts' dime for the rest of your life."

I let out a shaky breath. I didn't care about how Benjy and I would pay for our perfect life together—I just wanted it to happen. I didn't want to be Lila anymore.

But I wanted to help those people, too. Everyone who had heard me speak in New York, everyone who had been branded and oppressed, whose entire lives had been dictated by one test while others were able to coast by, receiving their marks because of the family they'd been born into and education lower ranks couldn't afford—it wasn't fair. It wasn't fair to the people, and it wasn't fair to society.

I'd believed everything I'd said in my speech. I was one person, a III in a world that thought people like me were worthless. I could make a difference with this face, though. I would have a purpose. I couldn't walk away from it now, no matter how badly I wanted to.

"No one's going to kill me when it's over?" I said. "What happens if Daxton finds out? What happens if he remembers?"

"You'll be safe," said Knox. He set a hand on my knee, and beside me, Benjy huffed. "I promise no one will touch you. Not Daxton, not Celia, no one. They'll have to kill me first."

"Me, too," said Benjy. I didn't see the look he must have been giving Knox, but Knox removed his hand from my knee and straightened. "She's my girlfriend, and I'll protect her."

I frowned. "I don't need anyone's protection. No one else is going to die because of me, all right? I mean it." I glared at Benjy. "Especially not you."

Benjy looked away, and I knew he wouldn't listen. And when Knox shook his head, I knew he wouldn't, either.

"We'll do what we have to do," said Knox. "And I'll do what I have to do to help you. For what it's worth, you have my word."

I stared at the floor. This was the only purpose I had anymore, and I couldn't live with myself if I walked away knowing I could have done something to help.

Just a little while longer, I told myself, and then Benjy and I would be free to live the rest of our lives in peace. All I could do in the meantime was make sure he and Knox didn't do anything stupid to protect me.

This time I would be Lila on my own terms. Not Daxton's, not Celia's. Not even Knox's.

"All right," I said. "I'll do it."

Benjy said nothing. This was my decision, though. He was a VI; he couldn't understand. I'd only been a III for a day—one miserable, rotten day—and it had changed my entire life. No one deserved to have someone else control their future, and I wasn't about to let my fear of Daxton dictate mine.

Knox smiled and took my hand. "Thank you," he said. "For everything. You won't regret this."

I wasn't sure I believed him, but at least now I had the chance to choose my fate, and I would do whatever it took to make sure everyone else did, too.

Augusta's funeral was held the day Daxton was well enough to leave the infirmary. It was my first public appearance with the family as Lila, and I slipped easily into the role.

No one told Daxton exactly how she had died, and he didn't seem to care. Even though we were in public, he showed a stunning lack of emotion. And why wouldn't he? Not only was he not her real son, but now he was free to run the entire country any way he pleased without a single person telling him what to do.

If I had anything to say about it, though, that wouldn't last long.

The funeral was held in a cathedral with vaulted ceilings and stained glass windows. Spots of color appeared on the ground when the sun broke through the clouds, and it was breathtaking. Mourners filled the pews, none of them ranked below a V, and not a single one looked sincerely broken up over Augusta's death. Plenty had crocodile tears in their eyes, but as we passed, their greedy looks and furtive smiles gave them away.

What was left of the family sat together in the front pew. Benjy was in the back with the others, leaving me to sit between Knox and Greyson, who had barely said a word to me since I'd killed Augusta.

As Daxton passed, he patted Greyson on the shoulder. "Such a shame, son," he murmured, but even I could see the glint of malice in his eyes. As he walked away to take his place at the end of the pew, the look Greyson gave him sent a jolt down my spine.

Greyson knew he wasn't Daxton.

I touched Greyson's hand, but he pulled away, and a wave of guilt washed over me. "When did you find out?" I whispered.

He furrowed his brow. "You know?"

I nodded. "I felt it when I..."

A muscle in Greyson's jaw twitched, and he leaned in close enough to put his lips against my ear. "The night my mother and brother died—I stayed behind because I was working on a new project. It had nothing to do with China. My father..." His voice hitched. "He was in the car with them. Grandmother tried to pretend he had survived, but I knew."

Of course he knew. I'd been an idiot to think he wouldn't have.

"I'm sorry," I said, and he looked away.

"Don't be. He'll be lost without Grandmother, and it'll only be a matter of time before it's my turn."

"That's not what I meant," I said softly, and he swallowed. As badly as I wanted his forgiveness, I knew it would be a long time before he was willing to give it. In the meantime, I'd do everything I could to make sure Greyson never had to be prime minister if he didn't want to. If I was stuck as a Hart, then I was damn well going to make it count.

I'd spent the days before the funeral speaking into an audio recorder, and after waking up in a cold sweat when I dreamed of Augusta's final moments again and again, I'd spent the nights doing the same. I created my own speeches, though none of them lived up to the one I'd given in New York. I talked about Celia and what had driven her to do the things she'd done; I spoke about the differences between the lives of those who weren't in charge and the lives of those who were. I said the words that had been building up inside me, waiting for release, and even though it took days, I thought they were finally ready.

I would make an appearance in Denver later that week, Knox told me. And after listening to my latest speech, he'd agreed it would be the one I gave. It would be fitting, I thought, considering Denver was the city that would have been my home had I accepted my role as a III. At the very least, I could look out across the audience and know I meant more to them doing this than I would have cleaning sewers.

As the funeral began I squirmed on the pew, the lace of my black dress rubbing against my knees. Daxton was the one to give the eulogy, and the mourners and members of the media who filled the cathedral hung on his every word. To my disgust, he used Augusta's eulogy as an excuse to talk about upholding her ideals. She'd wanted a world where everyone belonged, he said. Where no one wasted their lives. Where everyone had a purpose in society. Everyone was born equal and given a life where they would thrive, he claimed, but I knew that was a lie. For now I had to be content with knowing that I would have my chance at a rebuttal later.

When it was over, we lined up at the exit to thank everyone for coming. I'd never attended a proper funeral before, so I did what everyone else did: I shook the hands of strangers, and I said how sorry I was that the woman I'd killed was gone. Knox had whispered thank you into my ear when the service ended, and Benjy had flashed me a small smile as he left the cathedral with the other VIs. But like Greyson, I wasn't sure I would ever be able to forgive myself.

Once the line ended, we stood together in the entranceway, surrounded by guards while we waited to get into the limousine. With a tired look in his eyes, Daxton took my hands in his. He didn't have the strength to do this, but he'd insisted.

"As tragic as these events have been, I don't want them to interfere with your wedding plans," he said. "The end of the year is coming up quickly, and the country needs to move on. What better way than to see their beloved Lila happy?"

I forced a smile. The wedding on New Year's Eve. I'd nearly forgotten. "Of course." I glanced at Knox standing a few feet away. He seemed to be listening to Greyson, but his head was tilted toward us. "Knox and I will finalize the plans."

"That is wonderful to hear," said Daxton, pulling me into a hug. The feel of his body against mine made my skin crawl, but I didn't push him away. "I so very much hope this tragedy will bring us closer together, Lila. Sometimes I feel I no longer know you."

There was something in his tone that made me shiver. "Things haven't been easy lately," I said. "You still know me, though."

As he pulled away, he touched the back of my neck, and his fingertips brushed against the three ridges underneath my skin.

I froze.

"Yes," he said. "It seems I do."

He remembered.

He remembered everything.

All the air left my lungs, and fear crashed through me, seizing control of my body. He knew. He *knew,* and I was as good as dead.

Without thinking, I stepped closer and slid my hand up his

neck. He weakly pushed me away, but not before I felt the single V underneath his skin.

"It seems I still know you, too," I said, my heart pounding as we stared at each other. "I hear I'm not the only one, either."

Daxton stiffened. Whether he liked it or not, we both knew each other's secrets, and he had two options: kill me and run the risk of being revealed as an impostor, or trust me with his secret like I trusted him with mine. I had no idea which one he'd take.

After several seconds, Knox cut through the crowd to join us. "Everything all right?" he said, and I widened my eyes innocently.

"I'm not sure," I said. "Is everything okay, Daxton?"

He and Knox exchanged a look, and then an unforgiving smile curled across Daxton's lips. "Everything's fine, my dear. I'm tired, that's all. Though it seems the car is ready for us now. Shall we?"

Daxton offered me his arm, and I had no choice but to take it.

* * * * *

Turn the page for a sneak peek at
CAPTIVE,
the next book in THE BLACKCOAT REBELLION
by Aimée Carter,
available now at your favorite retailer!

I

FADING

Somewhere nearby, Benjy was waiting for me.

I could feel his stare as I made my rounds through the grand ballroom of Somerset Manor, greeting each new face with a smile that was becoming harder and harder to hold. They buzzed around me, vying for a few moments of my time, but we all knew they were only here because of my name and face. I was Lila Hart, the niece of the Prime Minister of the United States and one of the few VIIs in the entire country—which, in a roomful of VIs, made me more powerful than them all.

But I didn't want power or fame. If I had my way, I would be tucked away in my suite with Benjy, stealing as many moments alone together as we could. Instead, I was stuck celebrating my birthday with a roomful of my so-called closest friends, led around by a fiancé I didn't even particularly like, let alone love.

Except it wasn't my birthday. These weren't my friends. And Knox Creed was most definitely not my fiancé.

My name wasn't Lila Hart. It was Kitty Doe, and on my real seventeenth birthday in September, I'd been kidnapped by the Prime Minister and surgically transformed into his spoiled, rebellious, and supposedly dead niece against my will. He'd given me a choice: pretend to be Lila or wind up with a bullet in my brain. I wasn't an idiot, and even though it had meant giving up everything I'd known and everyone I'd loved, I'd chosen to live—and to fight. Three months later, after discovering a lifetime's worth of political conspiracies and secrets that should have stayed buried, here I was, with Knox clutching my arm as he led me through a crowd of people who would kill me if they figured out who I really was.

I glared up at him and tried to subtly twist my arm from his grip, but he hung on. I didn't care that he was handsome and tall, with dark hair and even darker eyes, and that most girls would have killed to be in my shoes. They didn't have to deal with his endless stream of instructions on how to impersonate a girl I hated, nor did they have to pretend to love him in front of the entire country when we spent most days in a constant tug-of-war.

Besides, I was extremely happy with the boyfriend I already had, thank you very much—a boyfriend who, with his infinite patience, had been waiting over an hour for me to slip away from these people. If I didn't find a way soon, the night wasn't going to end pleasantly for any of us.

"We had a deal," I whispered, leaning into Knox so only he could hear me. "I play nice for a couple hours and leave at nine. It's now almost eleven."

"Sometimes plans change," he said, his fingers tightening around my elbow. Even though he was speaking to me, his eyes scanned the ballroom. "Relax and try to enjoy yourself."

The only times I'd enjoyed myself in the past few months had been those stolen moments with Benjy. "Lila would have never stayed this long. Every minute I hang around, the more suspicious it looks."

"I know," he said quietly, bending down to brush his lips against my ear. The heat of his breath reminded me just how cold it was in the ballroom, and I shivered in my flimsy silk dress. "But sometimes even Lila had to do things she didn't like. Incoming."

I turned around in time to see a portly man amble up to us. Minister Bradley, one of the twelve Ministers of the Union who worked under the Prime Minister. I didn't know many of them on sight, but Minister Bradley's handlebar mustache was burned into my brain, along with the way my skin crawled whenever he was nearby.

"Lila, my dear, you look ravishing." He leaned in to bump his dry lips against my cheek, and it took every ounce of willpower I possessed to keep myself from shuddering. "After all you've been through, I expected something less…" He made a vague gesture, his eyes locking on my chest.

I didn't bother to smile this time. "Minister Bradley. I'm surprised to see you here. I thought your wife was sick."

He chuckled, and his gaze never wavered. "Yes, yes, well, I would never miss a chance to see your beautiful face."

"In that case, you might want to look up here instead," I said, and Minister Bradley turned scarlet.

"I'm sorry, Minister," said Knox quickly, and he hooked his elbow with mine. "Lila's had a bit too much to drink tonight. If you wouldn't mind, darling, I need a quick word with you."

He led me away, and I clutched my glass of champagne. We both knew I hadn't taken a single sip. I couldn't afford to drink, not when I needed every wit I had to survive the night.

Weaving through the Ministers and their families, along with several of the most prominent VIs in Washington, DC, Knox led me to a table laden with food and cloth napkins folded into the shape of peacocks. The people lingering nearby began to move in, but Knox shot them a look of pure poison, and they scattered.

"You know how important tonight is," he said quietly, once

we were alone. He handed me a small plate from the end of the table. "Do you really think insulting Minister Bradley to his face is going to make this any easier on you?"

"He was staring down my dress," I said. "Why do you expect me to smile and let him when Lila would've—"

"Right now I don't care what Lila would have done," he said. "I expect you not to cause a scene with one of the most powerful Ministers of the Union and make us another enemy we don't need."

"Everyone in this place is an enemy." I turned away and began to pile my plate with bite-size desserts.

"I'm not."

I hesitated, my hand hovering over a piece of pink cake. I was here because I trusted Knox more than I trusted most people, but some days I wasn't so sure he cared about me more than he cared about why he needed me in the first place. "If you don't want me to think you're an enemy, then stop treating me like a prisoner."

Knox sighed. "I wouldn't have to if you quit acting like you don't know how to behave in public. It's been months. You should know the rules by now."

"How can I when you keep changing them on me?" At the next table over, I spotted little bites of steak wrapped in a fluffy puff pastry, and my mouth watered. I hadn't eaten red meat since October. By now I was almost used to it, but there were days I would have given my right arm for a cheeseburger. Today was one of them.

If it was wrapped in a puff pastry, no one would notice, I decided. Edging toward that table, I tuned out whatever lecture Knox was whispering in my ear and casually picked up a piece. One bite. That was all I wanted.

It was half an inch from my lips when Knox's fingers closed around my wrist. "Lila, darling, that has red meat in it."

"Are you sure?" I said innocently, trying to tug my hand away, but his grip was too strong.

"Very."

I dropped the pastry onto his plate, and the last of my patience went with it. "If you'll excuse me, I need to pee." *And find Benjy before he gives up on me.*

"You need to freshen up," corrected Knox in a low voice.

"Minister Bradley is staring at me like I'm some prize pig," I said. "I need to pee."

Without warning, Knox wheeled me around toward an antechamber nearby, his fingertips digging into my arm, and he didn't say a word until we'd passed through the doorway. "Do you realize who's here?"

I glanced over his shoulder. Now that we had left, suddenly the buffet had become the most popular corner of the room, as Ministers, their families, and the clingiest social climbers in the District of Columbia milled around, waiting for us to emerge. They all had VIs tattooed on the backs of their necks—the highest rank we could earn after taking an aptitude test on our seventeenth birthday. The same one that decided the rest of our lives, including our jobs, where we lived, how many children we could have, and how long our lives would be. Their VIs meant endless privilege and put them at the top of the food chain. The III hidden under my VII had earned me a one-way ticket to cleaning sewers for the next four decades, if I'd managed to live that long with the few cruddy resources I would've been granted by our gracious government. "Yeah. Every bottom-feeder in Washington."

"Enough." Knox glared at me, and his carefully crafted facade finally dropped. He shut the door. "You can either play nice, or you can explain to Daxton why the entire country suddenly knows who you really are. Because those people out there aren't idiots, despite what you seem to think, and if you keep talking like this where they can all hear you, they will figure it out. Your choice."

"The only thing that's going to make them figure it out is if I act like I'm perfectly happy out there, pretending like I care about any of this," I said, my fake nails digging into my palms. "Lila wouldn't have stuck around this long."

Knox grimaced. Glancing at the door, he took a step closer, lowering his voice. "I know, Kitty. I'm sorry about that, I am. But if we slip away now, someone will come looking for us, and that's the last thing we need tonight, all right?"

"Then you should've told me that to begin with instead of playing this ridiculous game," I said. "I'm not completely unreasonable, you know. If you'd tell me these things—"

"I tell you as much as I can."

"You treat me like an object, Knox. Right now, in that room—I'm your prop." I shook my head, torn between seething and breaking down. All I wanted was to go upstairs and be alone with Benjy. With the only person left in the world who still cared about the person underneath Lila's face.

"You're not my prop," said Knox, his tone softening. "I'm trying to protect us both. What we're doing, dangerous as it is—it's the right thing to do. You know it is. Don't mess it up just because you're having a bad night."

A painful knot formed in my throat, and I swallowed hard. It was an argument we'd been having for the past month, ever since I had agreed to continue to impersonate Lila. Originally it hadn't been my choice; after Prime Minister Daxton Hart had bought me at a gentlemen's club, he'd knocked me out, and I'd woken up two weeks later to discover he'd had my body surgically altered—Masked, he'd called it—to be an exact copy of his niece, Lila Hart, whom he'd secretly had assassinated for leading a rebellion against him. I was supposed to take her place and stop it.

Instead, thanks to Knox, Lila was still alive and hidden underground. And as for me—turned out I wasn't okay with standing by and letting the government slaughter the people I loved.

That was the only reason I'd agreed to stay when Knox had asked me three weeks ago. It had been after an exhausting night and day, when Augusta Hart, Daxton's mother and the real iron fist around the country, had tried to kill not only me and Lila, but Benjy, too. Instead, I'd put six bullets in her. Now, with Lila seriously injured, it was up to me to pretend to be her until someone took the Prime Minister out of the picture.

That was easier said than done. I'd tried once before and failed—and as a result, Daxton had been in a coma long enough to miss the worst of the fight. When he'd woken up, he'd pretended not to know I wasn't Lila, but we both knew who I really was. I was nobody to these people. I had been raised as far away from the life of a VII as you could get, in a group home full of Extras born to parents who were only allowed one child. It hadn't been the most luxurious upbringing ever, but at least I could have had a cheeseburger without having to beg. And at least I'd known exactly who I was. The more time I spent as Lila, the less certain I became that I knew myself anymore at all.

"Think you can handle another hour?" said Knox, crossing his arms over his broad chest.

"One more hour," I muttered, trying to shove aside my frustration. Knox was right; I'd known exactly what I'd agreed to, and playing nice with the Ministers was part of it. "But Benjy gets to stay with me tonight after the meeting."

He raised an eyebrow. "You know the risks."

"I'll pretend I'm staying in your suite. You can tell everyone we had the best sex of your life—"

"It would probably be the worst."

I kicked his shin with my heel. "You're a jerk tonight."

He swore and rubbed his leg. "And you're going to get you and your boyfriend killed if you don't—"

The doorknob rattled, and without warning, Knox pinned me to the wall. His fingers tangled in my straw-colored hair, and his lips found mine as he kissed me with a burning hunger I couldn't escape. I didn't fight him. Better to be forced to kiss him every once in a while than to have someone catch us talking about my real identity—or worse, the rebellion against the government that we were leading together.

The door opened, and I broke away from Knox, trying my best to look embarrassed. "If you don't mind, we're sort of busy—"

I stopped, and all the air left my lungs. Even after two months of coming face-to-face with him on nearly a daily basis, Prime Minister Daxton Hart never failed to make my heart skip a beat. And not in a good way.

He loomed in the doorway, his bushy eyebrows raised in surprise. They were slowly going salt-and-pepper, matching his dark hair that was graying at the temples. "I apologize. I didn't mean to interrupt," he said in a smooth voice. "Lila, darling, your guests are anxiously awaiting your return."

I held his stare. His dark eyes met mine, and for several seconds, neither of us blinked. Knox had no idea that the Prime Minister knew who I was. Daxton had kept his own secret masterfully, only tipping his hand at Augusta's funeral in order to scare me into compliance. It hadn't worked. This was our own private game of chicken, and I wasn't going to be the first to blink.

"We'll be along in a minute, sir," said Knox. For a moment, I almost felt bad for him. He was the only one in the room who didn't know what was really going on. I should've told him Daxton remembered everything—that should've been my first conversation after the funeral. But no matter how much I trusted him more than the others, I didn't trust him completely, and I'd hesitated, focusing on rallying the people for the Blackcoats instead. Eventually time had passed, and I knew the fallout would be bad—the kind we would never recover from. So instead I'd selfishly held on to the truth as a trump card, to play when I needed it most. Or to never play at all.

Knox did know one thing, though: the secret that I had given up at the funeral, when I had brushed my fingertips against the VII on the back of Daxton's neck and felt the V underneath. I wasn't the only Hart who had been Masked. The only difference between us was that I still had my handler breathing down my neck. Now that Augusta was dead, the man pretending to be Prime Minister Daxton Hart had no one to stop him from doing whatever he wanted—including killing anyone who dared to step in his way. When everyone I cared about happened to be doing exactly that, it made things personal.

"One minute." Daxton raised a finger in emphasis. "I would hate for you to miss your birthday surprise, Lila."

I shuddered to think what he might have cooked up for me, but I forced a smile. "One minute."

As soon as he shut the door, I leaned in to Knox's ear and whispered, "How are we getting away for the meeting? He's not going to let me out of his sight."

"Leave that to me," whispered Knox, and he winked. Backing away, he ran his fingers through his hair and smoothed his black shirt and trousers. I tugged on my short purple dress. Three months ago, I would have never believed I'd be allowed to touch silk, let alone wear silk dress after silk dress custom-made for me. As nice as the wardrobe was—and the shoes, and the food, and the luxuries I could have never dreamed of as a III—it wasn't worth risking my life pretending to be Lila, and it definitely wasn't worth risking Benjy's by dragging him along.

I swore. He was still waiting for me. "I'm supposed to meet Benjy for a minute—"

"You'll see him after the meeting." Knox tucked a stray lock of hair behind my ear. "No matter how bad tonight is shaping up to be, don't do anything stupid, Kitty. I mean it. Whatever brief flash of joy you get out of it won't be worth being sent Elsewhere, and you know it."

Yes, I did. "Benjy and I. All night in your suite."

"All night, as long as I don't have to hear you." Knox smirked and opened the door. A round of applause met us as we walked arm in arm back into the throng of VIs, and several people I didn't recognize descended upon us, drinks in hand. I steeled myself for another round of pointless small talk. I'd long since stopped trying to remember names. Lila wouldn't have bothered, and I wasn't about to make the effort when all they wanted out of me was the power behind my VII. If only they knew what lay underneath it.

"Do you want another drink?" said Knox, even though I still held my full champagne flute. I shook my head.

"But if you can get me one of those puff pastry things—"

Bang.

A shot rang out, and in an instant, my mind went blank. All I could see was crimson against white, a stark contrast that wouldn't go away no matter how much I tried to block it out.

Bang.

The sight of Augusta's body going limp, and blood pooling around her on the carpet.

Bang.

The cold metal of a gun in my hands as I squeezed the trigger again and again, knowing that if I didn't, Augusta would kill Benjy.

Bang.

"Lila—Lila."

Knox's voice filtered through the haze toward me. I cracked open my eyes. Even though he hovered only a few inches away from me, he seemed far off, and his face was blurry. I sensed others lurking nearby, but the dull roar in my ears made it impossible for me to hear what they were saying.

"They're just fireworks," said Knox, his breath warm against my cheek as his hands gripped my shoulders. Cold seeped through my dress from the marble underneath me, and it took me a moment to realize I was on the floor. "See? Look over there."

I twisted around as another bang went off. Reflexively I ducked again, but Knox's hands remained steady. Bright bursts of color filled the grand ballroom, and I had to blink several times before my vision cleared enough for me to make out each one through the floor-to-ceiling windows.

Fireworks. Just fireworks. Not gunshots. No one was in any danger, except for Knox if he didn't get his hands off me.

"I'm fine," I mumbled, shoving him away. He took a step back, and it was then that I noticed the group of people who had formed a tight circle around us. Each of them stared openly, ignoring the display and instead paying attention to me. Terrific. Not only had I broken down, but I'd done so in front of the country's highest and mightiest. "I—" I began, racking my muddled mind for an excuse, but a familiar voice rang through the crowd, cutting me off.

"Lila!"

Benjy burst out from between Minister Bradley and his slack-jawed daughter, and he slid across the floor, kneeling beside me. As soon as I felt his warmth, the knot in my chest began to loosen.

"Are you all right? You were screaming." His blue eyes were wide and anxious, and his short red hair was disheveled. He reached out to touch my face the same way Knox had, but his hand stopped an inch away. Too many people were staring at us, and no matter how concerned he was, he couldn't give me away. He couldn't give us away.

"I'm fine, I promise," I said again. My cheeks burned, and I pushed myself to my feet, ignoring the way my knees shook. Birthday party or not, I had to get out of here. "I just—I just forgot to eat, that's all."

"Back up," said Knox to the crowd, and he began to corral them away. "Give her some air. Benjy, take her to my suite. I'll be there in a moment."

Benjy tucked his arm around me, and I shot Knox a grateful look. Aware of everyone staring at us, I allowed Benjy to lead me to the exit as the bang of fireworks echoed from the garden. Each one sent a shiver down my spine.

This wasn't normal. I'd never reacted this way before, and it'd been weeks since I'd killed Augusta. It wasn't as if I'd done it in cold blood. She'd had it coming, after what she'd done to me and Benjy—after what she'd done to her own family, trying to kill her daughter and granddaughter—but apparently my conscience wasn't interested in listening to reason.

Nor did I have any ends to justify my means. Killing Augusta hadn't done me any favors—it had only removed Daxton's leash completely, leaving all of us in grave danger. And that, I thought, was the worst part of all. I'd saved Benjy's life in the short term by pulling that trigger, but in the long term, we were both one whim away from death.

Daxton stood waiting for us by the double doors, his arms crossed as he regarded me with a look of mock concern. "I'm so very sorry, my dear," he said, reaching out to take my free hand. I made a point of wiping my sweaty palm against his. "I wasn't thinking. After all you've been through..."

"I'm fine," I said for a third time. "I just need to sit down."

"I'm sure your...friend will be willing to help you with that." He eyed Benjy up and down, and red-hot anger shot through me. Augusta may have been the power behind the throne, but Daxton was still the snake who sat on it.

Benjy cleared his throat. "Knox asked me to help her," he said. "I'll be down after."

"Take your time, boy," said Daxton, and he shifted his gaze to me. "The most important thing is that dear Lila's all right."

His slimy voice followed me even after Benjy and I walked away. I could feel his stare lingering on us, and though my knees still shook, I forced myself to walk faster toward the elevator. As soon as we were inside and the door closed, I let out a breath and turned into Benjy, hugging him tightly and burying my face in his chest.

"I'm sorry," I said, my voice muffled by his shirt. "I don't know what happened."

He wrapped his arms around me protectively, rubbing circles on my back, and the heat of his body warmed me from the inside out. If I could have stayed like this for the rest of my life, I would have. "You have nothing to be sorry for. Those fireworks scared me, too."

"Leave it to Daxton to figure out a way to terrorize me at my own birthday party," I grumbled. "How long do you think we'll have before Knox comes looking for us?"

"Not long enough," he said, and I sighed. It was never long enough.

The doors slid open, and together Benjy and I headed into the fourth-floor wing. My suite was down the hall from Knox's, and I would have given anything to drag Benjy inside and disappear for the rest of the night. But the party wasn't the only thing happening tonight, and I wouldn't have missed another Blackcoat meeting for anything. I was already behind enough—immediately after Augusta had died, Knox and the Blackcoats had seized the opportunity and sent me around to several cities across the country to rally supporters while Daxton was still too busy recovering to pay close attention. Denver, New York, Seattle, Los Angeles—I'd traveled for over a week, and by the time I'd returned, everything within the Blackcoats had shifted. Lila and her mother—Daxton's sister, Celia—had gone underground to hide, leaving Knox in control. Even now, weeks later, I was still catching up on the plans they'd come up with while I'd been away. I couldn't miss anything else.

The lights in Knox's suite turned on automatically as we stepped into the sitting room. Even though my knees had stopped shaking by now, I let Benjy help me to the couch, eager for as much contact as we could get before Knox returned. It had been days since I'd been able to steal as much as a simple hug from Benjy, who, as a legitimate VI, had earned his place as Knox's assistant. But with Knox constantly hovering over us, raising an eyebrow each time I so much as dared to smile at Benjy, it was next to impossible to find any time to just be with him. And that, above all else, was what I missed about my old life.

"I'm sorry I didn't find you earlier," I said, tucking my legs underneath me on the sofa. The navy leather was cool against my skin, and after spending hours in the sweltering ballroom, I welcomed it.

"Don't be. It isn't your fault." Benjy sat beside me and draped his arm over my shoulder, and I wasted no time curling up against him. "I nearly punched Minister Bradley for the way he was looking at you, though."

I grinned. "That would have made the whole thing infinitely more interesting."

"Until I was sent Elsewhere," he said. "Then it wouldn't have been as funny."

My smile vanished. I touched his cheek, turning his head until he was facing me. "You know I won't let that happen, right? No one's going to hurt you, not while I have something to say about it."

"I'm not the one you should be worried about." His gaze met mine, and he leaned in slowly until his breath was warm against my skin. "Promise me you won't take any more chances, Kitty. What happened tonight—"

"I couldn't help it," I said. "I didn't even know what was happening until it was over."

"That isn't what I meant," he said softly. "I overheard what you said to Knox. You're doing this for the right reasons, all right? I know it's hard sometimes—"

"You have no idea." My face grew hot, and frustration boiled inside me, threatening to burst the last ounce of self-control I had left. "Having to be someone else all the time—never getting to be me anymore, having my every move watched… I'm losing myself, Benjy. Sometimes I look in the mirror and forget this isn't my real face. And sometimes—sometimes I feel like Kitty Doe died, and even if Knox lets me walk away from this tomorrow, I'll never find her again."

Heavy silence settled over us, and Benjy's gaze bore into mine as he traced my lower lip. Lila's lower lip. "She didn't die," he whispered. "I see her every time I look at you. You are vivacious, and no one—not even Lila Hart—will ever drown you out. I don't care what you look like. The real you will never fade."

He had no idea how badly I needed to hear that right now—or maybe he did, and that was exactly why he'd said it. I slowly gravitated toward him, my entire body aching to be as close to him as possible. But before I could kiss him, he shifted and slipped his hand into his suit pocket.

"I almost forgot—I made you a birthday present," he said, and I sat back, disappointment washing over me.

"It isn't my birthday," I said. "It's Lila's."

"Then consider this a belated birthday present. Or an early one. Whichever you'd like." From his pocket he pulled a white cloth napkin, the sort that had been folded into peacocks around the buffet. He'd refolded it into a simple square, and I raised an eyebrow.

"It's...lovely," I said. "Thanks?"

He laughed, a deep, throaty sound I would never get tired of hearing. "Open it."

I unfolded the napkin, and my eyes widened. On the inside was a simple ink drawing of a house on a lake. Sitting in a field beside the lake were two stick figures—one with long hair, and one with Benjy's freckles. They cuddled together as the sun shone down on them, and a lump formed in my throat.

"I can't make this better right now," said Benjy, "but I can promise that it will be one day. We'll have our cottage in the woods, or our cabin on the beach—whatever you want. I'll go anywhere as long as you promise you'll be there with me. I'm going to spend my life with you, Kitty, and I don't care if the entire country tries to stop us. You're my future. It's always been you for me, and it always will be."

Finally he closed the distance between us and kissed me—a sweet, gentle kiss that held within it every single one of the thousand days I'd loved him as my everything, long after I'd begun to love him as a friend. I shifted into his lap, not caring whether or not someone could walk in at any moment and see us. I needed this. And after all we'd been through together, Benjy and I both deserved this.

He wrapped his arm around me again, safe and secure as I ran my fingers through his hair. He tasted like home. Like everything I missed about my old life, where we would spend the evening curled up together as he read to me. We would never have those moments again, but as soon as we were free of this place, we could make new ones. I'd spent so much of my time worrying about the present, worrying about being Lila, that I'd never let myself stop and think about what my future might hold. It seemed almost like asking too much—like I was challenging the universe by thinking about a life with Benjy as far away from the Harts as possible.

But Benjy had always been an optimist. He'd always seen good in the world where I wasn't so sure it existed. And this kernel of hope, this ink on cloth, was exactly the future I wanted. I knew in that moment, as I deepened the kiss between us, that I would do whatever it took to get it.

"Kitty," he whispered, breaking away long enough to glance anxiously at the door. "We shouldn't be—"

"I am so sick of being told what I should and shouldn't do," I murmured. "Everything will be fine. Trust me. Knox agreed to let me stay in here tonight. He's pretending I'm sleeping in his room, but he's going to let us have the night together."

Benjy's gaze snapped back to me. "You mean—?"

I nodded. "I think it's about time, don't you?"

Even though we'd been together for years, finding a moment alone in a group home with thirty-eight other kids hadn't exactly been easy, and neither of us had wanted it to be rushed. Now that we were both seventeen, I was Lila Hart, and Benjy was my fiancé's assistant. It was dangerous, but behind closed doors, with Knox willing to cover for us—we would finally have that freedom. I wasn't wasting it.

"The wedding's less than a month away," I said. "We might not have another chance before then, not like this. And I'll be damned if I'm marrying Knox without showing you exactly how much I love you."

Benjy blinked, looking torn between eagerness and confusion. "Is that why you want to do this? So Knox isn't—"

"If he thinks I'm ever letting him touch me no matter how married we are, he's going to lose his hand," I said. "I want to do this, Benjy. More than anything. If you don't, we can wait, but—"

"I want to." He sounded breathless, and he pressed his lips together, his eyes locked on mine. "Like you said, more than anything. I love you. I just don't want Knox to be the reason you're doing this."

"He's not, and he never will be." I brushed my lips against his again. "You're the only reason I need."

"Ahem."

I sprang apart from Benjy, my heart racing. Knox stood framed in the doorway, his arms crossed and his brow furrowed. "Ever heard of knocking?" I said, glaring at him.

"Considering it's my suite, no." He pushed off the wall and closed the door. "If you keep this up, it'll only be a matter of time before someone catches you. I won't be able to protect you then."

"So I'll tell them the truth—sometimes a girl just needs to be kissed instead of slobbered on." I tucked Benjy's drawing into the pocket of my dress. "Is the party over already?"

"No, but I couldn't very well stay down there while my fiancée was ill upstairs. Speaking of, how do you feel?"

"Better," I said, doing my best to look like nothing was bothering me at all. "When are we going?"

"*We* are not going anywhere." Knox moved to his desk and bent down to touch the screen. "*I* am leaving now."

"What? But—"

“Do you really think I’m going to let you come, after what just happened down there?” said Knox. “You need your rest.”

“That wasn’t my fault.”

He straightened. “Fainting aside, you’re having a bad day, and the last thing you need is a long night. The last thing I need is to worry about whether or not you’re holding up all right.”

“I’m fine,” I insisted. “Knox, please. We’re in this together. You said so yourself—”

“And right now that means I have to look out for you and your health. You’re exhausted. Your temper’s shorter than it’s ever been. Look at you—you’re practically shaking. You’re a liability, Kitty, and tonight is too important for me to take that kind of risk. I’ll fill you in when I get back, but right now, I need to go.”

I gaped at him. “You can’t just cut me out like this—”

“I’m not cutting you out,” he said steadily, but there was an edge of impatience to his voice. “It’s one meeting.”

“I’ve already missed three because of the speeches.”

“There will be plenty of others,” said Knox. “And look on the bright side—you’ll have even more time to spend with Benjy.”

Tempting as it was, staying behind meant missing the entire reason I had agreed to put up with this and people like Minister Bradley in the first place. I would have the rest of the night to be alone with Benjy—right now, I wanted to be a Blackcoat. I wanted to do what I was here to do: be the voice of a rebellion that, if successful, would mean Benjy and I would one day have that cottage by the lake. It would mean never looking over our shoulders again, worried someone might see us and catch on to who I really was. It would mean being Kitty Doe again instead of Lila Hart. It would mean finding myself and being the person Benjy saw when he looked at me.

The more meetings I missed, the more excuses Knox would have to dismiss my opinions and push me aside. I was here to fight. Not to be his prop or his mouthpiece. And no matter how much he insisted I wasn't, everything he had done that evening had said otherwise.

I cast a frustrated look at Benjy, and he slipped his hand into mine, giving it a reassuring squeeze.

"It's probably better if you relax tonight," he said. "I think you'll like this new book I bought the other day. I'll read some of it to you, if you'd like."

"Enjoy some time with your boyfriend, Kitty," said Knox. "I'll be back soon enough. If anyone checks on us, tell them I'm in the shower."

"Yeah, taking a cold one," I grumbled. He didn't rise to the bait, and instead he disappeared into his closet and up through the secret passageway that lay behind it. He'd shown it to me one of my first nights in Somerset, and it was the only safe way we had of leaving the property undetected.

As soon as he shut the door, I stood. "I'm going after him," I said, tugging down the hem of my dress. Not the outfit I would have chosen, but I didn't have time to change. "Cover for me."

Benjy stood as well, reaching out as if to stop me. "Kitty, you heard him—"

I twisted away from his grip. "If it wasn't for him, we'd have this by now." I gestured to the napkin sticking out of my dress pocket. "We wouldn't have to worry about the Harts or the wedding or fireworks driving me crazy. We'd be happy, and we'd never have to think about this nightmare again. Instead, Knox asked me to stay, and I did. Not for him, not for Lila, not for the parties or the jewelry or the private planes, but because of this." I jabbed my finger toward the closet. "If I'm not there, then what's the point of doing any of this anymore? I'm not his property, and he doesn't control me. I'm not letting him leave me behind."

Benjy sighed, but at least he didn't argue. "Then I'll go with you."

"Someone has to stay behind and make sure no one finds out we're gone," I said. He opened his mouth to protest, but I cut him off. "Please, Benjy. It'll be safer if it's just me anyway."

He gritted his teeth, and a muscle in his jaw twitched. "Okay. Just—be careful. And here, take this."

He shrugged off his suit jacket and draped it over my shoulders. I slipped my arms inside the sleeves, the fabric warm from his body. "Thanks," I said, softening. "Make sure no one discovers we're gone, all right?"

"I'm sure I'll figure something out," said Benjy, scowling. I stood on my tiptoes and kissed him.

"I love you. When I get back, I'm yours for the rest of the night. Okay?"

He nodded, and without giving him another chance to talk me out of it, I stepped inside the closet. Knox may have thought he owned Lila, but I wasn't her. Tonight, I was Kitty Doe again, and I wasn't going down without a fight.

QUESTIONS FOR DISCUSSION

1. Do you believe that your life's work should be determined by a test you take when you're seventeen?

2. What kind of job do you think you would be assigned if you took that test now? When you were twenty-five?

3. If your life was limited by restrictions—your job, the area where you live, having only one child and going Elsewhere when you turn sixty—do you believe you would be eager to achieve and succeed in life?

4. Kitty's dyslexia limits her future. Do you think children and teens today who have dyslexia are also under unfair burdens? Do you know people with dyslexia, and how they cope? How do their families and teachers react?

5. What would you give up to get out of the life that was predicted for you?

6. Do you believe that life in a meritocracy is "fairer" than one where your family or a lucky break benefits you? What happens if someone plays with the system?

7. One of the reasons why this America became a meritocracy was overpopulation. Do you think that the strain of overpopulation might lead us in this direction unless changes are made? What can be done to create a better future?

8. Instead of an elected official, this America has a prime minister, and the role is inherited. How does the idea of one family in power match with the meritocracy in this country?

9. Kitty gives up her own name and not-so-bright future to take on another girl's name and family. Would you be willing to give up your own life to live someone else's?

10. Even in an ordered society, there are those who find a way to rebel. Do you think Tabs was right to encourage Kitty to follow in her footsteps?

11. Almost everyone—except for Benjy—is keeping secrets in this book. Are you good at keeping secrets? How would you live with lying to everyone around you?

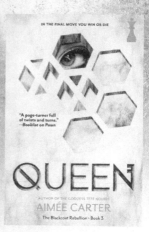